Built to Last

ALSO BY ERIN HAHN

You'd Be Mine

More Than Maybe

Never Saw You Coming

Built to Last

a novel

ERIN HAHN

ST. MARTIN'S GRIFFIN
NEW YORK

This is a work of fiction. All of the characters, organizations, and events portrayed in this novel are either products of the author's imagination or are used fictitiously.

First published in the United States by St. Martin's Griffin, an imprint of St. Martin's Publishing Group

Printed in the United States of America. For information, address St. Martin's Publishing Group, 120 Broadway, New York, NY 10271.

www.stmartins.com

Designed by Michelle McMillian

Library of Congress Cataloging-in-Publication Data

Names: Hahn, Erin, author.
Title: Built to last: a novel / Erin Hahn.
Description: First Edition. | New York: St. Martin's Griffin, 2022.
Identifiers: LCCN 2022013547 | ISBN 9781250827098 (trade paperback) | ISBN 9781250827104 (ebook)
Subjects: LCGFT: Novels.
Classification: LCC PS3608.A444 B85 2022 | DDC 813/.6—dc23
LC record available at https://lccn.loc.gov/2022013547

Our books may be purchased in bulk for promotional, educational, or business use. Please contact your local bookseller or the Macmillan Corporate and Premium Sales Department at 1-800-221-7945, extension 5442, or by email at MacmillanSpecialMarkets@macmillan.com.

First Edition: 2022

10 9 8 7 6 5 4 3 2 1

To my mom and my Tom.
Thank you for always supporting me and my writing.
Apologies in advance for pages (redacted) and (redacted)
and (redacted) and (redacted) and (redacted).

To my mother-in-law, Karen Hahn.
Thank you for sharing your love of romance with me
and for raising the best (bearded) romantic hero
a girl could ask for.

Built to Last

1

CAMERON

STITCHES

FIVE YEARS AGO

I've never loved flying. It's not only the lurching-in-a-claustrophobic-metal-tube-thousands-of-feet-above-the-earth part that bothers me, though that's . . . not great. I genuinely prefer watching the landscape zip past on land. I was meant for high-speed trains. Or low-speed trains. Any train, honestly. In fact, I'd take a wagon train rattling along the Oregon Trail, ditching dressers and flatware across the grassy miles, over flying.

Most especially, I'd choose train travel over this shit-storm of a bushwhacker held together with honest-to-God duct tape and flown by "Hal No Last Name" who reminds me of that crop-duster pilot from *Independence Day*.

And listen. I've traveled the world, and getting around is always iffy when you're working in remote areas, which is ninety-five percent of the job when you film documentaries for *National Geographic.* This feels infinitely worse. In part, because the three other passengers, members of a family from Anchorage, backed out at the last minute, leaving me the sole human cargo. Something Hal No-last-name barely seemed to register.

It's fine. It's for Shelby. No one dies in a plane crash on a flight taken as a grand gesture of a decade-long friendship.

I check my phone, which I refuse to turn off. It feels unwise to shut down the GPS just in case . . . well, you know. Surely, there's GPS on the plane. And a black box.

"There's a black box on this thing, right?" If I die out here, I'd like my mom to know why. No doubt, my dad would just grumble at the news and assume it was my fault for daring to leave ground in an "overblown, dramatic, Hollywood style—"

I shake off the morose thought.

Shelby. This is for Shelby.

Hal tugs one side of his headset away from his ear. "What was that?"

I decide to let it drop. Just as well I don't know about the black box.

I have two messages. The first is from my dad, asking if I'm coming home for Christmas.

It's from two days ago and I haven't answered yet. I probably *could* go home. I have a year under my belt at *National Geographic* and have never taken time off. I've earned the break. And every year I *say* I'll come home. But something inevitably comes up, and anyway, my older brother, Derek, is there. He and his college sweetheart, Michelle, were married two summers ago and have already started giving my parents grandkids. I doubt I'm missed. Me and my no girlfriend, no kids, not even a dog.

Add that to how the last time I was in Michigan, I was subjected to a thousand and one litanies of "the golden-boy prodigal returns," as if I'd spent my growing-up years in a cult rather than on a kid's show (not that my dad could discern a difference).

The second message is from Shelby Springfield, and it's why I'm making offerings to the goddess of fucking airborne disasters to save me.

SHELBY: CAM, THIS IS SHELB. I NEED U. PLEASE COEM. LYLE LIED TO MEE. PLS COME NOW.

I'm only guessing, but I think she might have been intoxicated when she sent it.

It's been years, but of course I still have her number in my phone. And apparently, she has mine in hers. When I called her, some stranger picked up. After confirming that I was, in fact, Cameron Riggs—*"Yes, that Cameron Riggs. Yes, thank you for saying so. I'm glad you liked the show."*—the answerer put Shelby on and all I could make out was that Lyle had dumped her and she was a mess. I got her address and hopped on the first flight out of Alaska.

. . .

Six hours and a mercifully uneventful flight from Anchorage later, I touch land in California. It's been five years since I left the West Coast behind for college, but it feels like five minutes. I don't bother checking into a hotel yet, catching an Uber to the address Shelby gave me instead. The sun is already setting, and I grimace at the grittiness travel and Alaska have left on my skin. My fingers twitch, nervously scrubbing over my pathetic three-day beard before uselessly smoothing at the scruff like I can make it somehow look less pitiful.

I didn't have facial hair when I was eighteen. I barely have it now.

Maybe I should have showered and cleaned up.

Too late. The door swings open before I can even reach for the bell and arms fling around my neck, smothering me in bleach blond hair and tequila fumes.

"Caaaaaam!"

Shelby chokes the breath out of me, but I relish the burn and immediately tuck her into my embrace. Her small shoulders tremble and I realize she's silently sobbing.

It feels unreal. Like the most familiar thing in the world, despite how long it's been. I kiss the top of her head before resting my cheek there, holding on. We're interrupted by three women in various stages of dress and readiness, sneaking out behind Shelby. Shelby releases me with a hiccup and waves them off. "Thank you *so* much, guys. See you later."

A too-long beat and one of them slurs, "Love you, babe!" I decide to give them the benefit of the doubt and assume they've been waiting for me to show up, rather than ditching Shelby all at once.

I nudge my friend gently backward through her doorway. She takes the hint and pulls me the rest of the way before leaning against the door to shut it. I'm surprised to see her building doesn't have a doorman or a gate or anything, but it's clear this residence is new. Like, brand new.

"He dumped me, and the fucker kept our condo," she explains. She leads me to the kitchen area. Her feet are bare, and I realize with a start she's not wearing any pants, only an oversized tee. My old Detroit Tigers tee, in fact. Like seven years old, *old*. Where did she even get that? Never mind. I know where she got it.

Why wear pants when you look like Shelby? Tanned, toned legs for days. Pants would be a shame.

"This place belongs to my assistant. She moved in with her boyfriend."

"It's nice," I say, not able to look anywhere but at her. She looks awesome.

Well, no. She looks like shit. Her navy-blue eyes are ringed in mascara and sleeplessness. Under her spray tan, her skin looks jaundiced. At twenty-two, she's got more sharp edges and hollow angles than I remember her having at seventeen. Five years have passed since I left, ending my contract with the hit children's show *The World According to Jackson*. Once upon a time, Shelby and I were costars, along with Shelby's douche-canoe ex, Lyle Jessup.

I shake myself. Regardless of history, she looks like a goddamn daydream, edges and all. *My* daydream, to be exact.

But that's not why I'm here. Obviously. She's a friend and she needs me. Friends always jump on deathtraps and fly thousands of miles when other friends drunkenly text them after five years of radio silence.

"It's not great digs. You don't have to lie. I just needed a place to hide, and paparazzi are camped out at every hotel from here to Tahoe."

I crack a small smile. "It's better than living in a tent with no plumbing and five grown men only washing with melted snow every other day."

She hands me a tumbler filled with straight Jose Cuervo. I take a sip to be polite, cough, and place it on the counter behind me. She drinks and I watch her throat work. She seems to notice me watching and smirks, hugging the glass to her chest. She also appears to have left her bra with her pants in the Place Where Pretty Girls Leave Optional Clothing.

"That's with *National Geographic?*" she asks.

I nod, impressed. "Yeah. How'd you know?"

She gestures around and then seems to remember where she is. "Fuck. Well, at my old place, I've got a collection of your articles. I know you do docs mostly, but I like the pictures best. I've gotten them framed and everything. I have a whole hall dedicated to your work." Her smile wanes. "Back at home." She shakes her head. "I mean . . . back at Ly—his place."

She motions at a small beige couch in the center of a stark white living room. I follow her to sit, perching awkwardly on the edge of a cushion while she folds her legs underneath her, taking an entire corner. I wipe my hands down my thighs, feeling fifteen and out of my league after only minutes in her presence. "You know, I could get you real copies of those, if you want. I'll replace the others."

"I would love that," she says. Her eyes seem to lose focus and I notice her glass is half empty. Yikes. I'd bet my new Nikon Shelby is seventy percent tequila right now.

"Tell me. What happened, Shelb? I came as soon as you texted."

She tries to straighten, but it comes out lopsided and her

shirt, *my* shirt, slips farther up her thighs, exposing the edges of her . . .

Focus, Riggs. *Why am I here?*

"Why am I here?" I try again. "Not that I mind. But it's been five years, Shelb. I was in Alaska." I'm pleased to report, I manage to sound irritated rather than flustered, and she might be drunk enough to buy it.

Instantly, her big blue eyes pool with tears and she gives a wet sniff. The sound strikes me right in the solar plexus—where I collect all my inconvenient feelings: Shelby, my dad, my brother, that one kid's dog I accidentally struck with my SUV in Sri Lanka . . .

"I'm a mess, Cam."

I grimace. "I'm sure things with Lyle—"

She shakes her head. The Cuervo makes it look almost like a wave. "No. Nope. That's done. He's sleeping with Marcella. I introduced them and now he's in love with her."

"Well—"

"And he wrote a song about it. A duet. They wrote a fucking duet about fucking behind my back. Except it's all sappy and makes them out to be these, like, star-crossed lovers, and I'm this horrible self-centered brat keeping them apart."

I sink back in the couch. "Wow."

"I don't want him back," she says.

"Okay?" It comes out like a question because I'm honestly not convinced. Shelby and Lyle have been together about as long as we've been apart. Five years now. For a while, they were the literal king and queen of the pop charts. Child stars who found love. They were everywhere. *Everywhere.* And it sure as shit looked real to me.

She narrows her eyes, looking mostly sober. "I *don't*. He's not a good guy. Everyone thinks he is. But he's *not*." I know this, of course. Out of everyone, *I* know exactly what kind of person Lyle Jessup is. She looks at me, closing one eye, probably to keep from seeing double. "But *you* are, Cam. Cameron Riggs. You're the bessst guy."

My cheeks feel warm and I clear my throat, uncomfortable with where this is headed. I stand up to retrieve the drink I left on the counter. I'm gonna need the tequila if this turns into another rousing round of Cameron Riggs versus Lyle Jessup. Even after half a decade, I don't feel like doing the calculations. "You barely know me anymore."

She shrugs, one shoulder slipping to escape the tee. *Fuck.* "You haven't changed," she insists. "No one could create such beautiful things and be a bad person. The guy that took the pictures of those children playing soccer in the desert is the same guy who taught me how to kiss in the rain."

I swear, Shelby Springfield is the only person I've ever known who can turn drunken ramblings into something poetic. I swallow a large gulp and feel it burn all the way down. Then I take another and try to pivot the conversation somewhere safe, in the opposite direction of rain-slick tongues, as I return to my seat.

"I'm sorry about Lyle and Marcella. You deserve better. What about your work? What are you doing now?" There. That was tactful.

She ignores my questions, instead lurching toward me and tucking herself against my chest, straight-up nuzzling me. "You smell like pine trees."

I chuckle nervously. "Better than sweat, I guess. I haven't showered yet."

"Maybe a little of that, too. You smell like a man. I don't mind." She curls even closer, her nose tracing my neck. I swallow. It's been a while since I spent time with any woman, let alone Shelby, but I am starting to suspect she didn't call me to help her pack.

"Shelb, maybe we should get some food. Are you hungry? I can order you something. Or you can shower and get dressed and I can take you out."

"I've missed you." Her voice is barely above a purr.

A purr. Jesus.

I sigh, the words pulled from somewhere in the vicinity of my heart. "Me, too."

"Why'd you leave?"

I squirm. "College. You know that."

She narrows her eyes and they accidentally cross and it looks stupid-cute. "Yeah. I'm jealous. Ada Mae insisted my career wouldn't wait for me to get an education."

Let the record show, I've never liked Shelby's mom. She was a nightmare on set. Total stage mom living vicariously through her kid. I'm pretty sure I read something about Shelby firing her a few years ago, but apparently it wasn't soon enough.

"How's that working out for you?" There's an acidic tone to my voice, but it's not toward the woman in front of me. She doesn't seem to notice, anyway.

"I'm burned-out. I feel a hundred years old and I'm tired of doing this."

"Then stop."

"I can't." She spreads her arms wide and flashes a self-deprecating half grin. "This is all I'm good at, Cam. I can't waste everything I've worked for."

Oh, man. She needs out, but I'm not one to talk. I've been running from real life since graduation. Going home means being an adult, and child stars have this weird quirk where they're never really kids to begin with, but they never grow up either. Or, at least, that's what my therapist told me. The one time I went to see a therapist.

But I'm concerned that Shelby won't get the *chance* to grow up if she continues like this. This situation has "tabloid tragedy" written all over it, and it's ripping my fucking heart out. Various bottles litter her counters, of both the liquor and prescription variety. Who knows what else she's been mixing in? And those women—her supposed friends—left her in the hands of a total stranger.

I'm going to murder Lyle. How could he do this? He's always been a selfish asshole, but he's known Shelby since she was ten years old.

Though, so have I. I draw her head to my chest with a sigh and hold her, thinking. I have two days before I need to be back in Alaska for shooting. Two days to figure this out.

• • •

Shelby is quiet, curled up against me. She seems lost in her thoughts, and sitting so close like this, I'm more aware than ever that I need a shower. I nudge her gently and excuse myself before grabbing my duffel from where I left it at the front door. With the amount of alcohol in her system, I wouldn't be surprised if she passed out. That'd be okay. She clearly needs the rest.

Still, I clean up fast, running a razor over my face, and get dressed in a pair of old jeans and a T-shirt while thinking about the one she's wearing. The one she stole from me back when we were something. Before the show ended and I left for college and she chose Lyle.

I run my hands through my hair and look in the mirror. I haven't seen much of my reflection the last few years. I could use a haircut and a good night's sleep in a real bed before I return to Alaska and my tent. I wonder if I can talk Shelby into sharing hers, for old time's sake.

Well, not quite like that.

I shove away the memories and pull open the bathroom door. Shelby is sitting up on the couch, a full drink in her hand. Her smile is blinding and sweet as she takes in my tall form.

"Good! You look all cleaned up!"

"I thought you said you liked my man smell," I tease, relieved to see she's stopped crying.

"Oh, I do," she says with a wink. It looks like she brushed her hair. And she's wearing pants. But she looks just as good in them. "I should probably test this smell, too. C'mere."

My heart rate ramps up as I drop my bag by the door and walk over to her. She stands, wrapping her arms around me easily. Too easily. Too familiar. And I can't help but hold her back.

"You smell exactly like I remember. My favorite."

"And you smell like more tequila," I say. "Why don't I get us some food?"

"I *am* feeling hungry," she admits. Then she reaches between us and slides her hand along the zipper of my Levi's, pressing in a way that has me instantly rising to the occasion. "But not for food."

A small groan escapes the back of my throat.

Fuck. This is *bad*.

"Shelb," I start, stepping back and reaching for her hand.

"Come on, Cam. It's been so long. Aren't you curious? D'you think we still fit like we used to?"

I exhale sharply, my blood surging at her whispered words.

We used to fit perfectly. So perfectly I had to travel to the ends of the earth to forget it.

I'm not doing this.

(I want to do this. I really do. But I'm *definitely* not.)

"Shelb," I try again. "This isn't what you want."

She straightens, her expression somehow both hurt and annoyed. "How do you know what I want?"

I glance around, noticing her glass is empty again. Man, she's a good actress.

She reaches for my face and smooths her body along mine, settling me against the wall. Her tongue slips past my lips and she tastes like everything I've ever wanted. Her softness melts against my hardness and *of course* we fit. I don't remember telling my hands to reach around her tiny frame, but they're sliding under her shirt, anyway. One hand is circling her waist and higher, the other dipping into the elastic at the small of her back and clutching at the smooth skin there. She bucks against me, grinding seductively, and sighs into my mouth. She reaches between us, her hand finding my zipper again. I don't know how to stop her or if I even want to, so instead I pick her up to get us away from this wall, and cooperative angel that she is, she wraps her legs around me.

"Bed," she pants, and I can't help but mindlessly oblige any and all panted requests.

At least for a minute. An entire blissful minute. I carry her down the hall and lay her on the comforter. I press myself on top of her and I savor it—both the feeling of fitting and the little gasps and whispered moans I manage to capture between my lips. This minute will take me years to get over, but right now, I don't care.

I cover her in open-mouthed kisses from her ear to her collarbone, memorizing the taste of her skin. Before, I didn't know it would be the last time. This time I do.

And then she hiccups, and I stand because the minute is over.

"I'm sorry," I say. "I . . . forgot something. I'll be right back."

She looks at me, dazed, and while I want to believe—need to believe, maybe—that I caused that look on her pretty face, it's obvious it's the alcohol and I'm feeling a little sick and a lot pathetic.

"Okay," she says, and she curls on her side, a sleepy smile lingering on her kiss-swollen lips. Her soft snores reach me before I even make it to the door.

I walk into the living room and drop onto the couch, elbows on my knees and my hands forking in my hair, willing myself to calm down—*all* of me to calm down. I'm not sure what to do. I can't stay. She's using me. It's not real, and I don't have it in me to decipher exactly why I came here, but it's clear she wanted a rebound and I stupidly flew in from fucking Alaska for the chance. I almost died in a claptrap modified hang glider to be her rebound—to be Lyle Jessup's replacement fuck.

Jesus. It doesn't get any more tragic.

While she sleeps, I clean the apartment, throw away empty bottles (and some of the more questionable full ones), and take out the trash. I straighten her things in the shower and on the bathroom sink and don't even spend that much time sniffing her shampoo like a lovesick idiot. I do all her dishes by hand and run a load of laundry. Most of this shit is probably dry-clean only, but beggars can't be choosers. I itch to leave, my entire awareness centered on her resting a few feet away, all while praying to the patron saint of boners that she doesn't wake up yet. I know when she wakes up, I'll be gone, and she'll hate me.

Finally, I call a car. It's minutes out, so I pick up a pen and find a scrap of paper and write her a note.

Shelby,

I had to go . . . Alaska is calling. Lyle never deserved your love, and he definitely doesn't deserve your tears. If you want to leave, do it. Start over. Don't let this town suck you dry anymore.

I'm sorry I left you. Both times. Turns out, I don't deserve you either.

Love,
Cameron

I finally work up the courage to slip into her room. She's breathing steadily, but blessedly deep asleep. I wonder how long it's been since she's really slept? I cover her with the edge of her duvet and press a barely there kiss to her forehead one last time. She doesn't stir and I'm torn.

Like always.

As I'm closing the door, my phone buzzes with the alert that my car has arrived.

I leave without saying goodbye.

2

SHELBY

IDGAF

PRESENT DAY

I have a confession.

I can't cry on command. Not in the impressive award-winning child-actress way, anyhow. I'm just sensitive. I cry all the time and can't help it. I even asked my therapist about overactive tear ducts once. She informed me it was a real medical issue and I didn't have it.

The thing is, like so many morally ambiguous stage moms, Ada Mae Springfield was a former pageant queen with a chip on her linen-padded shoulder. Before she could skip town, she'd fallen into bed with a local boy who had sawdust in the creases of his hands and found herself with a colicky baby nine months later. She named me Shelby after her favorite movie character, who unfortunately dies (but gives her mother one hell of a grief-stricken graveside monologue, winning Sally Field critical acclaim . . . which is an important footnote when talking about Ada Mae).

Feeling the pressure to make lemon martinis out of lemons, my mother enrolled me in every lesson, workshop, and camp that marketed the potential to turn me into some semblance of *darling*.

She cut and permed my hair like a late-nineties Shirley Temple, bought me tap shoes instead of the light-up jelly sandals I'd wanted, and made me practice my baton twirling every night before my prayers. I learned that we ate our salads with dressing on the side, only drank sparkling water so as not to stain our teeth, and that sunscreen "was for Catholics."

The morning of a particularly ill-fated audition, my dad snuck me a Boston cream donut. My dad was always doing things like that. Monday through Saturday, I was Ada Mae's project, Sundays belonged to Jesus, and my dad got whatever was left over. So, he'd sneak little things in. Like donuts while Ada Mae was in the shower or Johnny Cash while Ada Mae was snoring in the front passenger seat. I'd savored that donut. To this day, I can still picture the thick layer of gooey chocolate frosting, the feather-light layers of dough, and the smooth, cool custard filling. In my mind, it's like this delicious symbol of Before, but in that moment, I'd licked my fingers clean and then finished off the Ada Mae–approved apple slices before she'd made an appearance, none the wiser. My dad had smudged a whiskery kiss on our cheeks, winking over the top of Ada Mae's head at me, and left for work. Later, we did the same.

The problem wasn't the donut. I will swear to that until

the day I die. It was that I hated the smell in the casting director's office. Even now, I will tear up whenever I encounter someone who overdoes it on the Acqua di Giò. And I never really loved auditions in the first place—everyone staring at you, straight-faced and assessing. Even at age seven, I was uncomfortable with the scrutiny, and that's all it took for my throat to close up and my eyes to fill.

It was for some cereal commercial, but when I opened my mouth, no lines came out. Just sobs. Heart-wrenching, soul-shattering, earth-quaking sobs. And Ada Mae, queen of spin that she is, convinced them I'd done it on purpose. She said we'd interpreted the lines in such a way that we wanted to express our disgust with other cereals and, presumably, the utter tragedy that my commercial parents would feed me anything else.

It was a stretch, even for Ada Mae. I didn't get the job, obviously, but the casting director never forgot it. Three years later, they needed a girl who could cry on cue to play a running gag in a sitcom on a popular children's cable network. I'd done a little more work by that point. More commercials, and I'd won a few regional pageants. I'd even done a guest spot in a country crooner's music video that had seen decent circulation. Even still, Ada Mae saw a sitcom deal as the pot of gold at the end of the ever-loving fame rainbow. It would mean a consistent salary she could skim off the top of, an accompanying record deal she could micromanage, and most important, a way out of her marriage to my dad.

All because she told someone I could cry on demand.

Lemon martinis out of lemons, indeed.

Except, I can't cry on cue. Back then, I felt everything so

much it never took a lot of effort, but I couldn't just turn on the tears. I needed to feel first and there were always plenty of feelings to be had.

In short, it was exhausting but very real.

I emancipated myself from my mom and her lies when I turned seventeen, then I spent a good five years making a whole lot of mistakes all on my own. Drinking and partying all over Hollywood, until three weeks before my twenty-third birthday, when I had a massively public breakup. I'd been betrayed by my best friend and humiliated in the limelight. It probably didn't have to end my career, but I was tired, so I let it.

Totally alone and disgusted with my life and the people in it, I was fully ready to lie down in the sweet grass and let the fairies take me, when . . . I changed my mind. Or rather, I made up my own mind for the first time in my life. I was done with Hollywood and with feeling like garbage. I was finished giving and giving and giving. And I quit. Retired? Regardless, I packed up my things, rented a truck, and drove halfway across the country to my dad's place in Michigan.

Daniel Springfield gave me exactly five days to wallow in a second-story guest room, listening to his old Carly Simon albums on repeat, before he dragged me out of the house and made me go to work with him. He handed me a mallet, face mask, and goggles and said, "This wall needs to come down. When you're done, I have some cabinetry that needs tearing down next."

It was so much better than crying and the best kind of drained I've ever felt.

It took demolishing three more houses before I was ready

for the careful work of historic restoration. A lifetime of furious hurt and bitterness was a lot to reconcile.

By house number four, Dad took his time with me. He has an entire carpentry crew with various specialties, and he wanted me to figure out mine. I didn't need long. I knew what drew me. There's nothing in the world like tracing your fingers along the weathered edges of a beautiful piece of furniture, memorizing the creases, inhaling the sharp tang of history. Some people want to add their own flair to restoration. They want to remake it into something new.

Not me. Never me. I want to return it to what it was. There's such satisfaction and comfort in taking something apart only to make it completely whole once more. And I happen to be good at it. So good, in fact, I no longer have to join my dad on his jobs. I have my own state-of-the-art workshop, paid for with years of crying "on demand." Whenever my dad takes on a new home, I get first dibs. We walk through together and decide which pieces I'll restore, and whether I'll resell them or return them to the historic home they belonged to.

This piece I'm working on now is a floor-to-ceiling, wall-to-wall built-in I begged my dad to buy that came from a 1920s Craftsman. The entire thing had to be carefully dismantled and relocated to my shop for repairs, but I swear it will be worth it in the end. This is one of those heart-stopping kinds of pieces. The kind you buy an entire house for.

At least, that's what I told my dad. He was on the fence, but my pieces have upped the value of five of his last six flips in the past year alone, so he's willing to risk it.

I'm completely absorbed in my work, wunderkind country star Annie Mathers's new solo album blaring over my shop speakers, singing under my breath and smoothing the tip of my pointer finger along the newly sanded edge of a pocket shelf. I'm careful to use only the lightest touch, removing a near century of grime, but leaving the beautiful hardwood unaltered. My shoulders ache with the effort, but it's a good burn. The kind that feels like an honor to bear—a nod of respect to the original craftsman.

"I met Mathers once. Did I ever tell you that?"

I jump with a screech, the shelf thankfully safely clamped, but my woodworking tools clatter to the floor. I lurch back, my hand clutched to my chest as if it could hold my heart in place.

"Jesus H, Jones, it's called a doorbell." I suck in a breath and slowly release it.

"I used the doorbell. Twice. And I tried calling you." My best friend Lorelai Jones grabs my discarded phone from the bench where I'd tossed it. She's dressed up in dark-wash jeans, fashionably broken-in Western-style ankle boots, and a leather jacket. Her long brown waves are pulled back in a swinging pony, showing off high cheekbones and stunning dark eyes.

These same eyes are currently rolling at me in exasperation, because, shit, she's my ride to the airport. I surreptitiously check my varnish-speckled wristwatch and give a yelp.

"I got sidetracked." I wince and bend to hurriedly pick up my tools. "Sorry."

"Rough day?"

All that comes out is a grunt. I place the tools in their

rightful spots. It's a good thing Lorelai convinced me to bring my luggage to the shop this morning. "What was that about Annie Mathers?"

Lorelai straightens my stool and swipes some sawdust to the floor, which is already carpeted in a thick layer. She makes a face that plainly tells me she wants to comment on the mess but knows I don't care.

I *love* my mess. I could marry it, honestly.

"Nothing really. I just met her once is all. Way back when her momma was alive. We performed the same night at the Grand Ole Opry. Annie was just a peanut with gobs of star power back then."

I move to the coat rack and drop off my Carhartt, exchanging it for my North Face. "Isn't that what she is now?"

"Basically," Lorelai agrees.

I study my best friend's tone for bitterness, but there's none to be found. Back when I was attempting to erase my deflated child-star rep by exchanging it for a sexier bubblegum-pop rep, Lorelai was the reigning princess of the country music world. She used to front an all-girl band of Southern belles but went rogue one night on tour, playing some politically charged protest rock, and woke to the news that everyone south of the Bible Belt had turned on her, including her longtime superstar first love and fiancé, Drake Colter.

Lorelai and I met outside our mutual therapist's office in Grand Rapids. Neither of us kept the therapist, but we kept each other.

I'm fully done with Hollywood, but I'm not so sure Lorelai is. It's been nearly three years since things went sideways for her and I have a feeling she's fixing to make a comeback.

"Tide seems to be turning with some of these newer artists," I comment idly, pocketing my phone and reaching for my overnight case resting in the corner by the door.

She nods thoughtfully. "It might be."

"But I bet they could use someone with a little experience to show them how it's really done."

Lorelai's lips twitch. "Thinking of getting back in the game?"

I snort. "As if. I'm perfectly happy with my shop."

"Yeah, well, I don't think anyone is interested in my brand of experience."

"Maybe," I say with a shrug. We have this conversation once a month. So far, Lorelai has been content to play gigs at small-town bars while using her elementary teaching degree the rest of the time.

"So, why were you hiding from your phone?"

"I wasn't. Not really. It's just nerves."

Lorelai makes a sound of understanding in the back of her throat.

"The first time, I didn't really care that much whether it worked out or not. My dad was reluctant, and really, I was, too, when it came down to the inevitable press. But when they didn't pick up the pilot, I was disappointed. I'd kind of gotten used to the idea that this would be the best way to make sure my dad can retire comfortably." Six months ago, my dad and I were approached to do a pilot called *Home-Made,* one of those home-renovation shows. You know the kind: a couple buys up homes, fixes them, and flips them. We thought it turned out pretty well for a freshman effort, but apparently my dad is not meant for television. Go figure. The middle-aged contractor from Michigan doesn't have the ever-elusive "it" factor.

"That's not your responsibility, hon."

I huff out a breath, playing with the handle on my suitcase, extending it and collapsing it again. "It feels like it should be, though. And that was before his accident." My dad had gotten into a pileup on the interstate while driving to a worksite last fall. He came out of it alive, but his knee was crushed against the dash. It's been a slow road to recovery, not least because he's an ornery coot who's decided to be allergic to physical therapy. "He can't keep working on frozen jobsites. It's terrible for his joints. He basically saved my life and I want to be able to do the same for him."

I take a deep breath. "I'm going to have to say yes, Lore. To whatever they offer."

Lorelai freezes midstep and slowly turns to face me, her hand resting on the shop door handle.

"You aren't." She groans. "Shelby! I thought we agreed that you would take the free flight, hear them out long enough to be polite, and be home before the paparazzi even know you were in town."

"Right. I'm doing that, still. But also, I'm going to agree to it. On paper, *HomeMade* has merit. I can do this."

Lorelai's small hand finds her hip. "What if they want to swap your dad for your mom as your costar?"

My throat goes dry. "They wouldn't do that." She raises

her brows. "No, seriously, that would be a terrible idea. Ada Mae and I are oil and water. They aren't that dumb."

"Maybe not," Lorelai concedes as I follow her out into the last vestiges of early spring sunshine. "But she does have that book now and it's been sitting pretty on the *New York Times* bestseller list for months. Clearly there's interest and it's not only in her."

"Exactly, which is why it's also not happening. Not a chance in hell I'd costar with her. Never mind that she doesn't know how to renovate a home, doesn't live in Michigan, and I completely cut her from my life."

"Honestly, the fact that she wrote a fucking exposé of lies about you, calling you a drug addict and porn star is plenty enough reason not to hire her. One would hope, anyway. But this is Hollywood, Shelb."

Because even if I'm done with Hollywood, they're not done with me, and unfortunately, I need that to work in my favor for a little while longer. I wince, slipping on a pair of sunglasses as Lorelai tosses my suitcase in the hatchback. "She didn't *actually* say the words 'porn star,' did she?" I haven't bothered to read the book, but Lorelai has. She said one of us should know what's out there.

"She wrote that you sold sex tapes and nudes for drugs."

"First of all, everyone knows she didn't write that book herself. And second, *if* I'd had a sex tape in circulation, I wouldn't have had to release that embarrassing bubblegum-pop album of Courtney Love covers." I shudder, only half kidding. It was not my finest hour, but at least I fired my (second) manager after that.

"You can't work with her."

"I'm not! This is all hypothetical. You were the one who brought up Ada Mae." I wave my hand in front of me, as if to clear the air of bad vibes. "Stop putting that shit into the universe, Jones." *Note to self: pick up some sage next time you're in town.*

We get into the car and Lorelai runs a hand through her ponytail, setting it to swing, and snaps her chewing gum, thinking. She reverses in silence and I wait her out, knowing she has more on her mind and I'm her captive audience for the duration to the airport.

"Shelb, I think you're doing okay. Really, really excellent, even. And I know. I've seen some things," my best friend reminds me, her gaze taking in the rows of cornstalks sticking out of the still-frozen farm fields.

"*I* know I am." Honestly, I'm more than okay. I've got commissions enough to see me through the next six months at least, and I'm genuinely content living this quiet existence in northern Michigan. "But a single season of reality television could make my dad's retirement and pay off the rest of his medical bills in one fell swoop. You and I both know how he feels about capitalizing on my previous career."

Lorelai rolls her eyes. "He's the furthest thing from Ada Mae."

"Obviously."

"What makes you think he'd be okay with capitalizing on this, though?"

"Because one, I'm in a good place. I'm no longer vulnerable to a toxic power struggle. I'm a grown-ass adult who owns my own business and knows what I'm about. And two, because I'm going to demand they bring him on as a paid consultant."

Lorelai brightens at that and I can tell she's coming around. Sort of. "That's a good idea," she admits.

"I know, right?" I say, smug.

"You still don't know what you're walking into."

"It can't be any worse than Ada Mae. I'll survive."

She reaches for my fingers and squeezes them once. "It's what you do."

. . .

The following morning, I realize it *can* be worse than my mom. Two times worse, it turns out, because standing on either side of the sleek conference room table are my ex-boyfriends, and they look ready to murder each other. Just like the old days.

I give a long-suffering sigh before clearing my throat and rapping on the glass-paneled door with a knuckle.

"Please tell me I didn't fly all the way back to L.A. after five years of intensive therapy and hot yoga classes just to sit around a table with you two fuckwits again."

3

CAMERON

WHAT A MAN GOTTA DO

When I was thirteen, my dad took me out in this rusty old metal rowboat he'd camouflaged and repurposed for duck hunting. I didn't hunt. Didn't even know how to hold a gun. Anyway, it was summer, because I was on break from filming, so it was decidedly not hunting season.

He motored us out to the middle of this glorified neighborhood pond in the late afternoon. The sun was still high in the sky and there was a group of teenaged girls tanning on the dock. Once we managed to get to a point too far from shore for me to swim, he pounced.

"Cameron. Your mother thought it was time for me to talk to you about what happens in the bedroom between a man and a woman. You might've noticed the way your body is changing—"

I would pay a thousand dollars to exchange places with thirteen-year-old me right now. Two thousand. I would give my entire life savings for the chance to slip out of this conference room and away from Shelby's glare and return to the middle of that pond and my dad's booming baritone floating over to the high school girls sunning as he said, "It's normal to touch yourself, kid. Just quit leaving the evidence for your mom to clean up."

"As I was telling Cam before you arrived, Shelb. This—"

"Don't call me that."

Lyle sputters to a stop, his smarmy flow interrupted. His heavily groomed brows pinch together. "I'm sorry?"

"That's news to me," she mutters. "Nevertheless," she continues, louder, "as we are supposedly here in a business capacity, I'd appreciate you using my full name. And his," she adds as an afterthought, jerking her thumb at me, but not quite meeting my eyes.

I hide my laugh in a cough behind my fist and shift in my seat. "Yeah. I agree. Actually, I'd prefer you call me Mr. Riggs."

Shelby's full lips twitch in the corners. "Ms. Springfield, if it's all the same, thanks."

Lyle's shit-brown eyes dart between us a full ten seconds before he sinks back into his plush leather office chair with an exasperated huff. He turns to the other men in the room. There are two, Tiberius and Phineas (or something equally absurd). Presumably, they are unrelated, as they look nothing alike, aside from their overpriced slim-fit suits. However, it seems unlikely two separate couples decided to name their kids after ancient Romans and that they, in turn, worked for the same oily asshole, Lyle Jessup.

Said asshole gestures toward us but speaks as if we're not there. "What did I tell you, fellas? They're perfect."

"I can see it."

"Go on."

"Perfect for what?" I interrupt, my patience wearing thin. This room is about fifteen degrees too cold and every surface is reflective. It's like an experiment in discomfort and intimidation. "What are you doing here, Lyle? I flew in to speak with a Tom Franklin. Where is he?"

"Weird. I was told I was speaking with a Mary Swanson," Shelby says, leaning forward in her seat and folding her hands together on the shiny conference table. "I thought this was regarding a home-reno pilot. I'm not the slightest bit interested in a reunion show, Lyle. My agent could have told you that much on the phone."

"Reunion show?" I yelp, my temper flaring, and spring to my feet. "You've got to be kidding. Who wants to rehash that shit?" Shelby, Lyle, and I acted on *The World According to Jackson* together through our teens. It was the kind of cable network show where the kids sang and danced and mouthed off to sub-intelligent parent types, all set to laugh tracks. Lyle was the lead, Jackson, a kid who lived in his daydreams half the time. I played Carter Nelson, his nerdy, rule-following best friend, and Shelby played his longtime love interest with a penchant for the dramatic, Makayla Burns. There's a nostalgic following for the show a decade after it wrapped, but there's far too much history between us to even consider a reunion show. Case in point, the way the three of us can barely stand to be in the same room right now.

"Christ! Would you two settle down?" At our glares, Lyle sighs. "There's no reunion show. For fuck's sake, even *I* don't want to go back down that road." He scrubs a manicured hand down his face and gestures for me to sit down with a firm, "Please be seated, *Mr.* Riggs."

I sit.

Lyle swears under his breath but composes himself once more. "Look, forget ten years ago for a goddamn minute and listen to what I have to say. This is about *HomeMade*, the home-reno pilot, as *Ms. Springfield* suggested. I've been handed the project because they would like to give you, Ms. Springfield, a second opportunity. It's my understanding the test audiences didn't connect with your costar."

Shelby winces slightly but doesn't deny it.

"But I was also told they adored you."

I can tell this is news to Shelby. She gives a small nod for Lyle to continue.

"Clearly, you know what you're doing, but do you know enough to carry a show? Joanna and Chip, Erin and Ben, Christina and Tarek. They're all couples, Ms. Spring—"

She holds up a hand. "Okay, okay. Enough with the Ms. Springfield. Shelby is fine. I get it. You need two. But you're wrong, I don't always know what I'm doing. I do the finicky restorations, but my dad is the one who runs the projects from demolition to polish. I'm not sure I can do this without him."

"He can consult. I'll pay him a consulting commission on one project for the pilot. After that, we'll see."

Shelby narrows her eyes, taking in the suited men at the other end of the table and finally allowing her gaze to land on me for a half second without flinching.

Progress.

"Okay, that was too easy. What else? Flattery, acquiescence

with my dad . . . I know you, Lyle. You're far too slimy to just hand me those things. Why is Cameron here?"

"Mr. Riggs," I offer.

She glares, but it's not nearly as potent as it was fifteen minutes ago.

Lyle turns to me. "That's up to him. Like I said, you need a costar."

I inhale sharply and swallow wrong, hacking into the stiff sleeve of my button-down and finally wiping at my watering eyes. I'm not stupid. I'd figured out Lyle wanted me on the project in some capacity, but I honestly thought it would be behind the scenes. Sure, I'd been on camera in my teens, but after *Jackson,* I went to Columbia, got my degree in filmmaking, got an internship with *National Geographic,* and have since spent the last six years traveling the globe while filming nature docs.

I'd taken this meeting as a favor to my agent, Peter, who's forever asking me to accept some work Stateside for a change, complaining my across-the-world hours aren't conducive to a healthy sex life on his end.

(I called him *once* in the middle of the night. *Maybe* twice. Jet lag is a killer.)

Peter said he knew a guy, Tom Franklin, who was looking to class up some reality television shows and wanted to discuss an opportunity with me. Obviously, costarring with my first girlfriend on a reality home-renovation show is not what I had in mind. Furthermore, I'm beginning to suspect Tom Franklin doesn't exist outside of Lyle's brain.

"I'm . . ." Sorry? Lost? Uncomfortable in this too-small chair and mirror-glazed hellscape? Or maybe I'm shaken the fuck up because I'm here in L.A., somehow breathing the same air as Shelby Springfield, and all I want to do is drag her out of here like a maniac, beg her to forgive me for everything I ever did, then lay her down and make love to her every day for the rest of our lives?

I'm not positive, but I doubt that's the answer Lyle is looking for here.

Or maybe it is. Which might be worse.

I level Lyle with a look. "I'm not sure why I'm here, to be honest. I haven't been in front of a camera in ten years, and I don't know the first thing about home renovation. So, either you are looking for a spare cameraman, and I'll be honest, my going rate is outside your budget, or you and my agent are playing a sick joke."

Lyle's eyes roll to the ceiling. "Jesus, Riggs. I forgot how dramatic you could be."

"Oh, that's rich."

Lyle ignores the jab. "I already signed on Daniel Springfield to consult. He can teach you anything you need to know about home reno."

"You haven't signed him to anything," Shelby reminds him. "But continue."

"*My point being,* I'm not looking for experts. I'm looking for star power and chemistry, which is why I called you two to L.A."

"Under false pretenses, Lyle. We need to address that."

"Fine," Lyle says, shrugging. "I asked someone else to make the calls in order to hide my identity from you two idiots because I knew if I called, you wouldn't show up. But the fact remains, I'm the showrunner for Shelby's second pilot."

I open my mouth to respond, but Shelby beats me to it. "I'm not an idiot for *not* wanting to see you again, Lyle. You cheated on me with my best friend, wrote a song blaming me for it, then won a Grammy, all while profiting off the meltdown of my career and sanity. I have plenty of reasons to avoid you."

Lyle sighs and waves away the two older gentlemen in the room. "I imagine you've seen enough. I'll catch up with you later." Neither bothers to hide their amusement as they file out and close the glass door behind them with a *shisk*, leaving us alone.

With our audience gone, Lyle stands, leaning forward and pressing his fingers into the polished surface of the table. "You can hate me all you want, Shelby. I don't give a shit. Blame me for everything that's gone wrong in your life. You've always loved playing the hapless victim, and I would expect nothing less. But do it while hamming it up for the cameras because whether I like it or not, and believe me, I don't love it, the viewers want a comeback story featuring America's fucked-up sweetheart."

Shelby's jaw slips, but I'm on my feet again in an instant, my roller chair smacking into the wall and my hands shoving against Lyle's chest. "You asshole! Are you kidding me? She wasn't playing the victim! She *was* the victim and you made her that way!"

Lyle huffs, straightening his suit jacket. "Stay out of this, Riggs. You don't know what you're talking about. You've been in the fucking desert playing at your own self-importance."

"I *do* know what I'm talking about. I was there. Five years ago, when she called me and said you'd run off with her friend and left her humiliated and alone."

Lyle shakes his head, laughs, and sits back down. "Of fucking *course*." He raises his brows to Shelby. "Of *course* you called him the minute I was gone. Poor Hot Mess Shelby needs Cameron Riggs to come to her rescue. Probably fucked, didn't you? I should be surprised, yet somehow, I'm not."

"Good grief, Lyle. Way to be professional."

Shelby snaps. "Oh my God, stop. Both of you. You're embarrassing yourselves." I sit, feeling guilty, and she rubs at her temples. Finally, she turns to Lyle. "You are narcissistic and delusional, but I don't have the energy to spell out all the ways you're wrong. It doesn't matter, anyway, because you *know* you're wrong. You messed up and hurt me and you don't care. That's not my problem. What I need to know is: Can you be a goddamn professional and carry this show or am I wasting my time?"

"I can do it," Lyle says, without hesitation. "But you need him." He gestures to me.

Shelby turns to me, finally, meeting my gaze straight on. "Tell the truth, did you know I was involved when you came for this meeting? Even presuming you would be behind the lens, did you know?"

I swallow hard, knowing I'm caught. "Maybe."

Her face softens instantly, and she smiles in a way that feels like a gift.

"Cam." Her voice is a whisper.

"Fine. I didn't know about Lyle, but I heard you were involved, and I had some time between projects for *Nat Geo,* so

I took the meeting. My mom's been on me for years to come back," I hurry to add. "It's not just you." *Liar.*

"Excellent," Lyle says, pulling out a slim laptop and, after making a few clicks on the keyboard, spinning it to face us. "You want to know how I know it needs to be the two of you? This is how."

He's cued up an old episode of *The World According to Jackson* and it all comes flooding back, even though I haven't seen the show in a decade. It was the episode of the final season that went viral instantly, when the writers decided to play with the relationships on the show. They wanted to see if they could pull off a little teen drama.

Their gamble payed off bigger than anyone could have imagined, but it didn't matter. Shelby and I walked away after that—me to college and Shelby to a short-lived career as a pop star.

On-screen, Makayla and Carter are in Jackson's bedroom alone, part of one of Jackson's famous daydream sequences. Lyle's character was imagining that they had crushes on each other, and we were supposed to be acting out this fantasy as it played out in his head. We were instructed to overact. Pretend to *pretend* we were in love. Pretend to *pretend* to want to kiss. Pretend to kiss. It was supposed to be ridiculous.

What they hadn't counted on was that off-screen, Shelby and I had grown close. Like, really close. At that time, the *world* and the fandom wanted Shelby and Lyle to be together. Kids had grown up with them together. Cory and Topanga, Miley and Jesse, Makayla and Jackson.

Definitely not Carter and Makayla. Never them. But it didn't matter. The second our lips touched, it was like you'd lit a fuse in those two teenagers, and the result was a very believable, very chemistry-laden first kiss that the viewers never got over.

Shelby got an obscene amount of hate mail calling her a slut for cheating on Lyle and breaking Jackson's heart. It was unrelenting, and she couldn't take it after that. When she and Lyle started to date after the show ended, people never really stopped accusing her of cheating.

I concentrate on the kids on the screen, trying to see them through objective eyes. I barely recognize myself, to be honest. Eighteen-year-old Cameron was lanky and squeaky-voiced with longish dark-blond hair and smooth cheeks. There's definitely something there between Shelby and me, though. Outside of our characters, even. Of course, I know *what* that something was, but now I can see how obvious it was on-screen, once the writers put us alone together in a small space. We seem to circle each other's orbit and spark with chemistry. Shelby tucks a long blond curl behind her ear and bites her lip. I lean down and smile at her and she grins back, all moon-eyed. When I bend to meet her lips, she raises on her tiptoes and captures mine perfectly. On-screen, my cheeks are ruddy with the *wooooo!* coming from the "live studio audience." In the conference room, I'm grateful for the thick beard that covers my face these days.

The scene goes black and Lyle's grin is shit-eating. "Am I wrong?"

I clear my throat. "You're basing everything off an on-screen kiss?"

Shelby clears hers right after. "From a decade ago, no less."

Lyle narrows his eyes shrewdly and crosses his arms.

"First of all, fuck you if you think for one second that I didn't know you were together during that. Sneaking off after shooting, all those meaningful staring contests." He jerks his pointed chin at me. "I will hand you my net worth right now if you weren't making out with her in the closet during lunch breaks."

My heart thuds in my chest. For so long, everything was a secret. It's been years, but I don't feel like I can divulge anything yet. And especially not to Lyle. The fucker.

"Fine," he says, after a long silence. "Don't admit it. I don't actually care. But that"—he points to the screen—"is exactly how I know you can pull this off.

"You two, regardless of what you were *behind closed doors*"—he raises his eyebrows suggestively—"were peas in a pod and about as wholesome as two child stars could be, since neither of you bothered sticking around Hollywood long enough to spiral."

My skepticism is obvious. "Really? What would you call what happened to Shelby five years ago then?"

Lyle is unfazed. "We're back on this? It was a messy breakup. We grew apart."

"You fucking *ruined* her."

Shelby makes a noise like an angry cat.

He waves a hand and focuses his gaze on Shelby. "You would've come out of it fine. Instead, you *chose* to walk away from everything. You were looking for the chance to escape. I just gave you a reason."

"You let everyone shit on her!" I yell in a strangled voice. Lyle's eyes flicker to the doorway and back to my face. I lower my tone, but I can't seem to let this lie. "You didn't even try to defend her, even though you were the one in the wrong."

Lyle's expression hardens and his eyes glint. "Looks like she didn't need me, though. She had you. Just like she has you right now. So, tell me, *Mr. Riggs,* are you here for Shelby? Are you ready to prove you're the better man, once and for all?"

Shelby cuts in. "Oh, for fuck's sake. Quit it, Lyle. Cameron, don't listen to him. He's just bitter because he can't grow facial hair like you to cover his acne scars."

I know she's right. He's just goading me. Nothing has changed in the last decade when it comes to Lyle Jessup. He's the same obnoxious attention hog he's always been.

I let out a grunt, run my hands down my thighs, and clamp down on the words that are fighting to escape. I want throw it in his face that she called me, and I *did* come. That I took the first flight out of the motherfucking permafrost just to be there for her. That she kissed me and tried to make me stay, and instead of taking advantage of her, I left. That I would do it again in a heartbeat. I'll always come running for this woman.

Not that she needs me. She's not the same hurting Shelby who drunk-texted me five years ago. The Shelby sitting here is a far cry from that girl. This Shelby is fierce and endlessly patient and elegant in the face of Lyle's bullshit. I fell hard for the old Shelby, but this new version will absolutely destroy me.

I exhale, long and slow. "I'll do it. I have to confirm a leave of absence with *Nat Geo* and I want at least two weeks before the cameras arrive to shadow Daniel. But yeah. I'll do the show."

Like I even have a choice.

4

SHELBY

PIECES OF ME

"Fine. I'll admit the built-in was worth the trouble."

I stand back, hooking my thumbs in the tool belt slung at my waist, and take in my creation.

Well. My *re*-creation.

"And that's without a finish, Dad. Imagine it polished up and glossy. This room is about to feel a million times cozier. That soft LED Jasmine dropped off is a game changer."

My dad nods, his hands on his still-trim hips, and turns in place, taking in the entire space. This used to be a shallow living room with wood paneling and a rotting carpet that had questionable stains. My dad wanted to knock it all out and replace it with drywall, which is the simplest and least expensive option. Except for one problem.

The built-ins were in the way. I convinced him to give me those and I let him have free rein with the rest. He didn't disappoint. He removed a dividing wall, rebricked the fireplace in the center—opening it up to two rooms—and replaced the paneling with white car siding from the floor to the ceiling rafters. It's stunning. Everything is clean lines and natural surfaces and every bit of it points to the showstopper—my bookcases.

I'm giddy.

"You did good, kid," he says, approval clear in his voice.

"Thanks, Pops. You, too." I hold up a hand and his lips quirk under his salt-and-pepper mustache as he returns my high five.

"I'm gonna run. I told Jasmine I would keep healthier hours, whatever that means."

I hide my smile at his gruff tone. That man is marshmallow over his girlfriend, real-estate agent Jasmine Rodriguez. They've worked together for a decade, dancing around their two divorces and raising their three kids (her two, his one). But now we're all grown up and they're finally making a go of it. It's so cute, I could cry. (Surprise, surprise.)

"Sure. Thanks for the food." I gesture to the paper bag of calories sitting on a sawhorse in the corner.

"Don't let it get cold. It's not any good cold."

"I won't," I insist. "Now go."

"You sure you don't need me?"

I roll my eyes lightly. "Dad. It's only varnish. All I need is time and an empty workspace without sawdust flying in the air." I shoo him away with my hands. "Out. Give Jazz my love."

He leaves, shutting the door behind him, and I let loose a heavy sigh. *Finally.* I wander over to my cheeseburger and pull it out, wrapping the bottom half in the foil, and take a bite as I slowly pace the room. My work boots creak on the stiff new hardwood floors, and while it's still light outside,

I flip on the work lights to make sure I can see everything clearly. After I finish my burger, tossing the foil in the trash I'll be taking out when I leave, I walk to the kitchen sink and rinse my hands. No greasy fingers for this project.

I tug out my phone and connect to the Bluetooth speaker my dad allows on-site. Scrolling through my playlist, I pick Michael Bublé's "Sway" to get me moving and crank it.

I carefully lay a cloth along the new floors and crack open a fresh can of cherry varnish and prep my brush, making sure I have everything I need within reach. I did the first sanding and layer of varnish in the shop, but I needed more space to do the second and third layers, so now I'm at the house. Varnish is a magnet for dust and prints. I'll finish it tonight, and by the time the crew shows up tomorrow morning, it should be set enough to be safe.

I tug a pair of latex gloves and a face mask out of my jacket pocket before removing my coat, dropping it next to the soft drink I haven't touched. The heat isn't turned on yet, but it's March, and once I start moving, I'll be working up a sweat.

Sarah Brightman comes on singing "Time to Say Goodbye." I start to hum under my breath and can already feel myself relaxing into the work. My shoulders soften and any tension in my neck slinks away.

Dipping my brush, I begin at one end of the wall and work my way across, singing the Italian lyrics. Despite my bubblegum-pop reputation, I was classically trained.

Classically trained to sing Broadway standards in an empty old house.

It almost makes me want to record a clip and send it to Ada Mae with a text reading Warmest Regards.

Except she'd probably accidentally-on-purpose leak it to the press.

I'm really in my feels, belting out Hayley Westenra's cover of "Never Saw Blue," when the doorbell rings, nearly causing me to pee myself and spill varnish all over my dad's new floors.

"Shit!" I screech when the doorbell rings out again, but I compose myself enough to carefully put down the can and brush. I fling open the door with a scowl. "Who is—?"

"Hey, Shelby."

My breath leaves in a gust of "Cameron." If I hadn't seen him a month ago, I would still recognize those grass-green eyes anywhere. Even on a thickly bearded face.

"What?" I manage to croak out after.

I cringe. Jesus. Cameron Riggs shows up at my door five years after stabbing me in the ego and all I can word vomit is *"What?"* In L.A., I had this miraculous confidence, likely borne out of the thick layer of don't-give-a-fuck-ness I applied along with my sunscreen after landing at LAX. I scramble to regain that feeling, but I'm coming up short. The Midwest has made me soft. It's probably all that fleece we wear.

I clear my throat, dragging my mask off my burning face. "I mean, what are you doing here?"

My only consolation is Cameron looks just as uncomfortable, and at six three, two hundred pounds of plaid-covered masculinity, he wears it weird. I open the door the rest of the way and beckon him in. Last time I saw him, he was defending my honor at the top of his lungs, and the time before that, I was practicing my whole "numbness campaign," so seeing him sober and in this context is like a lightning strike.

I instantly feel the telltale tickle of emotion in my throat. I attempt to ever-so-subtly slow my heart rate and open my airways.

Inhale, exhale. I am a motherfucking yogi.

"I . . . was in the area," he says, hands in his jeans pockets. Like he's completely unaware that I'm on the precipice of tears, which is doubtful. Cam could always tell when I was about to cry. "Uh, in Michigan. Finally. So, I decided to come visit. I figured doing this off-screen was better for everyone involved."

"You heard I was here, at this unoccupied house?"

He grimaces, scratching at his heavily whiskered cheek. "Of course not. Daniel told me where to find you."

"Oh?" The question dangles between us. Because clearly there is more to it than that. Like how he found my dad's house? Or how he's been in contact with my dad, and my dad didn't tell me? Maybe even how I will be having some strong words with my father, after I figure out if I'm mad or happy to see Cameron.

"How about this?" he offers. "Let's rewind." He makes this ridiculous sound like a record scratch, rolling his hands backward as though he's reversing time. "To before L.A. and Lyle. Forget them for a minute." He steps closer, and I giggle, despite my nerves. With him, comes the smell of outside and spearmint gum. My eyes trace up his scuffed boots, long legs, and green-and-blue flannel shirt, sleeves rolled to the elbows. His beard is dark brown and tidy, his eyes are familiar and edged with laugh lines. His hair is shorter than I've ever seen it, but it suits him.

He looks good. Real good. Like a lumberjack spliced with young Paul Newman.

Well done, past me, I think. *You hit that.*

To which my inner self reminds me I also *did not* hit that *again,* so ouch.

"Forgotten," I agree. "Hey, Cameron Riggs. What brings you to the neighborhood?"

His answering grin is relieved and easy. "Heard an old friend was here and I wanted to see her."

I allow a small smile to slip out. "It's good to see your face, Cam. It's been too long."

"Five years," he says softly.

"Something like that."

"So, you're rehabbing houses." He gestures to the room at large and I realize it's not so much a question as an ice-breaker.

I close the door behind us and lead him over to my built-ins. "Well, my dad rehabs the houses. I'm a bit more specialized . . ."

His eyebrows lift. "You did this?"

"Yeah. It's not as impressive if you didn't see the before. Here." I pull out my phone and scroll to the old photos. To his credit, Cam seems to really study them.

"That's incredible. They're stunning. Is this the original oak?"

"Well spotted," I say, beaming. "It is. Nothing better than the original."

He runs his hand along an unfinished piece with a reverence I recognize.

"What about you?" I ask. "Where've you been?"

"Here and there," he says, and I know he's not being cryptic. He's honestly been everywhere in the last six years.

"How's *National Geographic*?" That's the spirit. We'll talk *around* the memories. Like friends without complicated pasts do.

"It's good. We just wrapped a series on the cloud forests in Ecuador."

"Wow. Interesting."

He nods, a little distracted. "It was, but I'm glad for the break. My mom's thrilled. She's been begging me to come home for a visit ever since she and my dad made their split official."

My heart jolts. Damn. "I didn't know about your parents, Cam. I'm sorry."

He shrugs. "It's okay. It was a long time coming. She moved not too far from here, actually, outside Grand Rapids, and I flew in last night to stay with her for a bit."

Weird how I'd somehow managed to forget Cameron was born and raised in Michigan, too. It was something of an inside joke with us on the set of *Jackson*—two Midwestern kids in the middle of all that glitz. (Lyle was a local, *of course.*) But in the years since, I guess I just always pictured Cameron in some exotic, worldly destination. He felt so far away from the comfort of evergreen-lined lakes and rolling green hills.

Not that I pictured him *that* often.

"So, what else? Married? Dating? Kids?" I ask, as casual as I can manage, which is admittedly not very casual.

"Not right now, no. You?"

"Nah. A few dates here and there, but I've been focused

on my work. Speaking of . . ." I pick up the varnish. "Do you mind? I need to get this done before the crew comes back tomorrow."

"Can I help?" he asks. I hesitate, and Cam notices. "It's okay, I don't have to—"

"No!" I say. "It's fine. Thank you. There's an extra brush and a spare mask over by my coat." I gesture toward the pile. "I'm not used to having other people around, but I can make an exception."

I watch him for a few moments, but Cameron is a quick study and has a steady hand, so I motion for him to take the higher shelves while I work on the lower. "Have you done this before?" I ask.

"Not really. But I'm capable enough." We work in comfortable silence for a few minutes and it's strange how *not* strange this is. Cameron Riggs is here in Michigan. Next to me. Varnishing shelves.

"I'm really sorry again, about your parents, Cam. I feel terrible I didn't know."

"How could you? It's okay." He takes a deep breath, obviously steeling himself for something. "While we're apologizing, I'm sorry for—"

I cut him off with a shake of my head. "Don't. It's fine."

"It wasn't. Please just let me say it, Shelby."

I really, *really* don't want to listen to this, but from his determined tone, there's no avoiding it. "Okay, fine."

He's still holding the brush, but he stops to face me and tugs down his mask. His eyes pierce my carefully constructed shell. I swallow hard. "I'm sorry I left. I didn't want to. You probably won't believe me but walking away from you that day was the hardest thing I've ever done. I just knew I couldn't let anything, um, like *that,* happen between us. *Again.* You weren't in the right headspace."

"And you were?"

He shakes his head wryly. "Not really, no. Timing always seems to be against us."

I let that sink in, taking his version of events and replacing it over the hazy version of mine.

"I wondered," I say. "Not at the time, of course. I was too out of my mind to wonder then. But since . . . I kept your note. Which is kind of a miracle."

He laughs self-deprecatingly. "I'm shocked you didn't burn it."

"I know, right? It was a dick move, Riggs, leaving while I slept. But not a complete waste. I got out before they sucked me dry, like you told me to. Packed my stuff, rented a truck, and showed up at my dad's door three days later."

He clears his throat, his voice a little hoarse. "I thought if I waited for you to wake up, I wouldn't be able to leave. But leaving you . . . I was no better than Lyle. I'm so sorry."

I feel the press of tears and I wave him off, pleading for him to stop. To stop being so nice. Stop being so caring. Stop being so *Cam.* "Forgiven, okay? I really, *truly* don't want to talk about that day anymore."

He nods in silence and we go back to varnishing.

"What are you listening to?" he asks.

"Il Divo."

He nods again, and we fall quiet. It's not uncomfortable or awkward. It's . . . nice.

"Do you want me to do the pilot, Shelb? Not just because you need a costar, but me, specifically? Is this okay? With our, um, past and everything?"

My hand freezes midstroke and I raise my eyebrows.

He rushes on. "I'm already committed. I'm on sabbatical and obviously I'm here and everything, but you were as shocked as I was in L.A. I know you didn't have a choice in the matter."

I can't help but feel stung at the idea Cameron was pulled from his thriving documentary career to swoop in and save my show. That, ultimately, Lyle had to beg him. Lyle's still pulling strings while Cameron runs defense, and all the while, I'm here, being pitiful.

"I didn't ask for Lyle to manipulate you like that."

"Of course not—"

I cut him off with an aggrieved slash of my varnish brush. "I didn't ask for him to do *anything*. I didn't agree to work for him, period. He inserted himself into the production, and he took it upon himself to interrupt your life."

"I was there, Shelb. I know."

I huff. "I know, too. It's just—I felt like I needed to say that. To be up-front with you, I haven't been pining for you. And I've been busy. I've made a career here. I'm content."

"I can tell. Honest. I didn't mean it to seem like I was swooping in to save you. I *want* to be here." He's so sincere that I'm baffled.

I turn to face him fully, my head tilting to the side, and I try to understand—try to put aside my irritation. "Why?"

"Why what?"

"Why would you want to do this? Why jeopardize your career behind the camera for a reality show? You walked away from television a decade ago. Why go back now?"

He releases a long breath. "I'm not jeopardizing anything. I haven't taken a break in years, Shelby. When I say I haven't been to visit since my parents' split, that's not an exaggeration. I've been on the road almost every day for the last six years. I needed to come home. See my mom. Stay in one place long enough to let the dust collect.

"But mostly," he says, "I want to work with you again." He hesitates, and then his lips quirk in a half grin. "And it would piss Lyle off that we'd be the center of attention without him."

Another huff escapes before I can stop it. "That's true, though I can assure you, he'll find some way to make it about him."

I dip my brush and we go back to work in silence while I think. Our arms and hands work in smooth synchronization, bringing the shelves to gleaming life.

Finally, I say, "Lyle has always been jealous of you."

"Me?"

"Yeah. I mean, I know I made that snarky comment about the beard, but it's more than that. At the time, I didn't understand it. But he was always trying to one-up you. I think that's really the only reason he ever wanted me."

"But why would he be jealous? Bearing in mind this was ten years ago and we were teenagers, but he *got* you."

I sigh softly. "I wish he hadn't in the end. But, Cam, *you* had me *first*. Anyway"—I shake my head—"you're right, that was a lifetime ago. So, now what?"

Cameron brightens and I'm struck all over again with how good-looking he's become. He was always cute—all swoopy hair and eyes twinkling with mischief—but now he's something else altogether. Sexy and self-assured. "I guess we're doing this, for real."

"I guess we are. In case I forget to say it later: thanks, Cameron. I know you have lots of reasons to come back, but I appreciate it, nevertheless."

"Of course."

We replace our masks and soon our brushstrokes are matching. I'm humming under my breath and a little surprised to realize how relaxed I feel with him next to me. I can't even work with my dad next to me most days. It's why I built my own shop. But somehow, Cameron's presence doesn't feel like a disruption.

"Full disclosure, and you can't ever tell Lyle this because he's a fucker, but that video clip he showed us may have played a part in my decision."

I snort. "You're joking. That was so cheesy! It reeked of desperation."

His green eyes twinkle with humor above his mask. "I know, but it worked!" Cameron runs his free hand through his hair, mussing the waves. "It reminded me of what we were."

I press my lips together, stifling a suddenly shaky exhale. After a beat, I scoff, "Two hormonal kids with a crush."

His expression is unreadable. "Be that as it may, it reminded me how well we worked together. And how much fun we have on-screen. And that we've always had a natural chemistry."

My heartbeat picks up. "You think?"

"I do." He puts his brush down and gestures widely. "Fine. Honesty time. Would I like to work with you again? I wasn't sure before," he says. "But ringing that bell and seeing you kind of clinched it for me. You've got stain in your hair, it smells like french fries in here, and you're listening to—is this Bryan Adams?"

"It's vocal standards!"

He cuts me off with a laugh. "It doesn't matter! This is the most at peace I've felt in years. *Years.* Listening to you hum under your breath. Staring at this piece of art you've created. It's . . ." He searches for the words, his hands dropping to his sides. "I like it. A lot. And I think we could be good at this. Maybe Lyle is in it for himself, but he's not wrong about us working well together."

I take a deep breath, letting his words sink in, and try to imagine it. Me and Cam working side by side, on camera, rehabbing houses.

"I still have to talk with my dad about it." I hedge. "I mean, I've been kind of a chicken about telling him. I don't want him to think I believe he's a charity case or anything. He'll be afraid I'm being taken advantage of."

"Ha. He didn't see you in action in L.A. like I did. If he had, he'd know he has nothing to worry about. Besides, I'm the one he needs to be concerned over. He has weeks to make me into a respectable general contractor."

"Respectable?"

"Believable, at the very least."

"We don't want you to embarrass the Midwest."

His head sinks backward with a groan. "Such pressure

to perform! We should also consider going to the historical society and the city council. The producers only care about ratings, but I was thinking about it on my drive over, and we have an opportunity to do something positive for the local economy and community with this. We can highlight local builders and tradesmen, like your dad. And we could stay within reasonable budgets to make sure that we aren't gentrifying the community when we flip. Improve, but not drive it into the ground, leaving nothing but a ghost town behind."

I can't help the smile spreading across my face. "Just a little thinking on the way, huh? I thought you said you weren't convinced until you got here?"

"Well, I might've done a little daydreaming."

"I like it, Cam. And if they want us bad enough, we can add those kinds of stipulations into our contracts to make sure things are on the level."

His eyes brighten at that. "They really want *you,* Shelby. So much I'm tempted to fuck with Lyle for a bit to make him sweat."

I laugh and it feels so good. "I've missed you."

Cam picks up his brush and returns to the shelf. "Me, too."

5

CAMERON

SUCKER

My mom moved last year from the four-bedroom, two-story Victorian she'd shared with my dad for twenty years to a cozy bungalow outside Grand Rapids. She no longer needed all the space, living alone, and the upkeep was a hassle to manage on her own. I sent her Zillow ads, arranged a real-estate agent, and gifted her the down payment, while my brother, Derek, did the legwork on the ground. I was filming in New Zealand and couldn't get away, but I wanted to do what I could to take care of her from afar.

Was I also trying to avoid confronting and subsequently packing up two decades of brittle history?

Probably.

I will admit to thinking the timing was convenient until a few weeks ago, when I showed up, the shame-faced prodigal son, on my mom's doorstep, needing a place to crash while I got settled in for my new starring role in a reality show.

Paul Riggs will shit a brick when he hears. I'm almost sad I won't get to see it.

At any rate, I wasn't exactly disappointed to learn her spare bedroom was full of enough exercise equipment to supply a gym. On the plus side, she's healthier than she's been in years. On the plus-plus side, I had to sleep on the couch. Which I did, happily, while coordinating with my old college roommate, Kevin, to find a rental in Le Croix, Michigan.

Classic Cameron Riggs. Make sure your exit strategy is in place at all times.

To be fair, I was raised by my mom. She was the one who lived with me in L.A. during filming for the years I spent on *The World According to Jackson,* and we've always been close. It's not that I want to be away from her so much as I need to escape the memories of *him.* Everywhere I look in this fucking (charming) house, he's there. His eyes follow me from every photo frame; his disapproval follows me from every trophy and yearbook, and the taxidermized deer head that bears his and my brother's names.

My mom missed the memo that said when you divorce your husband of twenty-five years, you're supposed to sell all their belongings in a yard sale.

Noticeably absent are any carefully clipped-out paraphernalia from my six years at *National Geographic*. I'll just assume my dad took those with him when he left. He probably wanted them close by so he can stare at them every day with pride in his cold heart.

It *almost* makes one think they shouldn't choose their career based on their jackass parent's wishes—as if they should stick to what (and who) makes them happy and say fuck all to the rest. Or at least it *would* make one think, *if* that line of thinking wasn't a one-way ticket into existential crisis.

It's obvious Paul Riggs has still got way too much power over my life. I'm man enough to admit this, but also, a college degree and six years of hard work is a big fucking commitment to just walk away from out of spite.

Walking away because of a woman? That might be worse.

• • •

I don't immediately drive to Le Croix, the quaint Lake Michigan beach town where I'll be living for the foreseeable future. Kevin isn't expecting me for another few hours, and I want to take the opportunity to study the area. I need to put on my research lens and tuck away my emotions. I don't bother with Google Maps. The sun has broken through the morning cloud cover, and while it's not warm, it's not freezing either, so I crack open my windows and drive. No radio, no voices, phone on Silent. All my senses are open and ready to take in the lakeshore of northern Michigan.

Everything is still asleep. The grass is brown and matted from repeat winter snowfall. Farm field rows are patches of spiky harvest leftovers. Bare tree limbs clack against each other, surrounding random outcroppings of centuries-old family cemeteries.

This is sacred ground. Families settled here hundreds of years ago and never left. They bore their children in these homes. They buried their loved ones in their backyards. Their blood, sweat, and tears—everything a sacrifice to their crops. Tiny, white clapboard evangelical churches sit every few miles. Wood piles rest on the side of the road, advertising warm homes. Farm-fresh eggs. Winter squash. Union pride. God's country.

I know what Lyle expects: dried-up and backward and slow. Bingo in church basements and chicken broils. Flea markets and livestock auctions.

And that's all here, but I vow with everything in me that I will give this area the same treatment I would the cloud forests of Central America; these people deserve as much. I'll seek out the vibrancy. Gingham-checked tablecloths. Smiling cheeks, freckled in the sunshine. The dark earth speckled chartreuse after early April rains.

I want viewers to smell the earthworms on long gravel driveways. I want them to hear the chirping of western chorus frogs. I want them to feel the moment when the grass beneath their bare feet changes from prickly to soft. I want their souls to lift in praise on Sunday morning and curse the early call of Monday morning's workload. I want them to feel like they know the good-bad-best-and-ugly about everyone in these towns, without revealing their secrets.

I want to do this right. Even if I'm not the one behind the lens this time, I can maneuver things to capture the big, brilliant heart of this place. My parting gift can be to cancel out whatever garbage Lyle has up his sleeve.

It's not long before Shelby creeps into my thoughts. I can't separate her from this. That's the nature of reality television. To make this work, we need viewers to tune in week after week. This needs to be binge-worthy and that's Shelby. She brings the story and the local connection.

By now I'm hitting the edges of Le Croix. The athletic

fields are sprawling, and the buildings are coming closer together and have a trendy, liberal tilt to their exteriors. Rainbow pride flags, Black Lives Matter signs, people walking their dogs and riding bikes and sipping coffee as they FaceTime with friends. It's still the Midwest, and we're only minutes from the farm fields, but it's like a whole different world.

I turn on my phone's GPS and it navigates me to my friend's building, just a block from Lake Michigan. I drive around another few minutes, looking for street parking, before giving up and pulling into a parking structure. If it were up to me, I'd drive around longer, looking for a cheaper option, but I'll happily bill this to Lyle.

Lake Shore Distillery is modestly full for a Saturday afternoon. It's dimly lit with soft recess lighting and warmed by a huge stone fireplace in the center of a wide-open sitting area. Everything is glass and hardwoods, and flames reflect off every gleaming surface. I head directly for the bar and settle myself on a white oak stool. A bartender places a napkin in front of me.

"I'm definitely going to have a drink, but I'm looking for Kevin VonHause?"

"Riggs!" a voice shouts from the doorway leading to a kitchen area of sorts. It's Kevin's wife and college sweetheart, Beth. Before I'm off the stool, she's in front of me, her arms wrapping me a warm hug. I stare at her growing belly. "Beth! When are you—"

She laughs. "Not for another four months or so. It's just so soon after the other two. These days, all Kev has to do is look at me and I'm knocked up again. It feels like I've been pregnant for years, honestly."

"You wear it well," I say. And I mean it. Beth's heart-shaped face is glowing.

"Kev's in the back on a call with a distributor." She waves a hand at the bartender. "Take five, Sven. This is Cameron Riggs. He's basically family and he's not going anywhere."

She slides behind the bar and starts preparing me something without asking what I want. I don't argue. It's four o'clock, but I'll never turn down a meal, so I grab a menu. "Anything to eat here?"

She rolls her eyes. "Obviously. Locally sourced, with vegan and gluten-free options."

I grin. "A cheeseburger is fine."

"How long are you here? Are you really staying for a while?"

I tell her about the job while she shakes my cocktail. "House special old-fashioned," she says, passing me the glass. "On the rocks."

I take a sip, and she walks back to shout my order to the cook before settling down on a stool next to me. "So, reality television, huh? That's a far cry from *Independent Lens.*"

This time I take a big swallow and relish in the burn. "Yeah."

She doesn't say anything more before Kevin walks out, wrapping me in a bear hug that fits his monstrous size. I'm large, but he's colossal. Six foot six and three hundred pounds of pure Viking, easy. While my beard is trim and neat, his is groomed but hangs to his collarbone. His thick blond hair is parted in a severe line to the side, and he wears thick red plastic glasses. He's wearing suspenders to match the frames over a plaid shirt and jeans. He's a hipster lumberjack banjo-playing distillery owner and I've missed the fucker.

We were roommates before either of us could grow facial hair. Kevin met Beth our freshman year and that was it for him. He worked for a few years painting houses with her dad before saving enough for prime real estate in downtown Le Croix, just off the boardwalk.

"I assumed it was you after I saw an order come through for a plain old cheeseburger."

"You can't take the Midwest out of the guy."

"After you're done, I've got a place for you to look at."

"Already?"

Kevin grins. "I know, right? One of our renters just wrapped on their residency. Moving to Seattle. Available at the end of the week."

"Sounds perfect."

"Well, look at it first. If it's not your deal, I have some friends who might have other options."

"Sure," I agree easily, but I already know I don't care what it looks like. I'll be taking it.

"Where's Shelby?"

Beth smacks his shoulder.

"What? Is it supposed to be a secret? He's been not-so-casually mentioning the woman for the last ten years. And they happen to both be here, in Michigan, where he's suddenly interested in filming a home-reno show, and less than a month later he's all 'Hey, Kev, guess what? In totally unrelated and irrelevant news, I'm quitting my illustrious career as world-traveling documentarian and moving to Le Croix where I have never mentioned wanting to live ever.'"

I swirl the ice in my glass and put it down. "I didn't quit. I'm on sabbatical. And I just saw her again for the first time in years, like, a month ago, and it was orchestrated by that fuckwit Lyle Jessup. To say it's complicated is a complete understatement."

Kevin's shit-eating grin widens at the mention of my former costar's name. "You fucker, Riggs." He takes a bottle off the shelf and pours me another two-fingers' worth straight into the glass. "You'll be apprenticing under her dad?"

"Starting Monday. A two-week crash course in home reno while the execs get their ducks in a row and hire a crew. They want to be ready to film as soon as the weather is stable and make sure they get an entire pilot episode's worth."

"I love it," Beth says after sidling up and listening to our conversation. "Those shows are my addiction. So comforting and adorable. I can't wait to see you two in action. I literally grew up watching you moon over each other every week for years. Be ready, Cam. People are going to go bonkers with speculation."

"I believe you're thinking of Lyle and Shelby. I wasn't part of that."

Beth rolls her eyes at her husband. Kevin holds his hands up, defensively. "I told you. He's in denial."

"It was ten years ago. And a kid's show. Not real life."

"And now?"

"And now we're on a reality show. Even *less* real than the scripted kind."

"Except you really are friends in real life, right?"

"Sure. At least, we used to be. I can see it happening again."

"Friends who also *love* each other?"

"Christ. *As friends.*"

"*I* love you as a friend, Riggs."

"Thank you."

"This is where you tell me you love me back, you dick."

I take in his hulking form. "As a friend who loves you, I beg you to rethink the suspenders."

He takes the cue. "As a friend who loves me, you should *respect* my decision to integrate suspenders into my wardrobe."

"But why should I when there are belts?"

"I'm three hundred and seventeen pounds of pure sex, Riggs." He rubs a thick hand down his chest, and I try not to choke on my drink. "I can't be contained by a mere belt."

• • •

The apartment is above Kevin's distillery, and I end up taking it. Kevin's questionable taste aside, the place is perfect. Simple, comfortable, furnished, close to my friends, and available immediately. There's a back entrance that grants plenty of privacy, but honestly, it doesn't matter. No one recognizes me on the street these days. I'm a little surprised Shelby knew who I was. The beard really throws people.

But she's exactly the same. Same long blond waves tucked under a ball cap. Same slim frame. Same legs for days. Same stunning girl-next-door looks. I suspect she deals with a lot of recognition, since she hung around the scene longer, but it seems like folks up here are plenty respectful of her privacy.

I'm counting on that to continue after we start filming. So far, so good. Her dad, Daniel, is a bulldog in Dickies. I don't think she notices. He plays the easygoing tradesman, but his grip on my outstretched hand was enough to make a lesser man weep.

I hope to God he's around when Lyle comes knocking.

Today, Daniel is introducing me to the Correct Way to Demo a Kitchen.

"It's not like they do it on those other shows," he grouses, gesturing at me with a mallet, and I'm immediately aware of why Daniel didn't fly with test audiences. He's a genius at what he does, but he doesn't give a shit if you like him. This, admittedly, makes me like him a whole lot.

"They're looking to demolish down to the bones. We're looking to restore. If you go too hard on your strikes, you could damage the integrity of the building. So often in these homes, they're covered in layers. Decades of restoration stacked on top of one another. Usually, those layers will preserve the original house deep underneath. If you're careful, you can reveal it, then reinforce it to make it safe."

"Like an archeologist," I say, stuffing my hands in my pockets. "I once filmed some ancient Mayan digs for *Nat Geo.* Tedious work, but the payout was awesome. To be the first person to reveal something since it was originally buried, sometimes millennia before."

Daniel chokes on a laugh, but his eyes are approving. "Well, hopefully these houses aren't that old and decrepit, but yeah. Just like that. We're the archeologists of these homes."

I can't wait. Daniel's enthusiasm is contagious.

We break for coffee and I ask, "Does it bother you that they're bringing me in? Instead of it being you and Shelby?"

Daniel shakes his head. "Hell, no. Better you than me. I'm too old to be worrying about being filmed while I'm trying to work." Daniel agreed to stay on for a consultant fee, with the caveat that he was never, ever in front of the camera.

"How do you feel about Shelby doing this?"

He hesitates.

"It's okay," I reassure him. "I want the truth. I wouldn't ask otherwise."

"I'm not crazy about it," he concedes. "I don't trust Lyle Jessup, and I don't believe they won't try to take advantage of her." I exhale, a little uneasily. I knew this already from Shelby, but it's still hard to hear.

He squints at me. "I remember you from back then, kid. I wasn't around as much as Ada Mae, but I still checked in from time to time." This is one of many differences between Daniel and my dad. Daniel turned up on set over the years, while L.A. may as well have been on the moon to Paul Riggs. Daniel continues, "And you were always around, even when you weren't in a scene. Just close enough, literally dancing around the edges in those tap shoes of yours, watching my girl."

I feel my face flame. What is it with *everyone* digging that shit up? I was a kid with a crush, and *by the way,* it was mutual.

"She showed me the letter you left her in L.A."

I wince at the memory, and thankfully, he lets it drop.

"I didn't want her to do this show," he admits. "But I'm proud of Shelby and who she's become, and she thinks she needs this. She wants to show the world that she's not that broken girl anymore."

I don't say anything. I want the same.

"But I'm trusting you to take care of each other. Watch her, like you used to, and let her look out for you."

"I don't think she wants me dogging her steps."

"You misunderstand. I don't want that either. Just be there beside her and let her be beside you."

I release my breath in a gust. That sounds okay. "That I can do."

6

SHELBY

GOOD 4 U

One of the first things I did when I moved into my own place and got a little acreage to roam was get myself some chickens and a few barn cats to catch the mice in my workshop. I've always liked animals, but Ada Mae claimed she was allergic, and my dad worked long hours. In California, my schedule was impossible.

Once I settled in Michigan, I converted a small, dilapidated shed into a roost and spent a determined Saturday afternoon putting up a chicken-wire fence that offered plenty of room to range. My first batch was only a handful of chicks, just to make sure I could handle the workload, but I shouldn't have worried. Chickens are pretty self-sufficient, and the fresh eggs are a huge perk.

I decided to take on another batch after the new year. I picked them up from the post office just last week and secured them under a heat lamp in the custom brooder I have at my shop, so I can keep an eye on them.

I've named at least half of them, even though my dad practically growled at me that they're livestock, not pets.

Judith would beg to differ. She's as elegant and stupid as a one-week-old poultry could be. I hold out a palm decorated with dried-up mealworms and click my tongue at her as she picks her way around her crate-mates, sidestepping Carla's recent wet mess and Maria's outstretched legs. I wait for her, hand steady and patient, and soon she gobbles up the worms.

It's a small accomplishment, but it's taken me days of diligent patience to get this far and I silently cheer to myself.

"Ooh, pretty girl. Who's gorgeous? You're gorgeous. Judith is a star. A queen among mortals, aren't you?" I coo into the dimly lit workspace. Seeing that my hand is empty, Judith ruffles her down with an adorable little shake and skips back to huddle under the heat lamp.

The room fills with the yellow light of early evening and the stocky figure of my dad lumbers down the steps toward me. He pulls a chair over to where I'm on the cold concrete floor.

"What are you doing, Shelby?"

"Oh, you know," I say with a casual shrug. "Night out with my ladies."

He doesn't smile, but the corner of his thick salt-and-pepper mustache twitches. I'm not kidding, though. I stopped working an hour ago, at least, and have no plans to leave. I could stare at these little balls of downy fluff and cuteness all night and I just might do it. So what if I'm tired? Live a little, Springfield.

If only *TMZ* could see me now.

"I can't believe you bought more."

"You mean, because they're so amazing?"

He snorts.

"Or because you really, really appreciate all the quality free-range eggs you get for nothing?"

He chuckles low. "Jazz does love your eggs. Insists they make her baking taste better."

"Happy chickens, happy eggs," I say, scooping Betty, a spotted dark-feathered beauty, into my hands and cupping her close to my chest so I can stroke the top of her head.

"Listen, I came by to warn you. While we were wrapping for the day, Cameron got a call from Lyle. He's in town. Well, in Le Croix, anyway."

I purse my lips, not stopping my cuddling.

"I figured he couldn't stay away for long," I say eventually.

"I didn't think producers were really involved in the day-to-day filming."

I shake my head, replacing Betty with the others. "They aren't, as far as I know. But Lyle's not the executive producer, he's the showrunner. It's complicated, but basically, he's the go-between for us and Hollywood. So, it's not that weird for him to be in Michigan, unfortunately. He's expected to turn up on-site before things get rolling and meet with the cast and crew and locals."

My dad sighs, rubbing at his mustache, and looks uncomfortable.

"Spit it out, Dad. What's on your mind?"

"I don't like it, Shelb. This is why I didn't want you to do the show in the first place. You don't need it."

"Technically, maybe I don't. But we've been over this. I

wanted the opportunity to show that I've grown. That I'm happy and doing well."

"And the commission for me means nothing, I'm sure."

I blink, feeling caught. He presses on.

"Look, I'm not an idiot, kid. I know you're worried, but you don't need to be. I'm going to be fine. I don't need you putting yourself through this just so I can retire early."

"I'm not. Not completely, anyway," I concede at his look. "I really do want to prove myself, and to do that, I need your expertise. You're doing me a favor taking on the commission. If it helps you, great. I'd love nothing more than for you and Jazz to retire and take long cruises to places neither of you can pronounce."

"I never liked how Ada Mae took advantage of you. I know I should have done more at the time. You deserved better from me. And this, here, feels too close for comfort."

I shake my head. "Not even, Dad. Ada Mae pissed away my money before I even knew what a bank account was. She used it on plastic surgery and her boyfriends. You gave me a home, a career, a loving family, and a future. All things I can never repay you for. And now you're making it possible for me, and by extension, Cameron Riggs, to start off fresh. Take the fucking commission and let's never talk of it again."

My dad chuckles, low. "Fine, fine. I'll take it. And only because you're right. Cameron is gonna need my help if he's going to survive flipping a house with you."

My jaw drops in faux offense and I shove at his shoulder. His face turns serious, though. "Speaking of, you should probably see what those guys are up to."

"They aren't coming *here,* are they?" I ask, afraid of the answer. It's not that I'm scared of Lyle, but I'm definitely dreading seeing him. And I'd like to avoid that moment of "Oh, so *this* is where you've been hiding since I broke your heart and melted your career?" if I can.

Not that he would say that, but it would be implied in every loaded look, gauging his power to hurt me still, and I already hate him for it.

"Well, Cameron went to meet with him. I get the impression he wanted to speak with you both, but Riggs cut him off and promised to meet him at some distillery in town."

I can't tell if I'm relieved or annoyed. Obviously, I'm grateful for the reprieve, but Cam has to know it's temporary at best. I pull out my phone. Two missed calls from Lyle. I really need to get used to turning the ringer on again. I scroll to Cameron's phone number and hit Call.

He answers right away. "Hello?"

"Hey, Cam, is Hollywood Satan there with you?"

Cameron snorts. "Yeah."

I release a slow breath and can hear Lyle asking about me over the sound of clattering dishes.

"Your choice," Cameron says softly.

"I'd rather get it over with."

"Want to meet us? We're at my friend's bar in Le Croix. It's called Lake Shore Distillery."

"Will you stay?" I ask, feeling extra vulnerable. I don't want to need a bodyguard, but Cameron has always been this perfect buffer for the inane fuckery of Lyle and me together.

"Of course."

"Okay. I need to get changed. I'll be there in forty minutes." I hang up and my dad is getting to his feet with a groan.

"You sure about this, kid?"

"Thanks, but yeah. I can do this. He's on my turf, Dad. And he needs *me* this time." I kiss his scruffy cheek and grab my coat. "Close up behind me," I say.

A few minutes later, I've crossed the yard to my farmhouse and am scrambling up the stairs inside. I don't have time for a shower, but I yank my ponytail out and spritz some pretty-smelling dry shampoo at my roots, shaking it all out. I turn on the flat iron and walk into my closet, looking for something to wear. I don't bother second-guessing and reach for a flattering pair of dark-wash skinny jeans and a white boho tunic. I kick off my work boots and get changed, finishing everything off with a pair of coral-colored Tieks and matching dangling coral earrings.

"Alexa, call Lorelai on speaker."

A moment later, my best friend answers. "Hello?"

"Where are you right now?"

"Specifically? My kitchen, staring at my pantry. Tell me you have a better alternative than gluten-free instant oatmeal."

I grin at my reflection and twist a long lock through my flat iron.

"Lyle is in town."

"Fucker."

I snort, kind of loving how that's everyone's first response to his name. "Right. Cameron's got him at some distillery in

Le Croix and I'm going to meet them. Can you be ready in ten? I'll swing by. Please," I add, not even trying to keep the pleading from my voice.

"Obviously. See you."

The phone disconnects, and I finish with my hair, flipping it upside down and shaking it out. I apply a second coat of mascara and some fresh lipstick, pocketing the tube just in case. I try not to think about how long it's been since I trimmed my hair or got highlights or a manicure.

Forget a manicure, I stare at my fingertips with a grimace. When was the last time I smoothed my nails with a file?

No, it's fine. So I'm a bit out of touch with a salon. I work on furniture, for fuck's sake. I have chickens.

Taking a deep breath, I smooth down my top and spin from side to side. I know I saw Lyle a month ago, but this still matters. I want to say I look better than I did at twenty-two. Healthier, anyway, despite the lack of expensive grooming. Leaving behind a diet of meal-replacement smoothies and juice cleanses will do that for you.

Gah. Fuck it.

I grab my keys and purse and slam the front door behind me.

. . .

Twenty minutes later, I'm holding the door open for Lorelai. This place looks new and is a trendy mix of rustic and environmentally responsible. I instantly like it. The gleaming bar is obviously well crafted and cared for but not in an ostentatious way. Exactly my jam. Overhead, there are plenty of lanterns glowing, casting everything in a flattering and cozy light. There's an enormous fireplace in the center of the room, putting off just enough warmth that I immediately tug off my jacket, and Lorelai does the same. She raises her brows at my tunic.

"What?" I mouth.

She grins. "Nothing. You look perfect."

I flash her a grateful smile and search the room for Cameron. He's so tall, I figure I'll see him first.

That's the *only* reason I'm looking for him. Obviously.

I spot him right away, sitting at the bar, his body turned to face the door. His face registers recognition, and I walk his way, tugging my best friend behind me and steadily avoiding looking at the back of Lyle's head. I slow to a stop in front of them right as Cam stands, his smile wide. Stage smile. Cameron might've left the business but putting on a happy front to smooth things over will always come second nature to him. Lorelai squeezes my hand once.

"Hello," I say in as offhand a tone as I can muster, impressing even myself. Particularly because the inside of my brain is shrieking at being this close to the man who humiliated me and left me for *tragic,* so soon after our recent meeting in L.A. Not just soon, even. This is going to be a regular thing. I need to get used to it. My greeting reaches Lyle midsip. His hand drops, lowering a glass glittering with something golden and undoubtedly expensive, and he turns. My breath catches, automatically. His cool brown eyes take me in, toes to crown, and I feel instantly used up.

Just like always.

The worst kind of familiar.

Cameron, bless him, circles Lyle, blocking him from view and breaking the moment, to wrap me up in a big hug, practically lifting me from my feet.

The best kind of familiar.

"I'm okay," I reassure him with a whisper.

"I'm not," he quips, releasing me. "That was for me." I catch Lorelai's shocked expression over his giant shoulder. I can already see the wheels spinning. The car ride home will be interesting. I've told her bits and pieces about my history with these two men over the years, but that was when I thought that part of my life was over and done. Clearly, I need to update her, but hell if I know how to explain this.

Lyle has risen to his feet and is watching us.

"Lyle," I say, clearing my throat.

He grins, overlarge and sappy, pressing in to kiss my cheek. I hold my breath. I don't need to be inhaling his expensive cologne. I'm half sick to my stomach and one whiff away from choking out nervous tears. "Good to see you, Shelby. I didn't get the chance to say it before, but you look all grown up."

My breath rushes out in a huff. Jesus. Could he be any more patronizing?

"And I didn't get the chance to tell you, you look just the same. Careful with that Botox, Lyle. I've heard it can mess with your testosterone levels."

"There she is," he mutters, rolling his eyes. "Classy as always, Shelb." He turns to Lorelai, who holds up a hand in front of her face.

"Fuck no," she says.

I love her.

"Cameron Riggs and Lyle Jessup, this is my best friend, Lorelai Jones."

Lyle's eyebrows climb with surprise and he whistles low. "I finally get to meet *the* Lorelai Jones. I'd heard a rumor you two were friends."

Lorelai scowls. "Of course *the* Lorelai Jones. You think I would purposely lie about my name just so I could deal with jackoffs like you every time I went to a bar?" She turns to Cameron. "No offense, I love it here. Shelby said your friend owns the place?"

Cameron's expression is a mix of bemused and appreciative. Excellent. She could use more decent guys in her corner. He recovers quickly and turns to the bar, raising his hand. A blond giant of a man comes over from where he's been taking in our group by the sink. He tosses his rag over his shoulder and rubs his beefy hands together. His shirt is plaid, his forearms are tatted up, his beard is bushy, and his suspenders are lime green. He's like the Brawny paper towel guy's hipster brother.

"Shelby, Lorelai, this is Kevin VonHause. We roomed together in college and I can't seem to shake him. He and his lovely wife, Beth, own this place."

I reach my hand out and find it encompassed in his warm palm. "So nice to meet you, Kevin. This is a great place. I don't get out much, but clearly I need to be making an exception."

Lorelai is already reading a drink menu. "What do you suggest, Kevin? Best of the best?"

Kevin leans forward and points to the menu. "The best isn't on there. I save it for special VIP guests. My wife is probably your biggest fan, and she would murder me if I charged you for something off the menu. I know just the thing."

Lorelai looks pleased and sits down on a stool. "Cheers, Kevin. I'm digging your suspenders."

Cam scoffs with a friendly groan. "Don't encourage him." He motions me over. "Here, you can sit in my seat. I don't mind standing."

Kevin pulls his suspenders with a goading snap. "What can I get you, Shelby?"

"A lemonade if you've got it?"

Lyle mutters something under his breath, then says, "She'll take a Long Island iced tea. I'll cover her tab."

Kevin freezes in his movements and raises thick eyebrows at me over his ruby-red plastic eyeglass frames.

I swallow back my frustration and hitch a friendly smile on my face. "I can pay my own tab." I turn to Lyle. "Please don't presume to know anything about me anymore." To Kevin, I add, "Lemonade with ice, please. And if you have any cherries, I'd love a few. Is your kitchen open?"

He nods, his eyes twinkling with respect, and passes me another menu before fixing our drinks. "Thanks," I tell him. "I'm starving."

Cameron leans down over my shoulder, close to my ear, causing tiny goosebumps to erupt across my skin. He points to the menu. "Last time I was here I had the cheeseburger, and it was incredible."

I breathe in his woodsy scent, feeling like he must've walked in straight from a bonfire, and have to force myself to concentrate on the words on the page.

It's occurs to me, this man used to make me forget my

lines when he was just a kid. And that was before he had forearms the size of whiffle bats and smelled like autumn.

I come back to myself and slap the menu shut. "A bacon cheeseburger sounds fantastic," I tell Kevin.

"French fries?"

"Please."

Lyle huffs cynically.

"What?" I ask, tersely.

"You're about to be on television after years living as a civilian. You might want to watch the french fries and bacon cheeseburgers."

Behind me, I hear Cameron growl under his breath, and I elbow him, catching him in the stomach. He coughs.

I take a long sip of my lemonade and pop a cherry in my mouth, chewing carefully before saying, "If you want me on television after years of not, then you will take me however you get me. I'll be sober, healthy, and boring, or I won't be on at all. Your choice." This is bold considering a month ago I told Lorelai I would say yes to anything L.A. offered. Lyle doesn't need to know that, though.

Lyle holds up his hands as if I pointed a gun at him. "Whoa, whoa, whoa, easy. I'm not trying to start something." He smiles at Lorelai and quickly rethinks it when she slurps her drink while fixing him with a glare. After all, there's no *I* in Team Shelby.

"When are you not trying to start something?" I ask, conversationally. "What are you here about, anyway?"

"The usual, Shelb, I swear. I'm checking on my project and that includes my stars."

"All right," I concede. "Well, we're here and we're in good

shape. Cam told you he's apprenticing under my dad, I'm sure. We're going out on Monday morning with a Realtor to eye up some potential projects."

"I want a camera crew on that," Lyle interjects. "And in the future, I'll need you to run any viewings by my assistant, Caleb."

I stop short. "Really? The viewings? Why?"

"Yes, really," he says in that patronizing tone. Or maybe it's not patronizing. Maybe it's only him. Is this how he's always talked to me? And I just used to think it was attractive?

To be fair, I was an oft-overserved teenager. My attraction meter was woozy at best.

"We'll want to roll footage," he continues, "on all the prep work and acquisitions so we can bring the audience up to speed on the property after the fact. I realize these things can take some time in real life. It'd be a waste of money to pay a crew for months of searching and deal-making and closings. I'll send a crew down to get some B-roll footage of you two and the properties. Then we'll use whichever you choose for the pilot."

Lyle's shift into producer mode is subtle, but my subconscious feels it nevertheless and it's prodding me to remember that I can be calm and collected in the face of Producer Lyle.

Despite.

"That sounds reasonable," I say. "Though, my dad doesn't want anything to do with this." I chew on the edge of my nail, considering.

"He doesn't need to come, then. Just you and Cameron," he says dismissively.

This instantly irritates me. Lyle is like a pair of too-small panties: sexier than you intend while cutting off your sanity every time you inhale. "Yes, I get that part. But you see, on and off camera, I still work for my dad. He buys the properties and flips them. I make them pretty."

Cam leans around me, his elbow cradling me on the far side, just as Kevin puts my plate in front of me. "Your dad and I've talked about it. He's been showing me what to look for, enough that we won't look like idiots on film. We can have him off camera giving us his thoughts, too. It'll be okay. I bought my mom a house last fall. It's not that complicated."

I sigh. "I know. I just don't want to mess this up. You realize how critically people will be watching me? Looking for me to mess up? And honestly, I couldn't care less if they don't approve of me, but my dad built this business from the ground up. I don't want to risk that." Particularly since I'm suddenly the face of his livelihood.

Cam turns me on my stool and lowers his voice. "Your dad trusts you. The community trusts you. I trust you. You know more about all of this than you probably even realize. You are the furthest thing from a flaky celeb."

Lorelai snickers into her drink. "Shelb, you bought your jeans at the Fleet Farm. You barely count as middle class at this point."

"Hey!" I say. "They're Levi's and they look great on me."

Lyle looks like he's in pain at the thought of me buying anything at a feed store, let alone clothing. "I'll be sending wardrobe and a stylist. You need to get a haircut, too. Just a trim," he insists.

"You're kidding me. You can't tell me how to wear my hair."

"I can if you look like a farmer."

"She doesn't look like a farmer!" Cameron says at the same time as Lorelai says, "Better a farmer than an influencer!"

"Enough," I say. "It's fine. I'll get a haircut. But it will be on my terms from someone I trust. I've been a little neglectful of late and would want to clean up before getting in front of a camera crew, anyway. But nothing impractical. This isn't just for show, Lyle. This is my life." I toss a fry in my mouth.

"What about romance?"

I swallow wrong and choke on air.

"Lyle," Cameron warns.

"What?" Lyle glares at Cameron. "Are we still pretending you two don't have a history?"

Lorelai leans in to listen, her eyes far too interested, and I throw her a glare.

Cameron's cheeks are red under his beard and it would be charming any other time, at any other place, and for literally any other reason.

"We're not pretending anything," I say, feeling my face heat as Cameron's eyes lock on me. "But we haven't seen each other in . . . years."

"Shouldn't take much time to get reacquainted. You two were always too close for comfort."

I snap, my maturity out the window. "Says the guy who I dated for five years, faithfully, and then dumped me for my best friend!"

Lyle looks at Cameron and points to him. "Pot." And to me. "Kettle."

"The hell?" I shout.

Cameron shakes his head, looking around at the people

staring at us, and lowers his voice. "Watch it, Lyle. We were teenagers. This is a business arrangement. Act like it."

"Seventeen or twenty-seven. I don't care. But for one minute, I wish you two would just be honest with me and admit you were together."

Cameron raises to his full, impressive height, and I catch my breath, reaching my hand to rest on his forearm. He looks at me. I don't know why I don't want him to tell Lyle. It's not because I'm ashamed. It's because I'm *not*. Because of all the seriously fucked-up things that happened in my childhood and adolescence, Cameron Riggs and our relationship was not one of them. It was *good*. The highlight, even. The only glittering, magical bit, edging out even Boston cream donuts with my dad.

And I don't want Lyle to touch it with his greasy suspicions.

"Please," I whisper.

Cameron releases a slow breath, and for a half second, hurt flashes in his eyes, but almost as quick, it's gone. He turns to Lyle.

"We don't owe you anything. Take it or leave it."

Lyle's eyes dart between us and he shakes his head with an exasperated smirk. "Whatever. I don't need you to confirm it. I know. I've always known. It's fine. You're what the network wants"—he points to me—"and he's the only way I could get you to agree." He points to Cam. "Which is pretty fucking telling, but you guys keep lying to yourselves."

Lorelai steals a fry from my plate, and I remember I need to eat. Cameron excuses himself to the restroom, and I eat in silence as Lyle signs autographs and takes selfies with a bachelorette party that's just arrived. When Cameron comes back, he looks normal, but the air between us feels . . . charged.

I pass Lorelai my plate and grab Cameron's hand, jumping off the stool. Lyle is still busy, so I lead Cameron out back onto a quiet deck area. It's still too cold for outdoor dining, so it's empty out here. Without my jacket, a small shiver goes through me, so I move us out of the wind. A sconce light flicks on as a space heater flares to life. Cameron waves over my shoulder at Kevin in the window, and I sigh at the warmth.

"It's okay," he says before I open my mouth. "I won't tell him, but I'm pretty sure he knows we were *something,* Shelby, and he's super hung up on it."

"Lyle thought he was the first," I say in a rush.

Cameron freezes. "The first?"

"Right," I say, my words infused with meaning. "The *first.* He thought I was a virgin when we dated."

In the barely-there light, I see Cameron's jaw clench. He scratches at the beard there, absently. My fingers itch to smooth it. "And you don't want him to know you weren't?"

I shake my head. "No, that's not—I don't care. This isn't, like, some kind of messy misogynistic thing, and I didn't lie to him. He assumed, and I never denied it."

"Because you were embarrassed?" he guesses, sounding deflated.

"What? No!" I say, quick to correct him. *"Never,"* I promise. "Jesus, Cam, you were the best thing to ever happen to me! You were my best friend."

"So"—he shakes his head—"I'm confused. Why don't

you just tell him then? At least the timing of it so he stops trying to accuse you of something."

I slump against the wall, and Cameron leans next to me, his hands in his pockets. "I just don't want anyone to know. Like, my entire childhood and teens and even my early twenties were an open book. Between my mom and Lyle, everyone exploited everything about me. It was gross how many people were obsessed with my virginity back then. What happened between us was this incredible secret that felt like a piece of the *real* me, you know? I gave Lyle too much. I don't want to give him this, too. It needs to stay between us."

Cameron runs a hand through his hair and rubs at the back of his neck. "Yeah . . . okay. I've never told anyone. Well, I told Kevin. But that was back in college and he won't tell anyone. Especially not Lyle."

"I'm not embarrassed it was you," I say again. "I'm grateful."

He shrugs, avoiding my gaze. "It's fine. It was a lifetime ago. And I'm glad it was you."

The breeze picks up and a stream of awkwardness grows between us, thick and roiling. Everything between Cameron Riggs and me has always felt at once insignificant and extraordinary. We were kids. It was only a crush. It was just sex.

I swallow thickly, knowing none of it was that simple.

"We should get inside before Lyle comes looking," he says softly, turning to go. Something in his tone is off and once upon a time I would have known what it was, but right now, I'm lost.

"Okay," I say quietly. But he's already gone.

7

CAMERON

GIRLS LIKE YOU

I wake up too early on Saturday, with a headache and a text from Lyle.

LYLE: On my way back to LA, looking forward to the b roll

I don't bother responding. We haven't even begun, and I'm already exhausted by his shit. More than anything, I'm annoyed that I subjected myself to this whole thing. I've spent years distancing myself from Shelby and Lyle, and in one fell swoop, I'm tangled up all over again.

In the basest of terms, I was apparently her practice fuck. Not only that. I was her *secret* practice fuck. At least it was only once. At least by the time I was in my twenties, I knew better.

Know better. I just need to follow through. Put some professional space between us. Remind eighteen-year-old Cameron that she's trouble for us.

It's only one pilot, I tell myself. Just enough time to renovate some dusty old home and patch things up . . . between me and my dad? Me and my brother? Me and Shelby?

Pick a number. I have a whole lot of patching up to do and not a lot of time, which may or may not be by design. How much grief and destruction can I cause in only a few short months?

I roll out of bed, setting a pot of coffee to brew, and start the shower, immediately turning it as hot as I can handle, letting the water pressure work at my pounding skull and shoulders. It's not that I drank a lot of whiskey last night, but I drank it for a long time.

I get out, dry off, and get dressed. By the time I pour myself some coffee, I'm calling my mom. She picks up on the first ring, even though it's barely eight.

"Hey, kid," she chirps through the speaker.

"Hey, Ma. I was thinking of coming out today. You gonna be around?"

To her credit—and my relief—her response is casual. Nothing like the machine-gun tears I got when I called to tell her I would be temporarily moving back to Michigan or when I told her I would be moving into Kevin's place.

"I'll be up to my elbows in my garden. Gotta get the plots ready for my veggies. What time are you thinking?"

I sip my coffee. "Midmorning?"

"Wonderful. Bring your muscles," she says. "I need you to move some timbers for me."

I groan, but she knows I don't mean it. Even still, she adds, "I'll treat you to lunch to sweeten the pot."

"You mean, you'll make me a sandwich," I say, grinning.

My mom's a lot of things, but she's not much of a cook. Whenever we were in Michigan, my dad fed us. When I was on the show, and my mom rented an overpriced studio apartment for me and her in L.A., we ate a whole lot of In-N-Out Burger while my dad and brother held things down in Michigan. Holidays were an experience focused solely on food. My dad would go all out, prepping and cooking for days, spoiling us and trying his damnedest to convince us to stay.

It's a credit to his cooking that he nearly did. (It's a credit to our forever-tumultuous relationship that he didn't.)

"Take it or leave it."

"I love sandwiches, Mom. I'll see you in a few hours." I hang up, shaking my head.

I lift my mug up to my lips, taking another sip as my phone lights up with a text.

SHELBY: DON'T LET THE DOOR HIT YOU, LYLE.

I snort, sucking coffee down the wrong pipe, and cough, trying to breathe through it. I didn't realize Shelby was on the text.

Figuring she's awake, I'm opening another text before I can stop myself.

CAMERON: You made me spit out my coffee.

SHELBY: Ha! Sorry. Too early for his shit.

CAMERON: Agreed. He needs a warning label.

My phone lights up a second later, and I'm grinning like an idiot, the weirdness of last night dissolving. This is reminding me of how we used to pass notes during tutoring.

SHELBY: CAUTION: Ginormous Ego Ahead. If you experience toxic masculinity and gaslighting, wash your eyes out with bleach.

CAMERON: And move to Michigan, presumably.

SHELBY: LOL NOT FAR ENOUGH though!

I'm suddenly struck with a mix of longing and a really, really stupid idea. My fingers hesitate over the screen for a beat while I decide just how masochistic I'm feeling today.

CAMERON: I'm heading to my mom's this morning. Feel like a visit? She'd love to see you.

CAMERON: And put you to work.

CAMERON: In her garden.

I glance at my watch and groan: 8:17 A.M. My convictions lasted almost twenty minutes. A new record where Shelby is concerned. Maybe she won't want to come.

SHELBY: I'd love that! It's been ages since I've seen your mom!

SHELBY: What time?

I sigh.

CAMERON: Can you be ready in an hour?

SHELBY: If you can give me an hour and a half, I'll make it worth the wait!

A shiver goes up my spine, and my groan echoes through my empty kitchen. *That's* not what she meant. Obviously.

Eighteen-year-old Cameron doesn't agree.

• • •

An hour and a half later, I'm pulling up the winding gravel road to Shelby's. I haven't been out here yet, and I slow to a crawl, taking it in. Thick rows of trees, evergreens and still-bare hardwoods, tower on either side of the long drive up. After a final curve, the property opens to several cleared acres. On one end is a huge state-of-the-art barn, likely her workshop. Opposite is a cozy two-story farmhouse complete with wraparound porch and a pair of mismatched rocking chairs.

It's amazing—and exactly perfect for her. At least for the new, independent, adult her I've been getting to know.

I park on the gravel in between the structures, and a large orange barn cat saunters past, giving me side-eye, before hopping up on the porch and perching on a railing, licking its butt.

Still perfect, I think. Maybe more so.

I climb the steps, noticing her front door is open behind the screen and a delicious smell is beckoning me in. My mouth waters instantly. She needed ninety minutes to *bake.* Sweet Jesus.

"I'll make it worth the wait!" she'd said. Not *that,* but almost better. It's been years since I had homemade anything.

I rap my knuckles on the door and her voice carries over, "Come in!"

"How'd you know it was me?"

She appears, hands on hips, huffing a long strand of blond hair out of her eyes. "Duh. I heard your truck coming up the drive. It's not like I get a lot of traffic out here, Cam."

"Nice cat," I say.

She grins. "Francine. She likes you. She hisses at the UPS guy. He's taken to dropping packages on the bottom step and fleeing in a cloud of dust. I don't necessarily mind. He's this guy I went to kindergarten with. Used to eat glue."

"Francine's clearly a good judge of character, then."

Shelby's eyes dance with humor. "If it didn't mean having him know where I live, I'd love to try her out on Lyle."

"Please call me if you ever do."

"First thing," she agrees and opens the screen door. "Sorry. Come in! Almost ready."

I step over the threshold, taking in her home. It's tidy but lived in. Blankets draped over couches, books and woodworking magazines stacked haphazardly across the coffee table, shoes and boots flung carelessly on a rug by the door. But there are plenty of what I'm figuring out are touches of Shelby's craft as well. There's a tiny Regency-era rolltop desk with lots of pocket drawers tucked in an alcove near a window. A low-lying blue sideboard behind her couch, painted in a Victorian style with whimsical wildflowers in varying shades of green and yellow. And the gleaming wide-planked oak floors, likely original to the house, though they look brand new.

"It's incredible," I say. "Feels like you in here."

Her cheeks take on a happy pink glow and something

squeezes in my chest at the knowledge that my praise still means something to her. She looks amazing in a pair of loose-fitting denim overalls and a slim, striped cardigan. Her hair is swinging in a high ponytail. The entire look shouldn't be as sexy as it is. She probably bought it all at that feed store Lorelai was teasing her about.

"Thanks. This way. I'm just wrapping up some cookies to take to your mom."

"I should probably test one out first. You know. To make sure she'll like them. She's picky."

"Oh, is she?" Shelby asks, playing along as she leads me into the kitchen. "Well, in that case, you may have *one.*" She pulls out another Tupperware. "From your own stack, though."

"You made me cookies, too?"

She blushes again. "Don't tell my dad. I usually send him home with my spares. I like to bake cookies," she explains, "but I can't eat them all by myself."

I crack open the container immediately, pulling out two. They're still warm. I take a bite and my eyes slip shut in ecstasy. "Holy shit, Springfield, these are good. My mom's going to adopt you."

She laughs, snapping the lid shut on the second container. "You're too easy to impress. But that's good to know. Baking is how I relieve stress, but I don't think chocolate-chip cookies are in my Hollywood-approved diet. You'll be helping me out if you take them off my hands."

I make a face, my mouth too full with a third cookie to say what I want, and she waves me off, seemingly unbothered. "Enough. I don't want to think about him. Let's go see your mom."

. . .

As I'm learning with most things between Shelby and me, the drive is comfortable. The years somehow melt away when we're together. It's sunny and almost warm this morning, definitely closing in on spring. Shelby's eyes are hidden behind a pair of aviators, and she's looking irresistibly cute in my passenger seat, cookies for my mom resting in her lap.

A pop song comes on the radio and I switch it off, scrolling for anything *not* boy-band adjacent. I land on some Vampire Weekend.

"Do you miss singing?" she asks.

"I sing all the time," I say, crooning along to "This Life" and obnoxiously snapping my fingers just off beat.

She swipes my hand out of her face and snickers. "You know what I mean. Of the *three of us,*" she says meaningfully, "you always had the best voice."

I shrug. She's right, but talent isn't everything. "I don't play any instruments. Can't write lyrics. Didn't seem like a solid career choice, honestly."

"Broadway?"

"Can't dance."

"Oh, please, Mister Taps Like Gene Kelly!"

"Used to, maybe. Who even knows, I haven't done a flap-ball-change in probably a decade. I just wanted out. Wanted to be normal for a while. Go to college. Have a roommate. Meet girls," I say, waggling my brows.

She grins at my expression. "And so, you met Kevin."

"I did. We were both ditched before the school year began. Our respective roommates dropped out and we were paired up last minute."

"Did he know who you were? Were you recognized in college?"

I nod. "Freshman year, I was. After that, everyone got over it."

"I bet it got you laid a lot freshman year."

My face grows hot, and I clear my throat.

"YOU DID!" she says, gleefully. "Shy little Cameron Riggs using a kid show to get some tail."

"Yeah, well. I guess the singing and dancing did help in some areas. I was always a hit at frat parties."

She shakes her head, still smiling. "I can just see it. Unreal."

"Kevin met Beth pretty much the first day of school, and they were inseparable. So, he spent four years living vicariously as my wingman. His favorite trick was pulling out 'Best Girl,' cuing it up, and then sitting back and watching the girls swoon."

"Swoon," she repeats mildly, a smirk teasing around the corners of her lips. I have the most intense urge capture it in my mouth.

Instead, I slowly lift a shoulder, my eyes flicking to hers. She arches a blond brow behind her mirrored frames.

"It had a solid return," I admit.

"I can imagine," she says, softly. Too soft, something delicate in her near whisper. "That song has always made me think of you."

I place my hand on her knee and squeeze, not saying anything, even though I know how she feels. There were times at parties when her new pop hits would come on the speakers. The sorority girls would jump on tabletops and sway their hips seductively, pretending they were her.

But they never were.

I go to remove my hand, but she grabs it. "Hey," she says. "Are we . . . good?" Her voice goes up a notch.

It's a loaded question, and had she asked me last night . . . the answer might've been different. "Yeah. Yeah, we are." I give her a small smile and something in her seems to settle.

"Good," she says, releasing me and turning up the music with a grin, both hands returning to the cookies on her lap.

Soon, I'm navigating us into my mom's cozy subdivision. It's close to my brother's place, so he comes over once a week in the mild months to mow for her. It's clear by the freshly cut lines in her tidy lawn that he's been here recently. It never bothered me that he's taken care of it before, but for some reason, today it does. I shove against the wave of guilt creeping up my esophagus. My mom understands. Of everyone, she's always understood—always believed in me and my dreams and knew that sometimes dreams took you far away from home—and that sometimes families weren't meant to be close.

I shake it off. Regardless, I'm here now.

My mom's in the front yard getting set up when I park the truck along the curb. She circles around to the driver's side, tugging me into her tight embrace before I can even manage to shut the door behind me.

When we were kids, my mom used to say she was trying to squeeze her love into us. Since my dad left, however, it's as though she can't squeeze tightly enough. Like she's trying to infuse it into my marrow.

The guilt monster surges, reminding me of the years I basically stole her from him while she was with me in California. Seven years they'd sacrificed our family for me, assuming they had their entire futures ahead of them.

I hear the truck door close behind me and my mom pulls back, surprise on her face, her hands flapping wildly. "Shelby! Is that you? Come here, girl, I want to look at you."

"Hi, Mrs. Riggs." Shelby ducks a little to hug my mom. "It's so good to see you."

My mom takes Shelby's face between her hands. "Mm, mm, mm, girl, you are as stunning as ever. I told you she'd grow up a beauty, Cam. Didn't I tell you? Stunning. Come here. Come sit on the porch. Can I get you an iced tea? Coffee?"

Shelby shakes her head, settling on the top step next to my mom. She passes her the cookies. "I'm so sorry about Paul," she says. "I didn't know you guys split up."

"Oh my goodness," my mom says, exchanging watery looks with me. "Thank you. It was terrible for a while, but I'm getting along much better these days. You brought cookies?"

"Not only brought. She *made* them," I say. "Fresh this morning. They're delicious."

My mom looks at Shelby like she can't believe she's real and I swallow hard, feeling my throat work. I shouldn't have brought her with me. Honestly, I shouldn't have even come.

I don't know what's happening with me. When I decided to come back to Michigan, I set off a ripple of consequences I'm not sure I'm ready to see through to the inevitable end.

"Well, I think I'll have one before we start. Did you bring your play clothes, Shelby?" she asks, as if Shelby's six and came over to ride bikes. "I've got a garden to get started."

"Yes, ma'am."

"Cam, there's a load of timber in the garage. I've outlined where I want the bed. Can you lay them out while Shelby and I edge?" She wraps her arms around Shelby, squeezing her from the side. "So good to see you, kiddo."

My mom always had a soft spot for Shelby when we were kids. I assumed she was just that kind, but seeing them together now . . . I'm not sure. Maybe she knew Shelby needed a little attention from a maternal figure who didn't have an angle. As far as moms go, I won the lottery.

I try not to linger on the sight of them—refusing to imprint it into my brain—knowing it'll only make things worse later. Shelby's just too easy to love.

8

SHELBY

THANK U, NEXT

On Sunday, I cut off all my hair.

Lyle said trim, so I get a bob. Not just because of Lyle. I wanted a definitive way to show the world I wasn't *that girl* anymore. I don't cry on cue, I don't take shots of tequila in club bathrooms, I don't flash my underwear on the red carpet, and I no longer let men make my decisions for me.

I make a last-minute appointment at my friend's front-porch salon and hand her a photo.

Maren's honey eyes widen. "You realize that's like a foot of hair coming off."

I nod.

"It's taken you years to grow it this length," she tries again.

"Probably a decade, honestly. But it's in the way. I'm always getting paint in it."

"Long hair looks good on you, Shelb."

I shrug. "So will short hair. I have the face for it."

"Just do it, Maren. She won't blame you if it turns out terrible."

I shoot a glare at Lorelai, who invited herself along. "It won't look terrible." I turn to Maren. "I trust you."

I've known Maren my whole life—long before stage moms, children's shows, public humiliations, and wicked boys. A million years ago, we were on the pageant circuit together. She always placed ahead of me, so my mother never liked her.

Too bad I loved her. She's one of a handful of people in the entire world who sees me as I am. If only Maren had been an overtly sensitive child, she might've had my life, and I might've had hers. Instead, I spent my teens as a pop star and she spent hers guiding muskie fishing tours in northern Wisconsin. I have to imagine her clientele was fifty-fifty sincere elderly fishermen and unruly bachelor parties.

Maren spins me around in the worn salon chair and pulls my hair close to my chin, tucking it in and biting her lip, considering.

"You do have the face for it. Round with high cheekbones. You'll look older. Short hair always makes you look older."

"I *am* older," I reassure her. "Besides, I'm not trying to look younger, anything but, honestly. Just . . . more like me. I want the outside to match the inside."

Maren nods, tucking her own shoulder-length auburn curls behind her ear and then, quick as lightning, twisting them up and securing them with a giant clip. Suddenly all business. Excellent. Maren doesn't really cut hair for a living. Her mom used to, so she has the tools. But years spent winning pageants have given her the skills she needs to make me look nice.

Plus, I want to keep this a secret. For a day at least.

"Okay." She gathers my long, golden strands in one hand, wrapping them carefully in a hair tie and holding the length out to the side so I can see it in the mirror.

"If you're sure, then I'm thinking all of it." She points to the nape of my neck and a thrill rushes through my belly.

"Perfect."

She squints. "Side part, maybe. Chunky and stacked in the back. So, longer layers around the face to frame the front and you can still slip it behind your ears."

Lorelai looks up from the outdated women's magazine in her lap and meets my gaze. She rolls her eyes, but it's friendly. "Jesus, Springfield, you're going to be so cute, he'll die."

I scoff. "Lyle can fuck—"

"I meant Cameron," she cuts me off neatly. "Obviously."

My mouth falls open as Maren asks, "Cameron Riggs?"

"Yes, *Cameron Riggs.* Cameron Riggs, who looks like a frigging Patagonia model and stares at our Shelby as if she put the ever-loving stars in the sky."

"Reeeeeally?" Maren drags the word out long enough for me to recover myself.

"No, not really. Well," I admit, "the Patagonia model part is true. He's stupid good-looking. But not the part about him staring at me." I narrow my eyes at Lorelai. "You know our history is complicated."

"Do I? Weird. I forget," she says casually, flipping a page and ignoring my glare. "Was he or was he not your first love?"

I feel my cheeks burn. "He was *mine,* as you well know, but I wasn't his. Practically the minute we had sex, he quit the show and left."

"And Lyle was there to pick up the pieces."

"It was a long time ago," I say, smoothing my hands down my leggings.

"So was my fiasco, but you like to dredge that up often enough," she mutters heatedly.

Maren snorts. "That's because you're too stubborn for your own good." She taps her chin with a pair of shears, winking at me in the mirror. "How does that new Drake Colter song go again?"

I grin, feeling smug. "The one where he waxes poetic about his many mistakes and is begging for his lost love to return to him?"

"It's a terrible pun," Lorelai grouses.

"It's called '*Jones*in'," I say, laying my emphasis on thick as syrup.

"We were talking about Cameron."

"We were talking about my haircut, actually," I say.

"Right." Maren snaps to attention. "But we will be revisiting all of that," she says, gesturing between Lorelai and me, "over some of those chocolate-chip cookies you brought after I'm done."

• • •

"What the fuck, Shelby? I said a trim!"

"Thanks, Lyle. I like it, too," I say on speakerphone as Rebecca, a friendly stylist, powders my face. She snickers under her breath.

"You don't even look the same! We asked for Shelby Springfield."

I roll my eyes at Rebecca. "Last I checked, I'm still her, for better or worse, Lyle. It's only a haircut."

"You look older."

"One of us should," I quip, pleased. "Besides, Cam grew a whole-ass beard, and you aren't up his butt about it."

Cameron smothers a smile behind his bear paw of a hand. "Don't you drag me into this," he mumbles low enough that Lyle can't hear.

"Listen, Lyle, we have an appointment with the Realtor in fifteen. I gotta go."

"Put Steve on!" he yells, referring to our director. Instead, I end the call.

"Oooh, he's gonna be mad at you for that," Cameron jokes.

"Ugh!" I say. My nostrils flare out, full of indignation. "He's such a jerk. How'd he even know about my hair?"

Rebecca grimaces. "Steve."

I glare over at where our director is talking with the lone camera guy, Darius. We'll have one unmanned camera in the car as we drive from house to house, with Darius following us while we do our walk-throughs and getting the talking head–style fillers as we discuss our thoughts on various properties.

"Traitor."

"I bet if you bake him some cookies, he'll be putty in your hands," Cameron suggests from his chair. Rebecca is rubbing some kind of waxy balm between her fingers and smoothing it through his beard.

I grin. "It's weird, isn't it?"

His white teeth flash in a wide smile. "Sort of feels like nothing and everything's changed all at once."

"I like seeing you in the chair next to me again."

"And I like your hair."

I blush.

Rebecca *tsks* at me. "Now I have to powder you again."

I wave my hand. "You don't. It's the Cam effect. I'm still getting used to him after all these years apart."

Cameron hops off his chair, brushing down his long legs. We're both dressed pretty closely to our typical style, just . . . more coordinated. But give that man a pair of well-fitting jeans and . . . somehow Cam isn't just Cam anymore. He's full-on *Riggs.* Gone is the boy who used to tap-dance into the hearts of little girls week after week (including mine). He's standing still, arms held aloft, as they hook up his mic pack. I can't keep myself from drinking in his powerful form, remembering the way he hefted timber on Saturday for his mother's garden, as if it was nothing.

Listen. It's been a while, okay? A bit of a drought, if you will—and in walks my first kiss, looking straight out of a Jack London novel, complete with a responsible brow and thighs the size of tree trunks.

Thighs that could easily support *me* against a tree trunk. If I was into that kind of thing and . . . I very much could be, if this man was offering.

(Confession: I've never understood the appeal of muscular thighs, but I've been converted. In fact, I am sorry for every minute before this that I didn't fully appreciate quads. Who knew Wranglers would be my kink?)

Cameron turns around, crouching to tighten the laces on his work boots, and I bite back a whimper.

Glory be.

Hallelujah.

Take me now.

"You ready?" he asks, guileless.

I hop off my chair, stumbling a step because of the high-heeled booties they've put me in. Sorry, Wardrobe, these will be the first to go after today.

"Not in the least," I say, my cheeks flushing. Not ready for filming and probably not ready for him. But when has that ever stopped me? "Let's do it anyway."

. . .

The first house is a dud. The second is better but not an automatic yes. I suspect Jazz was instructed to make the choice obvious for the benefit of television, because the moment Cameron pulls up to the third house, I know. This is The One. Full-body chills, Spidey sense, all that. Forgetting the camera is on us, I say, "Holy shit, this is it."

Cameron snorts and I shake my head, trying again. "Wow, now *this* has potential," I say with a little more decorum. *No bleeps, Springfield, this is a family show.*

"Fuck yeah, it does," Cameron says, flashing a blinding smirk right into the camera.

I snicker, undoing my seat belt and hopping out of the car. Lyle is going to rue the day he hired us. Jazz is already waiting on the porch. She's surprisingly good at this, never accidentally staring at the camera and perfectly natural while she tours the homes. I'm super impressed with my dad's girlfriend. He is, too, if the kisses he keeps stealing every time the cameras are off are any indication.

(Either that or he's just digging her new pantsuit. Maybe Talbots is *his* kink.)

The house is a 1920s Craftsman farmhouse on a parcel of

five acres. The property is beautiful. Sometimes these parcels are just square chunks of old farm fields. Still pretty, but almost zero shade and more work. Not this one. It's got a small pond, a grove of ginormous oaks, a cozy-looking shed, and a viable barn.

"I love it," I say with a sigh.

"Hold your horses, Springfield. What's the inside like?" Cameron says in a teasing tone and I can already see how the viewers will eat him up. So easy and handsome and rugged with his perpetual half grin cocked and ready . . .

Hold your horses, Springfield.

Jazz welcomes us to a very rickety porch, and up close, it's a lot clearer why this place is so reasonably priced. Cameron holds out a hand to help me skip the broken top step in my heels. He bounces on the decaying slats of the stoop, a beaming smile on his face. He looks like a kid.

"It's not supposed to do that," I remind him dryly.

"Built-in trampoline!"

I shove him out of the way with my elbow to follow Jazz inside and come to a hard stop the second I enter, my heart catching in my throat. Cam's hands find my shoulders from behind.

"You okay?" Jazz asks, concerned.

Cameron huffs in my ear, all minty breath and unrelenting humor. "I think Shelby needs a minute."

"It's perfect," I say wistfully.

Steve, the killjoy, says, "Okay, cut. I get it, Shelby, but we need something more than 'It's perfect.' Something positive *and* something negative this time. Build a little suspense."

My face burns. I'd forgotten I was being filmed, honestly.

"Sorry," I say. "This is just what happens whenever I step into an old house. Let me look for a minute and gather my thoughts."

I take a turn around the main floor, feeling the usual heady sense of reverence I feel whenever I encounter a nearly untouched piece of Americana. My fingertips dance along a chair rail, my gaze moving over the wide-planked oak floors and layers of thick, printed wallpaper. The kitchen is a mess. Usually are in places like these. Kitchen remodels are expensive and modern appliances aren't made to fit in the original layouts. My dad can fix it, though. Well, Cameron can, with my dad's help.

I climb the stairs and am relieved to feel them solid beneath my feet. My heart nearly thuds to a stop at the landing, though. From the top, the roofline crosses perpendicular in either direction. A bedroom in each wing.

But that's not what I care about. It's the long, planked landing with a built-in bookshelf running from end to end and lined with gorgeous, broad-paned windows. And it's *right there* in all its potential for glory.

I whimper for the second time in one day, but this time it's woodwork that has me yearning. I'm a simple woman. Give me a bearded man and a sun-soaked early-century Craftsman reading nook and I will love you forever.

Cameron prods me forward, but yells down, "We'll take the house, fellas."

"It needs work," I whisper.

"It does."

"That kitchen," I say.

I catch his grimace out of the corner of my eye. "It's bad. The second house is easier by far. Probably a safer choice for our first go of things."

I lick my lips and turn to him. He's so close, I can see the golden petals in his grass-green eyes. "But you just told them we'll take this one."

"Your dad would choose the second one. Solid investment."

"But you said this one," I press.

"I did."

"*I* want this one," I admit.

"I know." His lips curve into a full smile and my heart clenches. Other parts of me might, too. Parts that should not be in charge of decision-making.

"I can make something spectacular out of this," I tell him. "The potential is out of this world. This floor." I tap it with my toe. "The staircase. This built-in, Cam, I could seriously cry. This is special."

"Okay," he says.

"Okay?"

"Yeah, why not? What's the worst that could happen? I humiliate myself on television while Lyle rakes in his fortune at my expense?"

"Wouldn't be the first time," I joke.

He barks out a laugh.

"You won't humiliate yourself," I promise.

His eyes leap to mine, pinning me in place.

"You swear?"

"I won't let you. I can do this, Cam. I know I'm not my

dad, but I can do this. And I won't let Lyle humiliate you because I don't want him to humiliate me either. But *this place.* I can feel it. This is right. Trust me?"

His eyes never leave mine and he groans, softly, under his breath. "I'm not sure of myself around you," he admits, and I ignore the thrill that flares through me, white-hot, at his confession. "But I trust you. I always have. So, if you say this is it, this is it."

"This is it," I say. Praying all the while I don't mess this up.

He holds out his hand and it's warm and big and sure as I take it in mine, shaking once.

He exhales, pressing his forehead to mine, his lips barely a breath away, and says in a low voice, "Now. Let's do that all again, and for fuck's sake, try to look a little less terrified this time, Springfield. Our viewers await."

9

CAMERON

THERE'S NOTHING HOLDIN' ME BACK

We end up with the third house. Of course. There was no way, after seeing the radiant glow literally pouring out of Shelby on that landing, that her dad could deny her.

Or that I could deny her.

I'm so fucked. This is why I'm here, at zero dark thirty in the morning, waiting in my truck with two black coffees and a dozen donuts from Tim Hortons in front of Daniel Springfield's house. He's ready for me, shrugging on his coat in the yellow shadow of the porch light and limping down the steps, before pulling open the passenger-side door and climbing in. I pass him the coffee.

He sips once appreciatively. "Thanks."

As I'm pulling away, I grin. The curtains framing Daniel's large picture window sway back into place. "If I'd known Jazz was here, I would've gotten her one, too."

He scowls, but there's no bite.

"Where to first?"

"St. John's Street." After seeing the state of the kitchen at the Caroline Street house, Daniel grimly pulled me aside, no doubt sensing the sheer panic coursing through my amateur veins.

"Shelby has a helluva instinct for this, Riggs. She's a visionary. If she says this is it, then this is it."

I nod.

"But that doesn't mean it's going to be easy. This kitchen is gonna to have to be stripped to the subfloors and that upstairs has to have a bathroom. She won't like it, because she wants that nook untouched, but no one has only one bathroom these days. We'll have to make her see logic. Even if it means putting an addition over the kitchen in the back."

The blood rushes from my face and I feel like throwing up. This sounds like a whole lot more than I am capable of with my few weeks of experience.

He slaps my shoulder, undoubtedly intending the action to feel reassuring. "Monday morning, let's get started. I have some properties in progress. I can show you what I'm talking about."

This is why I'm here, chauffeuring around Shelby's dad before the sun rises, trying to absorb as much know-how as I can before filming. The thing is, I know I can fake it. I could very easily pretend I'm a knowledgeable contractor with years of cabinetry experience. And even the most skilled builders aren't experts in every aspect. That's why there are a dozen different people on a site at any given time. Inspectors and mudders and electricians and plumbers and designers . . . everyone has a place in the renovations and I'm not expected to know everything.

But Shelby has her specialty and I want to contribute. I don't want to only be the comic relief. That's part of the fun, and what sells, but I want her respect. I want to take this seriously. I want *to be taken* seriously.

But that would mean staying here, committing to this place and this life. Could I give up being a nomad? Could I leave the rat race behind?

What if I could be a master of *this?*

If it means following Daniel house to house, scribbling notes and growing hard callouses over blisters and enduring the snide remarks from the good old boys about my Hollywood history, I'll do it.

Whatever it takes.

"I wish you'd settle down," my dad used to say. *"Just pick something and give your whole self over to it. Instead of flying around God's green earth, chasing mirages."*

Is this another mirage? It doesn't feel that way. I think the extreme level of terrified I'm-gonna-fuck-this-up-itis keeping me up at night means I'm headed in the right direction. After years of swimming with the current, letting it lead me wherever, I'm finally striking out against it and it's exhausting.

But I like the look of the shore in this direction. I'm trying not to let that scare me. I have no less than four pitches from *Nat Geo* about potential projects in my inbox, and I can't bring myself to open them for fear that I'll grasp on to the easy out they offer.

That way lies the path of least resistance, but this way might lead to something real.

• • •

The days run together in a blur of binge-building apprenticeship. I can't tell if it's all sinking in, but I'm memorizing the jargon much the same as I used to memorize a script. The irony isn't lost on me, but I can confidently play a builder on TV. I won't know if I can pull off the rest until the camera rolls on Monday morning. This is probably why I'm sitting alone in the dark on a Saturday night, nursing a six-pack of beer at the Caroline Street house.

I don't want my first real day in this place to be caught on camera—I'd rather be familiar with this house that is either going to save me or make me into a giant idiot.

I crack open my second beer, taking a lingering walk around, reassessing everything with a more professional eye, noticing the soft boards where years of rot have ruined some of the original planks. My eyes skim the ceiling above, seeing the water damage that will need to be resolved, replaced, and patched over. I take a long sip from the bottle and swallow with a grimace as I turn the corner to the kitchen. After spending time in Daniel's other properties, this is worse than I remembered. The layout is a mess, with the tiny, outdated stove tucked against the outside wall and the tired stainless-steel double sink on the opposite end of the room. No space for an island, but it needs one. I pull some of the sketches out that Daniel helped me draw up the other day over lunch. I lay them on the counter and turn on the stove light, pleasantly surprised it works.

I take another sip from my beer and spread the papers out, smoothing the creases and turning them to fit the layout

Daniel and I discussed. It's nearly impossible to recognize as the same space, but for the window. We're keeping the lone window—soon to be a window with a large ceramic farmhouse sink tucked under it so the user can better enjoy the picturesque view of the rolling acres off the back of the house.

I grab the papers and pace out the kitchen, trying to place everything in my mind. I want this to be clear so I can paint the image on camera Monday. There's an entire wall that I think needs to come down. Daniel's not convinced, and I'm clearly not the expert, but it's not load-bearing and the single window struggles to provide much-needed natural light into this space. My instincts are telling me if we took down the wall, it would open things up and create plenty of room for a walk-in canning pantry.

With all this land, there's more than enough space for a solid garden, and gardens mean canning. At least, they do out here. Not that I know anything about it, but I'm learning.

I'm lost in my thoughts when my phone buzzes in my pocket. I take another quick swig and tap the screen. It's a text from Shelby. I finish the bottle, putting it down with a clink before turning to lean back against the counter.

I'm not sure what she needs at eight o'clock on a Saturday night, but I'm positive it's not what I want her to need, so I tamp down my expectations before I read.

SHELBY: Are you at the house? On Caroline Street?

CAMERON: Maybe.

SHELBY: Maybe I am too. Can I come in?

I freeze. She's here? Shit. I start for the front door. My phone buzzes again.

SHELBY: I have a key. I'm . . . I just realized you might not be alone in there.

I groan and swing open the door.

"I'm alone," I say. "I just . . ." I trail off in the dark. Shelby moves past me through the doorway. She smells like brownies.

She holds up a Tupperware. "I told you, I stress bake. I was driving by when I saw your truck in the drive. Is this okay?"

"You packed baked goods just in case?"

She grins, her white teeth flashing in the dim light coming from the kitchen. "I was on the way to my dad's. His loss is your gain." She looks around, no doubt seeing my beer and taking in the darkness, getting darker by the minute. "What're you doing?"

I scratch at my hair, tugging off my baseball cap and replacing it, feeling sheepish. "Nerves," I explain. "I needed to spend some time in the space, mapping it out, before the camera crews came. Daniel gave me the keys."

She puts the Tupperware down on the Formica countertop and spins to face me, tucking a strand of short blond behind her ear.

"I like to come to the houses, too," she says. "Before starting. Alone. Not always in the dark, mind you," she teases. "I usually turn on the lights because I fully believe in ghosts."

I lean a hip against the counter. "You do?"

She scoffs adorably. "How could I not, working in old

homes? In a way, I'm relying on those ghosts to help me reveal their stories. I need their blessing—to be worthy of their . . ." She searches for the word.

"Furniture?" I supply. She laughs.

"I guess, yeah. That sounds a bit insane, but you know what I mean."

"I do."

"So, lights," she says. "They chase away the ghosts."

"But you said you want their blessing."

"After the fact, Cam," she says pragmatically. As if talking about ghosts is even remotely pragmatic. "I don't need them breathing down my neck. No one likes a back-seat carpenter."

I snort. "Of course not."

"So." She straightens. "What've you got figured out so far?"

I show her the diagrams, and she studies them knowledgably, nodding occasionally and asking questions. After a few minutes, I've relaxed. I walk to the stairs, flipping on the light.

"Okay, that's what I've got. Your turn," I say, gesturing to the second level and trying not to think about how close I was to kissing her the first time we ascended these stairs together.

Dreamer Shelby is too damn tempting by a lot. It's good that we'll have camera crews recording our every move.

They're not here now, though. We're very much alone. Looking back, I probably should've held off on that second beer. I'm nowhere near inebriated, but I'm definitely loose.

Shelby takes the lead, hopping up the first steps. Her short hair bounces, wisps brushing at the nape of her long, pale neck. My mouth waters.

Then she's several steps ahead of me and I'm struck with an altogether different view of the gentle curve of her waist, the sliver of soft-looking skin just above the delicious slope of her ass.

She's wearing the hell out of those pants.

I shake off the thought, willing myself to cool down and follow behind her in a completely nonpervert way. Half a staircase between us is probably enough.

Christ.

I reach the top and Shelby's already doing a slow spin, her brilliant brain taking in the detail work. I settle against the door jamb of the far bedroom, crossing my arms over my chest and watching her.

Her long fingers skim the dusty shelves before she leans across to the windowsill, pounding once and trying to open the window. It sticks; painted shut probably. She tries again with the next one. And the next. She gets to the last one and huffs in silence when it doesn't budge.

"We might just have to replace them, Shelb."

She shakes her head. "Not if I can help it. They're still good. Airtight. Besides, they're custom to the house. If we replaced them, I'd lose the top shelf of the bookcase. It's all one piece."

I'm beginning to see what her dad was talking about. She's stubborn.

I sigh and move behind her, making a fist and banging against each corner as hard as I can without shattering any glass. She's right about one thing: the windows *are* airtight. I'm just not convinced it isn't a century of lead paint making them that way.

I reach down, a hand on either side of her and tug up, pretending not to notice the way her breath catches at my nearness or how I can feel the heat coming off the bare skin of her neck.

The window slides open with an almighty creak, cool evening air rushing in, and she gasps in pleasure. The sound shoots straight to my core, burning me alive.

A window for Christ's sake. Imagine the sounds she'll make when I take down that wall downstairs.

Fuck. No. Don't imagine that. Not while only millimeters from being pressed against the sweeping curves of her back.

I take a giant step away. "There. That wasn't that difficult. I bet the rest will open with a little elbow grease."

She spins slowly to face me, color high in her cheeks and her blue eyes full of something that's definitely not what I hope it is.

"A little elbow grease?" she asks, a smile teasing on her lips.

I try to look casual. "It's a bit cold to test the theory tonight."

"Weird," she says softly. "I'm not even a little bit cold."

I clear my throat awkwardly. "All done up here?"

"Almost," she says, back to business. "My dad thinks we need another bathroom." As predicted, she sounds unconvinced.

Right. Dad. Business. TV show. Lyle, that fucker. "Yeah, it's a three-bedroom, four if you count the den conversion. We need at least one more bathroom, up here, and ideally a second one off the master downstairs. For resale value."

"Where, though? I don't want to give up this nook."

"So," I say. "I've got two ideas. One is easier, but would affect your windows . . ."

"And the other?"

I make a face. "Don't you want to at least hear the easy one?"

She grins. "Nope."

"Fine. The other option is to extend out this way." I point backward over the other side of the stairs, parallel to the bedroom. "This is over the garage and the laundry room. Which means we could run the water and electric straight up."

"That doesn't sound hard."

"That's probably because I don't know what I'm talking about."

"It feels like you do," she says, her eyes doing that sparkling thing again.

I shift my ball cap and replace it. A nervous twitch. Like letting the steam out of a boiling pot, except the boiling pot is me whenever she looks at me like I'm more than I am.

"I've talked to Daniel about it. He wasn't against it, exactly. Just concerned."

"Concerned about what?"

I chuckle humorlessly under my breath. "That I'm in over my head. Under time constraints, production deadlines, financial ruin, that kind of thing. Particularly," I remind her, "since this is a flip, and we aren't building it for us."

"Us?"

"*You,* really. We aren't building it for you," I say, feeling inexplicably like a jerk.

"I know we aren't," Shelby says with a shrug. "That's the

business of flipping. You might fall in love with aspects of a place . . . and you should, but in the end, it's a gift for someone else. And I want to give them *the best* gift."

I take a deep breath and release it. That's the part I'm struggling with, I realize. *We're* building this for someone else, but I'm still building it for *her.*

"But why not do it the easy way?"

She presses her lips together a moment before responding. "Just because they're strangers, doesn't mean they don't deserve the best. Whoever makes this their forever home deserves a whole hallway full of bold windows teasing in sunshine or freshly mown grass or . . . whatever. They deserve bookshelves lovingly restored to house their favorite books or collectibles. They deserve a cozy nook for a respite from the world, and I can give it to them. *We* can. All we have to do"—she wraps up her impassioned speech—"is build a bathroom over there." She points to the invisible space next to the bedroom.

"All *I* have to do, you mean."

"Right." She deflates, shaking her head and exhaling sharply. "You're right. It's asking too much, especially with that shithole of a kitchen . . ." She turns slowly, taking everything in. I can practically see her rearranging everything to fit. "I can compromise," she says finally. "We can do it the easy way."

I should feel relieved. It's not for her. It's not for me.

It's not for us.

But I don't feel relieved.

I feel . . .

I groan. "We'll do the bathroom off the back."

Her fine blond brows scrunch under her bangs. "Cam, you don't have to—"

"You gave one helluva TED Talk about how it's a gift for strangers and not for us, but that's the thing, it's *from* us. You know? Shelby Springfield and Cameron Riggs. Our names are going to be on this house. *HomeMade* is ours. And I want it to be perfect."

"Nothing is ever perfect, Cam."

"Maybe not the outcome, but the effort will be. All in, right?"

Her smile is blinding, and I'm staggered. She is going to murder me. Just like she did when we were kids and again when she called me to come save her five years ago . . . and now. I don't think I'll recover this time.

I don't even think I care. I'll die happy.

"All in," she repeats and suddenly she's closer than she was before. "What did you mean, the last time we were here, when you said you're not sure of yourself around me?"

Ah.

"Did you mean," she continues, "you aren't sure about this project or did you mean something else?"

I could lie. I want to lie.

I don't lie.

"Something else. Well"—I hesitate—"both. But at that moment, I was talking about something else."

Please don't ask for details.

"I'm . . . not sure about myself either. Around you," she clarifies. She's so close, I can see the ring of black in her navy eyes and the dusting of freckles across her nose and cheeks. I will my hand not to shake as I brush soft strands out of her eyes and skim the line of her jaw. Her breath catches and her red lips part, opening and inviting.

I've kissed those lips before and I wonder if I do it again, will she taste like I remember?

Like I've never been able to forget?

"I'm not sure about this," I say, still closing the distance between us. "But I can't seem to stop wanting it anyway."

She swallows, her eyes searching mine. She reaches a hand to my face, her fingertips delicately tracing my beard before sliding farther down my jaw and settling against the pulsing place where my neck meets my shoulder, setting fire to my skin. "The thing is . . ." Her voice is barely above a whisper, yet it still echoes through the dim space, where only her ghosts can hear us. "I'm not sure of myself around you, but I've always been sure of *you*. Nothing in my life but you."

My hand slides around to that teasing nape, her hair silk between my fingers, and I bend down to capture her lush bottom lip between mine. She doesn't resist, pressing herself fully against me and sliding her soft tongue against my lips, seeking entry. As if I could stop her. My other hand grips at the back of her shirt, fingering the edges and tracing the warm skin of her waist as I open my mouth to her, devouring. She moans, the sound sending shockwaves south, and I step my leg between hers as if I could press us impossibly closer.

Her hips slide against me in a slow buck and I'm halfway to seeing fireworks from the simple friction. Her fingers reach into my hair, knocking my hat clear off and tangling in the short length, pulling as her talented tongue curls along with mine.

This is what I've been missing. For years, what I've been

trying to replace. Who finds this at eighteen? I've tried for a decade to convince myself that this wasn't what I thought it was—that *she* wasn't who I thought she was—and I was crazy to think it was so special between us.

But I've kissed other women. I've tangled with them and woken up in their beds and none of them, none of *that*, compared to this one searing kiss.

Shelby pulls back, her harsh breaths echoing in the silence between us. My heart is nearly thudding out of my chest, but it calms when she smiles, wide and gorgeous.

"I should go. I don't want to," she admits, her cheeks flushing. "God," she licks her bottom lip. I lick mine in reaction, glorying in her taste. "I don't want to leave."

"Then don't," I say, lust making me bold.

She shakes her head, slowly, as if dragging through quicksand. "I . . . Cam. We can't do this."

Her words are like a bucket of ice water poured over my head.

Of course we can't. What was I thinking?

I step back, putting even more space between us. This time, a chasm.

"Right. You're right. We can't do this. It would be a mistake," I say in a rush and for a split second, I think I see hurt flash in her eyes, but just as quick, it's gone.

"I wasn't—I don't think it would be a mistake. Do you think it would be a mistake?" she asks, her voice softer. Maybe even uncertain.

I exhale, trying to read into what she's not telling me. "I don't know. It seems like I'm always making an idiot out of myself, chasing you."

Her eyes widen and suddenly it's as if a light switch has gone off and she looks . . . mad. Furious. "What are you talking about? *You* left the show. *You* left me to go to college."

This makes *me* furious if I'm honest, because what the fuck? "And you waited a whole five minutes before hooking up with Lyle!"

"I was hurt and a kid! And you were gone, presumably forever."

Nuh-uh. She's not getting off that easy. "No. Not forever. The second you reached out, saying you needed me, I came back."

Shelby inhales sharply, her face reddening. "And then you *left me again.*"

"I apologized!"

"I know, and I forgave you!" Her aggravated shout echoes off the ceiling. "I don't want to be some wall fuck, Cam."

"That's not what I was saying." Even though, it kind of was. What am I even thinking? I'm not staying in Michigan. I'm here to flip this house and record the pilot. Just long enough to make sure Shelby is okay. And kissing her and igniting things between us . . . that's the opposite of making sure she's okay.

I'm a dick.

She tilts her head, blond strands escaping from behind her ear. "Really? What were you suggesting then?"

My mouth opens and closes, before opening. And closing. I can't bring myself to say it. The three words, "I want you," won't come. They strangle in my throat, tied up in guilt and grief and obligations.

The truth is, I deserve for her to say no.

I left her. Twice. Even if I had reasons and those reasons

felt like good ones at the time, I still left her. Why should she accept me?

I don't want to be some wall fuck. Jesus.

I do the only thing I can.

"You're right. I don't know what I was suggesting. I should go. I'm tired. It's been a long week for both of us." I start down the stairs ahead of her, scooping up the last of my beer on the bottom step and grabbing my truck keys. I need to get out of here. "You can lock up?"

"Sure," she says, uncertainty infusing the word.

I reach for the door and turn the handle before stepping back and turning a last time. In the dim light, it looks almost like her eyes are shiny, but I don't want to know for sure.

"The thing is," I say, my voice a croak. "It's not the same, but it *feels* like it is. With us, it always feels like the same old missed connections. Maybe we should listen to them for once."

For better and for worse.

I step out into the cold air, feeling it sharp against my burning skin, and shut the door behind me. Leaving her again.

10

SHELBY

TEENAGE DREAM

I found a place.
—C

My stomach does a flip-flop as I read the note before searching out his eyes on the crowded World According to Jackson *set. I find them instantly, summer green and loaded with intention, and nibble my bottom lip, nodding once. His answering smile is blinding even across the room.* My smile, *I think. The secret smile Cameron Riggs reserves for me.*

Our on-set choreographer, Jackie, pulls him aside to review the coming dance sequence and I tuck his words into my back pocket, keeping them safe. I'm in the next scene, so I slide in front of the glowing hair-and-makeup mirror, practically dancing in my seat, unable to sit still. My makeup artist, Shandra, is busy yelling over her Bluetooth to one of her three kids and I tune her out as she fixes me up, automatically covering my flushed cheeks and blemishes. She can't do anything to dim the wild look in my eyes, though.

Tonight, *I think with a giddy kick. It's going to happen tonight. Cameron and I have been stealing kisses for months, hiding out in dressing rooms and trailers. It's been all laughing whispers and fumbling hands between us, and it's been perfect. He's perfect. So sweet and cute and talented. God, his voice is like buttercream frosting and ice cream and everything yummy.*

I wonder if it will hurt; I've read it sometimes hurts.

My face flushes at the thought and I squeeze my knees together. Even if it hurts, it will be worth it. I want to do this with him. Take this step. Give myself to him—lose myself to him, completely.

The set has been unbearable today. Lyle's been flubbing his lines a million and a half times in the daydream sequence, and I swear he's doing it on purpose. Even ever-patient Cam seems frustrated with him.

Or is that sexually frustrated? *I wonder with a jittery zing that goes straight to places hidden from everyone but him. Cam's hand brushes against my arm and I almost jump out of my skin. He shoots me a surprised glance that quickly turns to a smirk. I stick my tongue out and his eyes zero in on my mouth.*

It's another agonizing hour before the director finally calls it quits for the day and I may as well have sprinted to my trailer for my stuff. My mom is sitting at her computer, headset in place like she's at frigging mission control. Which, in her mind, she is.

"All done for the day," I say, heading for the bathroom and pulling out the makeup wipes to remove the day's work off my skin. Experience tells me I'm less recognizable in public without Makayla's face. I slip out of Makayla's quirky uniform of super stylish jeans and artfully draped scarves and bangles, exchanging them for

simple khaki shorts and a white tank top. I step into my flip-flops and brush out my long hair, combing through the hair spray as best as I can. I don't know where we're going this evening, but I want to go as myself.

Tonight is about Shelby and Cameron.

There's a knock on the trailer door and I pull it open with a ready smile. My smile falls just as quickly. Lyle.

"Oh. Hey. What's up?"

"Nothing," he says, looking bored and also boredly attractive, if there's such a thing. Straight from a Ralph Lauren catalog. Classic all-American looks and a perpetual smirk, like he knows he's better-looking than you. I fully admit I used to have a crush on him. For like a minute. Before I fell for Cameron. "Thought I might hit the town tonight. Want to come out?"

"I hate those clubs," I tell him for the hundredth time. Lyle used to hang out with Cameron and me after work. We called ourselves the "trifecta of awesome," getting ice cream and skating at the skate park. But then Lyle started dating this movie actress Ashley Sparks last summer and she introduced him to the L.A. club scene. I don't even know how he gets into these places. He's barely eighteen, the same age as Cam. "You're going to get into so much trouble when you get caught."

His expression is dubious. I swear he practices looking like a jerk in the mirror. "If I get caught," he scoffs. "Dinner, then?"

I'm already shaking my head, my eyes darting around. Please don't come right now, Cam. *"Not tonight," I say, leaning against my trailer door and crossing my arms over my chest. "What was your deal today? You forget to study your lines?"*

He shrugs. "Maybe."

I scowl at his indifference. "Well, quit it. It's annoying when everyone else is prepared." He rolls his eyes, pulling out a cigarette, and I tug it from his fingers. "Not here. Gross."

Lyle snatches it back. "Call me when you change your mind." His expression darkens. "Oh, hey, Cameron. Surprised to see you here," he says, his tone oozing sarcasm. Lyle doesn't linger, though, slinking off toward whatever pack of girls he's hanging out with this week.

We watch him leave in silence, the sunny California air charged between us. "Ready?" Cameron asks in a low voice that sends goosebumps across my skin. He's changed, too, out of his Carter Nelson uniform, and his cheeks are ruddy.

"Sure," I say, a little breathless. "Mom! I'm headed out for some dinner."

She doesn't even acknowledge I've said anything. At some point she'll notice I'm missing, probably between her personal training session and her nightly massage, and she'll text me.

Cameron holds out his hand—my lifeline clothed in cargo shorts and a shy smile. I grab ahold with all my might and he leads me away.

An hour later, after we've grabbed some food so we're not technically *lying, he's pulling into a small, deserted grassy field, the sun sinking fast. "Dark Sky Reserve," I read.*

"Completely dark. No lights allowed. It's where you come to go stargazing away from the city," he explains.

"Won't there be other people around?"

He shakes his head. "Nothing to see. No planets or comets tonight."

A thrill rushes through me at his words. All alone. He reaches behind us and pulls out a backpack. "I brought us some drinks. And, um, other stuff." He stops, sinking back into his seat, unsure. "Is this okay? I thought this might give us the most privacy, but if you don't like it, I can get us a hotel room or something . . ."

I reach for his face, pulling him toward me and pressing a kiss to his lips. "It's perfect."

"Really?" He exhales in a gust, relieved. Gah. So cute. "Great."

He comes around the car, opening my door and making me feel like I'm in the movie Sixteen Candles. *I'm a dizzy Samantha and he's the grown-up senior, Jake Ryan, with a car.*

Except these butterflies beating around inside of me are so much more than a crush. They're almost suffocating.

He reaches for my hand and leads me to a quilt. There're a couple of pillows there, already. I wonder when he had the time to do this. The idea of him driving out here alone, setting this up, is so sweet.

The sun has quickly sunk low on the horizon, and I'm surprised at how dark it is out here. Living in L.A. means almost never seeing the stars. This view reminds me of back home in Michigan—an endless indigo expanse of glittering galaxies pressing down from above.

He passes me a water, and I take an automatic sip, but find I'm not very thirsty. He isn't either. Cameron leans back, kicking off his sandals and stretching his long legs in front of us. Then he reaches over, gently tugging me to him so that I'm laying snug against his chest, my head cradled between his chin and his shoulder. I press a soft kiss to the warm skin of his neck and his breath catches, his hold on me tightening ever so slightly.

In the last bits of light, his bright green eyes search mine. "I really like you, Shelby." My heart bursts into a million hummingbirds at the sincerity in his whispered words, and I'm too overwhelmed to speak. Instead, I turn myself in his arms, getting to my knees and stretching them on either side of his slim hips, taking his face between my hands and kissing him with everything I have.

We try to go slow, but we're not very good at it. Once I'm straddling him, feeling him strain against me, hard where I'm soft, and his hands are tugging my shirt over my head, his fingers dancing inside my bra, cupping me, before his tongue is flicking against my fevered skin . . .

I whimper and crush against him and he barks out a surprised laugh before hungrily pulling me closer. He flips me gently onto my back, hovering over me and slipping my shorts down my legs, revealing me to him. The dark hides his features, but the way his breath catches thrums through my veins, and I swear I can hear his heart beating.

Soon we're both bare and he's digging in his pack for a condom. He fumbles for a moment before shakily lowering himself next to me on the blanket.

"I want to take care of you first," he whispers, low. "I'm afraid I won't last."

"But . . ."

"Please, Shelby. I want to be good for you."

His long fingers splay across my flat stomach and purposefully glide down to my center, dipping and swirling, drawing me out. He captures my whimper between his soft lips and in them, I feel his smile. I'm so close, so close, *and he can tell. We've been here before, but it's never been quite like this, bringing me to the brink and for the first time, not stopping, not hesitating. Stars burst behind my eyelids and I crush in on myself, overwhelmed, calling out his name to the smothering sky, my fingers wrapped in his hair, until eventually I slip, boneless, against the blanket.*

I release his hair and feel his mouth against my collarbone, masculine and proud. I pull him up, kissing him.

"Are you ready?" I ask.

"God, yes."

I nudge him over me, guiding him. My knees fall open, shaking a little and he hovers, before gracelessly taking me all at once.

It hurts, but I'm still buzzing from his fingers and it's mostly a good kind of hurt. Like he's branding me to my very bones. I trail my fingers down his smooth back as he sinks into me, stretching me, burning me alive. My breath catches, and I force myself to release it.

"Are you okay?" he asks, before groaning, "God, Shelby, I'm sorry, I'm—"

He jerks on top of me, and I bite my lip to keep from crying out at the stinging between my legs as he comes, but as his forehead sinks to my shoulder, I can't help but press a soft kiss to his neck. I'm feeling overwhelmed. Tender inside and out.

Because right then, under the stars, he's mine and I'm his. Two halves becoming a whole.

• • •

Sunday morning finds me staring at the four walls of my bedroom, cursing the brilliant yellow sunshine for searing into my seething brain.

I'm such an idiot.

First-class, last-class, *no-class idiot.*

Five years. *Five years* I've spent putting up boundaries and one stupid kiss undoes them all.

And then he calls it a mistake?

Hot tears flood the corners of my eyes and I swipe at them angrily, throwing off my covers and stomping out of bed before I can get any more pathetic. Though, waking up from a wet dream about losing your virginity is pretty much as pathetic as you can get, if we're keeping track.

Of course, it was a mistake. Getting involved with Shelby Springfield is always a mistake. But in my defense, this time, he started it. He kissed me. He pulled me against him.

Didn't he?

I shake my head, stepping under the shower spray, not bothering to wait for it to warm. I grit my teeth against the hiss in the back of my throat. Fuck, it's freezing.

Good. Ice to match the cold shoulder he gave me.

Christ, Springfield. Don't be so dramatic. He's your friend and business partner.

And first love, a tiny voice admits, originating somewhere around my fractured heart.

You don't find your soulmate at ten. Besides, soulmates go both ways and Cameron Riggs has now walked away from me three times.

The first time, we were basically kids. The second, I was a sloppy tequila-infused mess. Third time, though? I'm sober, I'm consenting, I'm an adult.

And I know, I *know* he would have taken me against the wall at the Caroline Street house. His eyes were pure sex. Even now, I can still feel the steely length of him pressed against me, ready. It would have been easier than breathing.

But is it too much to ask for a bed? To be taken back to his place? Or mine? To have someone hotly whisper sweet things in my ear? To hold my hand in his and tug me along, laughing like some fucking rom-com montage? To have my clothes peeled off one piece at a time while he covers every bit of exposed flesh with hot kisses?

To be worshipped with his tongue?

I know he has it in him. He did at eighteen, so it stands to reason now would be even better.

My eyes slip shut with a frustrated moan. The water is warm against my sensitive skin, but I refuse to give in to the temptation of pretending my hands are his. I switch the knob back to cold and jump out, toweling off.

Throwing on some leggings and one of my dad's hand-me-down Fair Isle sweaters, I pour myself a cup of coffee and plop on a stool right as Lorelai and Maren help themselves at my front door.

I frown. "No knocking?"

Lorelai glances around before pointedly tilting her head. "Do we need to knock?"

"No," I say. "It's just polite."

"Uh-oh," says Maren, helping herself to coffee. "I take it we're not doing yoga this morning?"

I make a face. I'd forgotten. "Not in the mood."

Lorelai sits on a stool next to me. "Fine by me." Lorelai hates yoga. She giggles through the entire class, saying the instructor's soothing tone reminds her of Mister Rogers having intercourse. (Yeah, I don't know either.)

My knee bounces in the silence and Maren and Lorelai exchange looks.

"Breakfast?"

"Not hungry," I mumble.

"Oh, she's hungry," Lorelai says, smirking.

Maren is a half beat too late in raising her mug to hide her smile.

I huff. "I'm not good company this morning. Raincheck?"

Maren shakes her head, her auburn ponytail swaying. "I don't think so. You're clearly upset."

Lorelai pulls open a package of Pop-Tarts, eating a frosted cherry one cold, like she was raised in a barn. She leans a legging-clad hip against my counter. "What she means is you have your 'I need to go fuck something up' face on."

"But in a sweet, cozy kind of way," Maren offers, with a nod at my sweater.

"My skin itches," I admit.

"Rash?"

"Cameron Riggs," I say on a sigh.

Lorelai makes a sound in the back of throat, her mouth full of tart.

"We kissed at the Caroline Street property last night."

Maren squeaks, lowering her cup to the island with a clink. "How was it? As good as you remember?"

"Better." My skin flushes remembering the way his calloused hands slid under my shirt. "But," I continue, rinsing my cup at the sink, "I don't want to have sex on a job site like I'm some kid sneaking behind my parent's back."

"Or like a kid sneaking behind a producer's back."

"That," I agree.

"And he *does* want that?"

I shrug, nodding my head, feeling a renewed sense of humiliation. "When I tried to stop us, he got upset. Said it was a mistake. Practically leaped out the door, leaving me there in the dark. Again." I bury my burning face in my hands, mumbling, "I'm such a fucking idiot."

"Oh no." Maren's hands come around me. "You aren't."

"Jesus, Maren. I *am*. This is the third time this man has walked away from me. I need to have some fucking self-respect. Or self-preservation. Whatever."

Lorelai looks shrewd.

"What?" I ask. "Spit it out. You're wrong, though."

She shrugs a single shoulder. "Maybe," she says when her tone is so obviously "But I'm not."

"What am I missing?" asks Maren, her eyes darting between us. "I haven't met this guy yet. You have to spell it out for me."

Lorelai purses her lips.

"Go ahead," I say. Lorelai says a lot of things I don't want her to, but she's also an incredible judge of character. She sees under the surface. It's part of what makes her such a powerful songwriter. Her takes are gutting, but usually in a good way.

I have a feeling this is not going to be one of those "good way" situations, though.

"You keep saying he's leaving you behind—" she says, leading.

"Yeah. We had sex, he quit the show, and moved back home. We didn't have sex, he left me, hopping the first flight out. We kissed, and I *didn't* want to have sex against a wall *at our job,* and he rushed out of the house like his pants were on fire and I was holding a spray bottle of lighter fluid."

Lorelai spreads her hands along the countertop. "I guess I'm not sure he's leaving so much as running."

I scowl.

"Same difference."

"Is it, though? Cameron Riggs doesn't strike me as someone who's careless with others' feelings. Lyle? Sure. Definitely. And since the two of them make up your entire dating history . . ."

"Hey!" I say, defensive. "I've dated other—"

Lorelai pins me with a skeptical look and continues, "I don't think you have a real healthy understanding of the difference."

"And you do?"

"Oh." Lorelai's smile is sardonic. "I know the difference. This isn't about me, but believe me when I say, Drake Colter knew the difference, too."

Maren nods. "Have you and Cameron ever actually talked about what's happened between you in the past?"

"Of course."

"So," Lorelai says, folding her arms across her chest. "You've told him he was your first love?"

"Not that. It makes me sound like a kid—"

"But you've told him how you ended up with Lyle because he left you?"

"It wasn't like that. I *did* like Lyle, too, at the time—"

"Or about how hurt you were that he left you in L.A. without saying goodbye?"

"I definitely mentioned it last night at one point. I was a pathetic mess, and he apologized for that, which is maybe worse—"

"And last night when you kissed and it was looking like more might happen, you explained that you weren't turning him down, you were looking for more?"

"He didn't even let me!" I shout, frustration strangling in my throat. "He didn't even try to make his case. He just shook me off and said it was a mistake. He said, and I quote, 'It's always the same old missed connections between us, isn't it, Shelby?'" Tears leave a burning trail down my cheeks.

Maren comes and wraps me in a firm hug from behind, but Lorelai stays put. She, like me, doesn't do shows of emotion very well. Her small smile is sad.

"He should have stayed."

I nod, sniffing uselessly. "I just wanted him to *try*. I want someone to prove I am worth the effort, you know? Not someone. *Cameron*. Because I've somehow built him up in my memories as this . . ." I shake my head and clear my throat, taking a deep, cleansing breath. "That's not fair. He *is* wonderful. I haven't made him up. He's kind and funny and respectful and loves his mom and . . . I want him to try."

"But isn't he eventually going to run again? Like, not from you, but he's not staying in Michigan, Shelb," Maren reminds me. "He hasn't committed to anything but the pilot, right?"

I sigh. Like I could forget. Cameron was clear with Lyle that he would only sign on for one episode. Technically, one whole-house renovation, but a renovation per episode means he's only committed to the pilot. As far as anyone knows, he fully intends to return to globe-trotting with *National Geographic* after things wrap on the Caroline Street house. Missed connections, bad timing, always leaving . . . all of it should be a giant, flashing neon relationship deterrent, but it's not.

My best friends stare at me: Maren, compassionate; Lorelai, assessing. Lorelai speaks first.

"So, what are we going to do, Shelb? You look like hell

and have to be in front of the camera tomorrow. You need to sleep tonight. So . . . ?"

Maren sighs dramatically. "Fine, then, not yoga, but what about canoeing or kayaks?"

Lorelai hops off her stool. "Better go with kayaks. Shelby has energy to burn."

For the second time that morning, I wipe at my face, clearing away the misery. "Sounds perfect, actually." This is one of my favorite things about these two. They're not much for letting me smother myself in pity. We've all got our shit. They move for the door and I offer to pack some lunch in a cooler while they run home to change and grab the kayaks.

"Don't forget sunblock," Maren says, ever the girl scout. "It's gonna be in the sixties today. Pure vitamin D, baby."

They leave, and I head upstairs to change. On my bed, my phone is lit where I left it. My heart jumps, but it's only the director, Steve, with last-minute details. Cameron has already responded with a thumbs-up.

SHELBY: Thanks, Steve. See you all tomorrow.

I sigh and wait a full minute to see if Cameron responds, even though I don't know why he would.

I just want him to try.

• • •

That evening, I'm completely wrung out from a day on the water. I get Alexa to play me something soft and melodic and crawl under my covers with a cup of tea and a romance novel before turning the lights down low. I end up sitting in the quiet, holding the book, still closed, on my lap. While kayaking, I buried myself in the work of propelling through the waterways, relishing the burn in my shoulders and the sun on my skin. I let Maren and Lorelai distract me from tomorrow and my not-quite-relationship woes. It was exactly the right thing to clear my head. But now that I'm alone, it's flooding back to the forefront of my mind. Particularly the argument between Cameron and me.

Because Lorelai's right. Cameron didn't really leave me. Instead, he returned to me, again and again. It's not perfect, but it's a starting point.

I'm self-aware enough at twenty-seven to acknowledge I deserve someone who will try, someone who will *stay.* And I can admit that Cameron Riggs deserves someone who will give him a real chance to prove himself either way. Our fight stung, and my pride took a hit at the rejection, one that is going to take some time to get over, but I'm secure enough in myself to know I *will* get over it. And if Cameron can get over it, too, maybe we can make this work.

Clearly, jumping into a kiss-slash-wall-fuck wasn't the best approach. We're a little rusty at things, I imagine. After all, we dated a decade ago, and even that was more like covert sneaking around than an actual relationship. We were babies, practically, and while young relationships can last forever, they usually have the benefit of two people growing together. Cameron and I grew up on our own terms. We don't really know each other anymore.

I'd like to get to know him, and I want him to know me.

A fresh start.

Decision made, I sip the last of my tea and place the mug

on my nightstand before flipping off the light and cozying down into my covers. Tomorrow we begin again. And this time, I'm determined to go in with my eyes and heart wide open.

11

CAMERON

TIMBER

Monday morning comes early and sharp as nails. Demo day on Caroline Street.

I arrive at the site before everyone else and unlock the front door. In the stark light of day, everything looks worse, which suits my mood just fine. No ghosts here; only dusty sunbeams and rejection. My empty beer bottle from the other night is still on the counter, so I collect it to throw in the giant trash receptacle out back. I wish I could blame the kiss on the two beers. That would be a minor redemption for my pride.

Unfortunately, I wasn't under the influence of anything other than Shelby.

I spent most of yesterday ignoring phone calls from my agent about my future with *National Geographic* and trying to reformulate all the plans to fit the bathroom addition on the second story instead. I don't completely know what I'm doing, but I'm learning. I wanted to have something to show

Daniel, at least; some prices and a modified timeline for the build. I also binge-watched an entire season of *This Old House* and three episodes of *The Pioneer Woman*.

The Pioneer Woman doesn't really touch on home renovations, but her meals remind me of the good parts of my dad. I ended up so inspired that I ran out and bought the ingredients to make myself an elaborate dinner of chicken-fried steaks and green-bean casserole and then brought the leftovers down to a grateful Beth and skeptical Kevin.

Turns out Shelby isn't the only one who stress bakes.

Maybe we should host a spin-off cooking show if this is successful.

I mean, maybe *Shelby* should. I won't be here, obviously. Probably. According to my agent, Peter, my sort-of rival Dominick Rivera is sniffing around my next project focusing on coral reefs, set to film in Fiji in the fall. Initially, I claimed the project, knowing I would be done filming the pilot of *HomeMade*. But just because I'll technically be done filming, doesn't mean I'll be ready to head up a new documentary. Projects take months of research, planning, scheduling, and interviews. You need to scout sites in advance and make face-to-face contact with the locals.

None of which I can do while filming a reality-show pilot in Michigan.

And that doesn't even begin to tackle what happens if the show ends up ordered for an entire season. Initially, I wasn't planning to stick around. I thought I could do the pilot and then they could replace me, or even better, let Shelby carry it. She's plenty capable. But that was before I started apprenticing under Daniel—and before I kissed Shelby.

All of which should bother me. If for no other reason than Rivera is new to the documentary scene. He's another Columbia grad chock-full of ambition who's been breathing down my neck the past year. If I lose the project to him, it could be a pretty huge blow to any progress and credibility I've earned over the last half decade. Things are *that* precarious in our field.

And yet, Fiji feels really far away from Michigan and Shelby. Too far to worry about when I have a house that needs rebuilding.

Before long, the rest of the very real crew arrives, both film and demo. Daniel and I go over the plans I made yesterday, and he seems impressed, offering to talk to a few of his contractors this morning to price things out. Then, I do a practice walk-through with him, explaining what we have in store for viewers this episode. He makes a few suggestions, but by the time I finish, he's slapping me on the shoulder.

"You're gonna do fine, Cam. You're a fast learner."

I slip off my cap and run my fingers through my hair before putting it back on. "I don't want to embarrass you and Shelby."

"You won't. I wouldn't let you," he says, and I'm struck with how closely his words echo his daughter's. Makeup arrives and starts messing with my face, so Daniel makes a run for it, probably to dig up where the donuts and coffee have landed today. My stomach rumbles, loudly. I already ate, though my breakfast of scrambled eggs and three cups of coffee feels like an age ago. I glance at my wristwatch. It's been a lot of hours since I gave up on sleeping and went for a run instead.

Wardrobe looks me up and down and passes me a bold cherry-red down vest. "For the talking head out front," she says gesturing out the front window, where Shelby is already waiting, stomping her feet in the cold and cradling a steaming foam cup. Hair and Makeup flutter around her, dusting her with brushes and sponges. My stomach clenches, my coffee churning. This is new territory. Usually whenever Shelby and I get *involved*, one or both of us takes off for a few years before we have to confront things. And by one or both of us, I mean me.

This time, I am contractually obligated to work with her in front of an audience of contractors and film crew. So, this should be fun.

I slip on the vest and walk out the front door, meeting the crew. The early-morning air has a damp chill to it. Our breaths are puffing out around us in the misty sunshine as we listen to our director, Steve, explain his plans for filming today. We'll be starting with off-the-cuff talking heads introducing me and Shelby, giving them a taste of our chemistry. I elbow Shelby.

"You hear that?" I ask, determined to restore some balance. "They think we have chemistry."

Shelby doesn't miss a beat, grinning at me conspiratorially. "They'll learn the truth soon enough."

Steve exchanges a knowing smile with one of the production assistants and we pretend not to notice like the chemistry-laden professionals we are.

"And then," he continues, "we'll get to the initial walkthrough. This is where you'll paint the picture of the planned reno for the audience. We'll come back and lay down a voice-over and some computer magic on our end after edits. Shelby," he looks to her. "I'm going to focus on the upstairs here for a bit . . . I want to hear some of the nitty-gritty on those shelves and why you two are choosing to build the addition rather than tear them down. Go for broke here."

Shelby glances at me, lowering her voice before she asks, "Are you sure about the addition? It's not too late to change your mind."

I nod. "I'm sure."

"But—"

I cut her off with a finger to her soft lips, before quickly removing it and tucking my hand into my vest pocket, curling it into a fist, feeling branded. "I already modified the plans to accommodate the addition. Worked on it all day yesterday. Your dad has them and is double-checking my figures as we speak. We're doing the addition."

Her eyes search for the lie in mine. She won't find it. The kiss between us may have been a mistake. But that doesn't change the job, and it doesn't change my feelings. I can safely say, even if only to myself, that ten years is a long time to care—too long to be crushed by a single night (or three) of fucking up. I said I would do it, and I will.

"Okay," she says at last.

"Okay." I turn to Steve. "And then the demo?"

He nods slowly. His expression is unreadable as he studies us. "Yeah." Whatever has him thinking, he shakes it off. "Yeah, demo this afternoon." He focuses on me. "That's your department."

"Excellent," I say. "I've been looking forward to ripping out those cabinets."

"I've been looking forward to watching," Shelby quips and turns pink. "I mean, because I hate those cabinets. They're super gross."

I smirk, crossing my arms over my chest. Her cheeks are lit up like a Christmas tree as she turns to Steve. "We should get going on those talking heads, I think."

• • •

It's quickly apparent that working with Shelby is still easy as pie. She's got the kind of down-to-earth charm that will make people from all walks of life happily fall in love with her. The girl next door you watched grow up on TV. The one you can never forget.

I knew this already. It's what I've been craving and avoiding in equal measure. But there's one part I hadn't counted on, especially after the mess from the other night. We've always been one step forward and three skips backward, but this time, while everyone is busy falling in love with her, she's got her starry blue eyes on me. It's the same look on her face when I make a joke as the one she wore the night I drove us to a blanket in the middle of an empty field for our first—and last—time together. The same as when I flew down from Alaska to land on her doorstep when she asked. And when I told her I would do the more difficult renovation.

It means something hopeful, that look. And, I think, it means something *more* that she's letting me see it now.

I don't understand. I was so nervous heading into this morning. I fucked up and we fought. She should hate me. Just like before.

Except, before, I hadn't stuck around for the aftermath. I don't actually know what her reaction was to my absence.

It's fucking with my head. What if all this time, I've been beating myself up for leaving, assuming I'd broken her heart, and she's been fine? Maybe she didn't care as much as I thought? As much as I did? Do?

Shelby glances over from where she's waiting to get started, a shy smile on her face.

And it hits me.

I have to know.

While the camera crew is working with Steve on lighting, I pull Shelby into the backyard. There's an old concrete slab for a porch that I mentally add to my list of fixes. This view is screaming for a proper deck. Ten to one Daniel already has it budgeted.

Shelby tucks her hair behind her ear, her expression open. "Everything okay?"

I shake my head, glancing nervously at the sliding door. I don't want anyone to notice us out here. "Not really, no. I mean." I take a deep breath and start over. "Yeah, everything seems great. Perfect, even. Which, I fucked up, Shelby. The other night. I'm sorry. I shouldn't have said what I said. I didn't mean it."

She holds up a hand. "Me, too. I was, well, pretty humiliated, to be honest. I know you didn't ditch me for college, Cam, and I promise I'm not mad about that."

"I'm sorry I kissed you."

She winces, tilting her head. "Are you really? Because," she rushes on, "I'm not. I'm . . ." She exhales. "I'm not sorry at all."

My chest squeezes and I feel like I can't quite catch my breath. "You aren't?"

"No. And I don't think it was a mistake. Maybe not great timing, but I *liked* kissing you." Her eyes shift to the door and back. She lowers her voice. "I'm not fragile, Cameron. You don't have to keep protecting me. I can make my own choices. It's not that I didn't want you. I . . ." She straightens, standing taller, her eyes full of emotion. "I just didn't want it to be like it was before. Sneaking around, led by our hormones. We're adults. We have homes and beds and walls of our own. *That's* what I meant."

What little air I have in my lungs escapes, and I feel lightheaded. My hands are tingling. I might be having a stroke. When I speak, my voice comes out strangled. "*That's* what you meant?"

Suddenly there's a tapping on the glass door. Steve is there, gesturing emphatically at his Apple watch. Shelby presses her lips together and holds up a finger before turning back to me.

"Yeah, Cam." Her voice is soft. "That's what I meant. Maybe our timing isn't as bad as you think. Maybe"—her lips quirk and I'm taken off guard by her mischievous grin—"our communication is the problem. Stop running and let me catch you, and I can tell you all about it next time."

And with that, she spins toward the house, leaving me gaping in her wake.

A little later, we're in front of the camera, strolling room to room, taking our prospective audience with us. I talk through the kitchen renovations, picking up a mallet and not waiting a single second more before putting it through a cabinet and revealing the nesting mice inside. Shelby screams as they scatter, jumping up on the countertop in her Chucks, her short hair practically standing on end while I laugh so hard, I cry. Steve looks like he can't tell if he wants to murder or kiss me. Daniel has to leave the house altogether.

A short while later, Shelby highlights the upstairs, her voice captivating and dreamy as she describes what will become of the nook. I share the plans for the addition and Steve prompts me about my choice to go the hard route with the renovation. I know what he's angling for, and I give it to him, pulling Shelby to my side and explaining what the lady wants, the lady gets. After all, "I've never been able to tell her no."

When the camera turns off, Shelby leans in and arches a brow. "Never?" Meaning is suffused into her words and I know she's remembering five years ago in L.A.

"Never," I repeat. Her chin dips a small nod of acceptance.

Because, I didn't say no in L.A., I left before I could say yes. There's a difference. It's not the right time to talk about it, but after today, after all those loaded looks and the earth-shattering conversation on the patio, I won't forget to bring it up.

Regardless of what my plans are in five months.

We finish the walk-through after repeating the upstairs bedrooms for the lighting guys and move on to demo. They won't be getting all the demo on camera, obviously. We'd be here all week just trying to dismantle the kitchen. Instead, they film as I break down the cabinetry, and Shelby, true to her word, makes a show of watching. I've pulled off my flannel, stripped down to a gray tee and damn if that girl doesn't follow my every move. I can feel her stare burn along my skin, licking at my neck and caressing my forearms. I stop to look at her, swiping at sweat and offering the mallet. She shakes her head, lips spreading in a salacious smile, well aware the camera's rolling. "No, thank you. I'm just happy to supervise." Shelby winks in an overtly cheesy way, the camera eating her up.

Oh, she's gonna get it. I let the mallet drop near my foot and swipe again at my forehead. She narrows her eyes in challenge. Without overthinking it, I grab the ends of my T-shirt and tug it over my head in one swift motion, tossing it at her.

She shrieks, catching it deftly, and laughs, full-bodied. I replace my goggles, pick up the mallet, and continue to work on demolishing the rest, thanking every deity that I've kept up on my running routine over the years.

Soon, the camera crew breaks for lunch, and I'm lost in the work of dismantling everything. My arms and shoulders burn with exertion, but I relish the feeling. Layers of blisters on my hands, sweat trickling in my eyes, covered in drywall and years of dust. It's not that I haven't had to work hard before. I've tracked indigenous tribes across the desert and climbed mountains and slogged through jungles. I spent hours a day learning choreography and performing lines on cue and producing emotion out of nothing from the time I was ten years old.

But my dad was always on my back to find something of my own to be proud of. *"You spend all your time observing and re-creating,' Cameron. You need to make your own way—settle down and start taking yourself seriously."*

Of course, he meant something outside of the entertainment industry. TV wasn't serious. It wasn't real. It was flash and camera angles and clowning around. To him, it wasn't me. I couldn't claim any of it as mine. Not even documentaries, as important as they can be, were important enough for him.

Home, family, and hard work. Those were the only things that mattered, and I'm only halfway there. Likely, as close as I'll ever get, if there's a camera aimed at my face.

Still, this is a whole new kind of meaningful. Renovating this home is a service and I find myself, for the first time in a long time, really enjoying myself. It's taking all my strength, skill, and energy to accomplish this and I'm crazy for the feeling.

I get it. I understand why Daniel and Shelby do this, over and over. I haven't even gotten to the part where we are rebuilding something better, and already I feel more challenged than I have in years.

It's a good feeling.

It's even better when I think about how I'm here, doing this, with her. I haven't made a lot of good decisions in my life, but this feels like it might be one of the best.

• • •

It's a few weeks since I've arrived in Michigan before I find myself in Shelby's personal workshop. I haven't felt right asking to see her shop ever since I walked in on the argument between (virtual) Lyle, Steve, and Shelby about her refusal to allow filming in her barn. But tonight, on our way out of Kevin's bar where we'd been having drinks with the crew, she finally offered, and there was no way I could refuse. I've been dying of curiosity to see where she spends her time—the place she found for herself after leaving L.A. behind.

We leave everyone at the bar, and I drive us over. This feels familiar. Only this morning, Steve sent us to look at some countertops for the kitchen, on film. The difference now is that it's just us. Cameron and Shelby. No one around to flirt for. No one to convince of our chemistry. Not that it's a hardship to do those things, but at the end of the day, it's still a job. And it's hard to parse real feelings with an audience.

Shelby settles back into the passenger seat with a long, drawn-out yawn and a minute later, I'm echoing it.

"We don't have to do this tonight," I make myself say. "I'm happy to just drop you off."

She shakes her head. "I'm good. The schedule's been a bit grueling, but I don't mind showing you. Probably better," she says. "No cameras. And I've been meaning to invite you for a while. It's not a secret or anything."

"But no cameras."

She huffs quietly. "Okay, it's sort of a secret. I don't want Lyle or the crew in there. It's my refuge. I don't feel like they deserve to see that part of me."

"Well, then, thank you in advance for showing it to me."

The corners of her lips turn up in the streetlight. "You're welcome."

She's quiet for a long moment and I'm about to turn on the radio to fill the silence when she speaks in a low voice.

"I'm not very good at sharing parts of myself, in case you haven't noticed."

"You've been hurt. It's understandable."

She nods. "It is." This time her smile is full-blown and edged with cheerful self-deprecation. "It took me a lot of therapy to be able to admit that."

"Is this the therapist you shared with Lorelai?"

She snickers softly. "Nah. The only thing I got from that particular therapist was a new best friend. Worth it, but the therapist herself was high-key weird. Lots of crystals, little substance. Not my jam."

"I saw a therapist after *Jackson* wrapped. When I got back to Michigan."

Her eyes dart to mine in the dark. "Really?"

I nod, watching the road. "Not for long. Actually, only once. My mom insisted. My dad and brother and I kept fighting. Like, not small fights either. They were these giant, knock-down, drag-out shouting matches that would rattle the rafters."

She shakes her head. "I can't imagine that, honestly. You're always so . . . even-keeled," she finishes finally.

"It was a lot of testosterone in a small house. We weren't used to living together. I lived in L.A. for most of my growing-up years. And my dad wanted me to be more like Derek. Small-town athlete with college ambitions."

"I overheard you tell my dad Derek still lives nearby?"

"He does. Between here and my mom's. I haven't been to see him yet."

"We've been busy," Shelby offers.

I grimace in the dark. "Not that busy."

She doesn't press. "You didn't want the same things as your dad and Derek, I take it?"

I shrug. "I didn't know what I wanted, honestly."

"Except you didn't want L.A." I hear what isn't being said. That I didn't want *her.* Which isn't true. It's never been true. No time like the present to work on those communication problems.

"I couldn't *compete* with L.A.," I correct.

She presses her lips together and seems to be contemplating a response. "Did therapy help?"

"Not really. You have to want to be better, and I didn't. I wanted out. So, I left for college in another state and then for *Nat Geo.* I rarely came home, was avoiding the fight. Didn't need to hear how settled Derek was or how much my mom missed me. For all our issues, my dad is one of the best men to ever exist and I just can't live up to his expectations."

"Couldn't compete with home either," she offers softly.

"I didn't even try. I should have tried."

Her eyes meet mine. "It's not too late to try."

She doesn't elaborate, but I nod, swallowing hard, understanding what isn't being said. Soon we're traveling down her long drive and I park in between her house and workshop. I round the back of the truck as she's getting out and follow as she leads us to a giant barn with a single light on over the door. She unlocks the door and shoves, swinging it open and flicking the lights on.

I walk in and my jaw drops to my chest. Where Shelby's house is cozy and carefully pieced together, her workshop is all business. State-of-the-art tools, benches, rows of furniture projects, walls of finishes and paint cans. She's got an entire hardware store in here.

And a small enclosure with a red heat lamp in the corner that's making a lot of peeps.

"Ah," I say. "I'll just be over there with the baby chicks, holding on to the last shreds of my dignity."

She laughs. "What are you talking about?"

"Are you kidding?" I ask. "This is incredible. I'm . . . fucking intimidated, Springfield. Here I am playing at being a home flipper and you have your own Home Depot in your backyard."

12

SHELBY

THE GOOD ONES

I've dreamed about this. In the years since I moved from L.A., I would practice my craft on old garage-sale dressers and nightstands and imagine Cameron beside me, watching me, proud of what I've accomplished.

Looking at me pretty much how he's looking at me right now.

I laugh again at his outburst. "A dirty and disorganized Ace Hardware, maybe. More of that hometown charm, if you please."

He spins around, taking in all the angles of my life's work. "It's incredible," he says, making the little hairs on my arms stand up.

"Thank you."

He moves for one of the aisles of commissioned work. "May I?"

I gesture for him to proceed.

His long fingers trail over each piece and I tell him what

they are, who they belong to, the plans I have for them. He listens like I'm the only person in the entire world, asking questions, tugging on drawer pulls, and tracing cracks I intend to fill and smooth over like new.

We stroll down one aisle and move to another. He comes up to my current project. A dining room table for the Caroline Street house. I don't usually make original furniture for the homes my dad and I flip, but Steve and Lyle commissioned me to do this one. As with the nook on the second story, they wanted to add an element to the show where I include a handcrafted creation for each home we sell.

"You made this from scratch?" he asks, running his palm along the freshly sanded tabletop.

"Yeah," I admit wryly. "I didn't have anything big enough in stock, for the newly renovated open-concept kitchen, that is," I say, grinning. "The wood is recycled barn wood, though. Locally sourced. It hits on the key points."

"I can't believe you made this." He shakes his head. "I mean. I can believe it, actually, but I'm so impressed."

"Thank you," I say, pleased. More pleased than he can possibly know. "It's intimidating, free-handing something, but I've been remaking pieces for years, so I had the basic idea."

"The basic idea," he says dryly. "I'd say so. This is art."

"Thank you," I repeat, my face warm.

"Do you miss acting?" he asks suddenly, not meeting my eyes. "It's just . . . I thought you were a lifer, you know? You and Lyle. I figured you would do Hollywood forever."

"I like how you and I both pretend we're not doing Hollywood right now."

He makes a face at the reminder and I laugh in commiseration.

"I don't miss it," I tell him, skirting the table and idly feeling for rough edges. I just sanded the top this morning. I make note of a patch I've missed, pulling out a carpentry pencil from the bench and making a light circle. "Not the way you mean. I should have left long before I did. I would have, even, if my mom hadn't been the one pulling the strings for so long. She really got into my brain, even after I fired her. I love my dad, don't get me wrong, but he shouldn't have left me in her care growing up."

His eyes are smiling. "That sounds like therapy, too."

I concede, laughing again. It feels like it's been years since I laughed this easily, especially talking about my past. "It is. Though, I skipped the part where I should have written a letter to him and burned it. I just straight-up yelled at him instead."

"I can picture it."

"To his credit, he took it. I was something to behold."

"You usually are."

I press my lips together and he busies himself looking under the table at the legs I'd turned. "These are pretty ornate for barn wood."

"Cam," I plead softly.

He straightens, sighing. "Sorry."

"For what? For being sweet and making me blush?"

"It's just . . ."

But I'm not done. "For learning how to restore houses for me? For treating my father with the utmost respect? For running to my rescue five years ago? For being my first lo—"

I swallow the word. "*Real* friend growing up? What on earth are you apologizing for?"

He looks pained. "What about when I took your virginity and then left you? Can I be sorry about that?"

My breath catches in my throat and he grimaces. "Fuck. Sorry," he says again. "That was . . ." He exhales sharply. "That came out harsher than I meant."

I have to ask. "Are you sorry that we had sex?"

"What?" He looks so surprised I almost laugh. "No! Not at all." He shakes his head. "But I am sorry for deserting you after. You were my first *friend,* too," he continues with a knowing look and my face heats. "I hated leaving. But I had to."

"You had to go to college, Cam. It's okay. We talked about this. I understand. I'm not upset."

"It's not just that," he insists. "I mean, yes, I had to go to college. My dad had been on my case. He hated everything about L.A. and my acting. He ragged on me for years, resented my mom living with me, resented my paychecks getting the family through rough patches. All of it was repellant to him. He insisted I go to college like my brother, and he was right. It was a solid decision. But it was rushed, and I was angry at being forced to choose. It was as though I didn't have a say in my own life, even though, ultimately, I did. I left everything in L.A. behind, and I didn't really miss any of it. Except you. I should have told you what I was going through. I should have tried to make things work between us."

"You should have said goodbye," I whisper.

"That." He's resolute.

"I thought maybe I cared more than you did. I didn't

understand how we went from crazy for each other to nothing in the span of a few weeks."

"I know. I was immature and stupid and"—he winces, rubbing at the back of his neck—"wildly jealous."

I can't imagine Cameron being jealous of anything, ever. He's always been the epitome of confidence. "Of what?"

He's sheepish. "Of *who,* you mean. I watched the news. Read the tabloids. I didn't want to, but I couldn't help but notice how quickly you hooked up with Lyle after me."

My face burns under his scrutiny. He's the opposite of accusatory, but I still feel guilty. After a moment, I say, "I don't have a defense to that except to say, I was a kid who was sad and lonely, and Lyle paid attention to me."

Cameron rolls his eyes. "You didn't do anything that needs defending. We weren't together, and I was the one who walked away. It hurt, but it was my own fault. Anyway," he sighs, his hands falling to his sides in resignation, "I'm sorry, for what it's worth."

I reach for him, not sure what my plan is until I'm wrapping my arms around him and squeezing. "Stop apologizing for being a good man. For fuck's sake," I finish dryly.

He chuckles, low, and squeezes me tighter, lifting me in the air, once, before placing me on my feet.

We pull apart, our eyes meeting and saying things we aren't ready to vocalize yet.

"I should go. It's late."

I nod and lead him out. We make it to his car, and I hug him once more, this time pressing my lips to the spot just above his whiskered cheekbones.

• • •

I haven't seen my mother in years, but that doesn't mean I'm the least bit shocked when she turns up at the Caroline Street house after lunch, right as the cameras have started rolling. Ada Mae making a surprise appearance, days into shooting, feels pretty par for the course. It's like she has a sixth sense that alerts her to when things are going well for me and Ada Mae *cannot* have that.

"Yoo-hoo!" she says, removing her sunglasses and poking her way through the sawdust and tarps in her snakeskin kitten heels.

"Sweet Jesus, here we go," I mutter under my breath.

"Shelby!" she says, her face quite literally painted in Clinique and careful surprise. "Why Shelby, baby, this is wonderful! So rustic!" She pauses a step, facing the camera crew, her manicured hand pressed to her unmoving breast (that I paid for, mind you). "Oh my! What have we heeeere?" She waves at the camera, aghast, as if she's been beamed down from a spaceship right into this wonderous half-finished living room.

Her faux-shocked expression isn't even the weirdest thing about her, honestly. The weirdest thing you need to understand about Ada Mae Springfield is she speaks with a Southern accent, but she was born and raised outside Detroit. It's as though she's willed herself to be a Southern belle and if you didn't know any better, you'd think she was.

Some people have plastic surgery to become someone new; my mother also adopted an entire geographic culture.

"How'd you find me?" I ask bluntly, moving to the sink to rinse the sawdust from my hands. I make a motion to cut the camera, and Steve shakes his head apologetically.

It's then that I realize no one seems surprised by my mother arriving except me. Well, until I take a quick look around and see Cameron and my dad peering into the kitchen. My dad looks halfway between resigned and ready to bolt, and even though he's half hidden behind a pair of goggles that make him look fourteen and bug-eyed, Cam is definitely furious. Maybe I *can* imagine him getting into arguments with his dad and brother. Given the proper motivation, he's plenty capable of anger.

Ugh. Fuck Lyle.

We've been moving right along on the Caroline Street house. Demolition done, electrical and plumbing updated, the plank floors stripped and replaced where necessary. My dad knows how to run a home reno like clockwork and Cameron is relentless in his pursuit to do this justice. They're a (nearly) unstoppable force, despite Lyle throwing as many curveballs as he can into the mix.

The last month has been a blur of hard work and preparations. And flirting. Lots of on-camera flirting. So much so that I told Steve I needed to take some time in my shop to work without distraction. This, I can assure you, was never an issue with my dad's renos. Before, I might've worked alone because I didn't like my dad's crew getting smudges in my varnish or sawdust in the joints. Now I'm hiding from Cameron's too-capable hands and the way he likes to tuck a pencil behind his ear and then spend the rest of the time looking for where he left it.

Cameron seems determined to break down my defenses one mallet swing at a time and he's doing one hell of a job. He still doesn't realize how much he doesn't need to convince me. I'm there, man. I've been there. I practically live there. RIP my sanity, send your regards to 1234 Shelby Is Pathetic for Cameron Street.

Everything is working too well, and Lyle can't have that. Locally, people seem genuinely enthusiastic for our potential return to the screen and encouraging about whatever it is that's happening between Cameron and me. It's all so pure and Lyle hates that shit because it doesn't require anything of *him*. He's determined to disrupt the wholesome with his special brand of drama. Always. And who is the Queen Bee of Drama?

"Baby, what a ridiculous thing to say. I'm your mother. *Of course,* I know where you live."

My eyes roll to the ceiling and get lost there. "Except I don't live here, Ada Mae. I work here."

She waves me off with a jangle of her twenty-four-karat gold bangles, clacking toward me with her arms outstretched. After a moment's hesitation, I return her bony embrace. It's about as warm as a walk-in freezer. I don't think Ada Mae has intentionally touched me since she squeezed me out the birth canal.

And I lost any longing for maternal affection the minute she released a memoir detailing my joke of a childhood.

"Are you here to help?" I ask, my skepticism oozing.

"Please, no. You know I don't know a thing about all this. I'm just so proud and wanted to take you out on the town! To celebrate!"

I glance over at Steve as if to ask, "Are you serious?" and he only shrugs again, mouthing the name "Lyle." I break character and storm off-camera toward our director, so he's forced to stop filming.

"What am I supposed to do with her?"

"I have a name." She pouts.

I ignore her. Steve's gaze shifts from her to me and he sighs, removing his headset. "This wasn't my idea, and I don't technically have enough room in the pilot for it, but it's been suggested that we aren't doing enough to remind the audience of your fame."

"What fame? I don't have it anymore. On purpose."

"That's debatable. Nevertheless, it wouldn't hurt to embrace it for the sake of your viewers. Just take her out to dinner or something."

"Take her out to dinner?" I repeat dumbly. "I can't take her in public."

"Oh, for heaven's sake, Shelby. Don't be so dramatic. Look at you. You're an instant from tears."

I attempt a deep breath. She's right but I'd die before admitting it to the crew and my dad and Cam. Barely five minutes in her presence and it's as though my lungs can't hold any air.

"Stop it, Mom," I snap. "I won't do anything public. She can come to my house and I'll cook for her."

"The cameras will only be there a minute. Just long enough to capture you together."

"I'll come, too," my dad says, protectiveness thick in his tone. He wraps an arm around my shoulders. "Ada Mae. Good to see you."

"Danny." She sniffs, before turning to me. "That would be grand. I'd love to see your home. Seven thirty okay?"

"Fabulous," I mutter.

"I'm doing keto now," my mom says, slipping on a pair of sunglasses, even though we're still inside. "Make sure you prepare for that."

"Of course you are."

"Well, darlin'." She waves her manicured hand around dismissively. "This is all very cute. Text me your address, please."

And she teeters the fuck out of my life. Well, until tonight, that is.

• • •

"You could've brought Jazz," I say, passing my dad a salad bowl to place on the table. I rushed home from the Caroline Street house early and called up Maren to help me brainstorm keto recipes. We came up with a butternut squash spaghetti with prosciutto and brown butter and a garden salad. I honestly can't tell if the droopy, orange-squash noodles look good or not, but if it's got butter, it can't be that bad.

He shakes his head. "She sends her love and promised to drop by later with some pie. But this is a family dinner."

I nudge his elbow. "You're my family, Dad, you and Jazz, even. Ada Mae's . . ."

"*Your mom,* for better or worse."

The doorbell rings and I smooth my hands down my long peasant dress. It's pretty and floral with cap sleeves. It's everything Ada Mae hates and I love. I make my way to the door, passing the camera crew.

"Just a few minutes," Steve had said. I can manage to be the old me for a few minutes. I take a deep breath and catch my dad's reassuring wink before pulling open the front door.

Ada Mae is a whirlwind from the second she crosses the threshold. She shoves a bag of takeout into my arms.

"I cooked for us," I remind her.

She titters. "I don't think so. I also brought a bottle of rosé. I know it's not tequila, but I'm sure a little class never hurt anyone. You're nearly thirty, you know."

"I don't drink anymore, Mom."

She sniffs at my sharp tone. "Don't be ridiculous, what are you, Quaker? It's the Midwest, Shelby, not the Vatican."

I sigh and carry the bag of takeout and wine and whatever else and pass it to my dad's waiting arms. "Why don't you show her around, kid? I'll just put this away for now."

My mom is standing in the center of my living room, looking at my furniture the way one might look at art in a museum: objective, cold, bored. I pretend not to notice. "Can I show you around? I mean. This is mostly it, besides the kitchen and the upstairs, but that's not really . . ."

"I have the gist. You made these?"

"Well, I didn't *make* them. I refurbished them. They were made a hundred years ago, and I made them new again."

"And people buy these refurbished things?"

"Um. Yeah. Quite a few people, actually."

"It's quaint. A sweet hobby."

I work at unclenching my jaw. "More than a hobby, Mom. It's how I make my living."

"Danny, be useful and crack open that rosé for us, please."

"Dad, don't—"

"Ada Mae, why don't you come and sit down. Our daughter spent the last two hours making a nice dinner to celebrate your being here."

I swallow a smile. My dad has never acted so hard in his life. I didn't know he had it in him.

"Kitchen's this way, Mom."

A minute later, the camera crew follows as we sit around my small dining room table.

"Should I say grace?" my dad asks, an ironic twinkle in eye.

"Jesus Christ," Ada Mae mutters.

"Amen," I finish.

I sip my iced tea as Ada Mae tries to make heads or tails of the pasta. "I checked, Mom. It's all keto friendly."

"Right. This is lovely." She picks up her fork and beams at me, all white teeth and perfectly lined lips. "Thanks, baby."

I swallow and blink and settle back in my chair, thrown off guard. Because for a split second—barely the space between breaths—I'm given what I've always yearned for. A family. A proud mom, a present dad, and me, all sitting around the dinner table. That's the picture the film crew captures.

And in the very next instant, everything evaporates. Conversation, history, affection, expectations. All of it, *poof,* gone. This is the end of the end of the line. The film crew packs up in silence, and we sit awkwardly, shuffling squash noodles around on our plates. They leave and I release a long breath. So does my dad. My mom finishes her entire glass of wine and pours a second.

"Now that they're gone?" she asks, plaintively, waving the bottle.

"I don't drink. I mean it."

"Cut the crap, Shelby. You sit here in your cozy thrift-store house and your thrift-store dress and your middle-aged hairstyle and you expect me to believe you're happy? And not only that, but sober? What a waste of a future. You could be making millions and winning awards and getting VIP treatment and instead you're playing *Little House on the Prairie* with your high school boyfriend."

My dad clears his throat gruffly. "That's enough, Ada—"

"And don't even get me started on you, Danny. Twenty-eight years and you haven't changed one bit. Still the same old roughneck construction worker, feeding her excuses and chocolate donuts."

I thought she couldn't hurt me anymore. If you had asked me two hours ago if I could handle my mother's sharp tongue, I would have laughed in your face. I would have told you I'd spent decades with her biting criticism. That "you should have" and "you aren't even" and I are practically siblings.

But I was wrong.

A loud, messy sniff escapes before I can prevent it and the sound draws my parents' attention like a magnet. My dad's shoulders sink. My mom rolls her eyes and stands.

"Not this again. God, you're such a victim. Lord knows I tried to make you tough, but some people aren't cut out for success. Some people rise with the cream, others sink with the custard."

I shake my head, swallowing hard against the fury strangled in my throat. What is *with* everyone calling me a victim in that dismissive tone lately? As though I'd tattooed the word "victim" underneath my eyeballs in curlicue letters like Post Malone and asked to legally change my name to Vic-Tim.

I'm exhausted. Twenty-seven years of piled-on and largely unmet expectations have worn me down. "There's nothing wrong with being a victim, Mom. I didn't do anything to deserve that title. If I'm a victim, it's *you* who made me this way. I'm not responsible for the way you treated me, neglected me, and took advantage of me, making money off your lies about me. You need to leave."

Ada Mae opens her mouth, but I'll never know what she was going to say. Instead, my dad cuts her off. "No more. She asked you to leave."

I stare, unfocused, at my untouched plate and listen as my mother's heels clack across my wood floors, the door slamming behind her. Her rental-car tires skid on the gravel of my drive and she's gone.

She's gone.

I breathe out a sigh of relief.

"Do you want to talk about it?"

I shake my head. "Not really, no."

"You're not a victim, Shelby. You're a survivor."

I look up. My dad's eyes are piercing blue and shiny with unshed tears. "You are the best part of me and the only redeemable part of her. I don't tell you that enough, but it's the truth."

I manage a small nod. "Thanks, Dad. I'm okay." Or at least I will be after I read Lyle the riot act later tonight. Siccing Ada Mae on me. For fuck's sake.

"Good. Should I text Jazz that the coast is clear?"

"Yes, please. This is disgusting." I shove the plate away from me. "I could use some pie and maybe one of her hugs, too."

My dad chuckles. "Me, too, kid."

13

CAMERON

HOT IN HERRE

After Ada-gate, Shelby announced she was headed to the Upper Peninsula for a long weekend to check out some enormous flea market outside Munising and asked me to come along.

"If you want," she hedged. "It can be a little overwhelming, and definitely features equal parts garbage to gems, but it's a nice change of scenery and there's this super cute B&B where I always stay, and it serves a Scandinavian menu and has an outside sauna and there's, like, zero Wi-Fi and . . ."

"I'm in. When do we leave?"

She smiled, relieved. "Tomorrow?"

I was concerned about the time away from shooting, but it turns out Steve has plenty of residual guilt from Ada Mae's surprise visit and he waved me off. "I could use a day or five in the editing room, anyway."

Daniel practically packed my overnight bag for me. "Take my truck. It's only a five-hour drive, give or take, and my

F150 is a lot older than that fancy new lease of yours. She'll want to bring home her finds and they're messy. Trust me."

This is how I found myself driving a rusty pickup across the Mackinac Bridge with Shelby Springfield snoring softly on the bench next to me. The last of the spring weather is still pretty cool up here. Midfifties in the sun, and the breeze off Lake Michigan is at least ten degrees cooler, but I still have my window cracked, teasing in the fresh air to keep me awake. It's been a long week. Between Ada Mae's disruption and the subsequent fallout between Lyle and Shelby and, well, Lyle and everyone, on top of the usual work of rehabbing an entire house for the first time ever, I'm feeling a little burned-out. Not that I haven't faced this kind of fatigue before. *Nat Geo* isn't exactly a walk in the park, but this is an unforeseen level of emotional exhaustion I've managed to avoid.

It's been more feeling than I've done in a very long time, if ever, and a weekend away with Shelby probably isn't the reprieve I'm seeking.

There's no exit plan, here.

And yet, I can't think of another place on earth I'd rather be.

Especially when Shelby cuddles closer to me, wrapping her arms more tightly in her oversized knit cardigan and nuzzling the pocket where my shoulder and neck meet. I crank the window closed and reach for the blower, aiming it in her direction before turning up the heat. Then, I turn on the radio. The only thing I can find on the radio is soft Christian hits or classic rock. I choose classic rock. There's only so much Michael W. Smith a man can take.

We make it over the bridge and into the Upper Peninsula, and I pull off the road to a Scandinavian-themed diner. Everything up here is Scandinavian. Kevin would fit right in. I maneuver Daniel's truck around a still-melting pile of snow and nudge Shelby as I remove my seat belt. She wakes up, stretching, and looks around, momentarily confused.

"We still have an hour and a half to go, but it's getting late, and you said there wasn't anywhere else to stop after we're past the bridge?"

Shelby nods. "Yep. Just Lake Michigan to your left and pine trees to your right for the duration of the Seney Stretch."

"Well, before we get to all that, I'm hungry and could use a bathroom break."

Shelby tugs on a knit hat that covers her ears and makes her look ten years younger. "Oh! I bet this place serves Swedish pancakes with lingonberries."

The restaurant is cozy and resembles a log cabin, its walls laden with deer heads and skis and black-and-white pictures of old Swedes. Our server's name is Marta, and she has a thick northern accent, reminding me of the movie *Fargo*. The Swedish pancakes are thinner than your typical flapjacks, but they're filling, and the lingonberries are so tart and delicious that it would be a disservice to cover them with maple syrup. (Even though, as a proper native Michigander, I could easily eat pure maple syrup with a spoon.)

The best part? No cameras, no directors, no Lyle. Only two old friends eating pancakes. Two good buddies, sitting across from each other in comfortable companionship and definitely not thinking about the other buddy naked. And most definitely *not* fantasizing about the B&B calling to say they messed up the reservation and only have one room available instead of two.

Shelby heads off to use the restroom and my phone buzzes with a notification, shaking me out of my reverie. I'm half expecting it to actually be the B&B, but it's Kevin.

KEVIN: Slow night if you want to come down and watch the Tigers/Sox game on the big screen.

I grimace, scratching my beard while considering how to respond.

CAMERON: Can't. Last minute trip to the U.P. w/ Shelby to check out some massive flea market.

After hitting Send I mentally count to ten and sure enough, my phone lights up. I glance toward the bathroom.

KEVIN: What?

KEVIN: Wait. What?

I inwardly groan.

CAMERON: It's not a big deal. It's a work thing.

KEVIN: You're on a weekend getaway up north to go antiquing. It doesn't get cozier than that, my friend.

KEVIN: Beth just smacked my arm and asked, "Why don't you ever take me antiquing?!" Case. In. Point.

My face flushes hot under my beard and my eyes dart to the bathroom. Still no Shelby.

CAMERON: It's for work. For the show.

KEVIN: Are they filming you?

CAMERON: No.

KEVIN: Are you being paid?

CAMERON: Obviously not.

KEVIN: Are you staying in a hotel? Separate rooms?

CAMERON: Separate rooms, yes. Hotel, no. It's some B&B Shelby likes that she ALWAYS stays at.

KEVIN: . . .

KEVIN: . . .

KEVIN: I'm sure the B&B is very "professional" and you will be very busy not having sex for the duration of your business trip. May God have mercy on your gonads.

CAMERON: You're a dick.

KEVIN: Sorry.

CAMERON: No, you aren't.

KEVIN: No, I'm not. Beth made me say that.

CAMERON: I have to go. Shelby's back and we have a ways to drive yet.

KEVIN: I'm not there to be your wingman, but I have it on good authority few girls can resist when you sing "Best Girl," it has at least a 90% success rate.

I swipe the screen clear before Shelby makes it to the table. Grabbing for the bill, I rub my eyes tiredly as she walks up.

"Do you need me to drive?" she asks.

"Only if you want."

Shelby holds out her hand for the keys. "I don't mind. I slept almost the entire way. Plus, I know the way to the Northern Nook." I pass them over and she pockets them, checking her phone. "I have a message. I'm just gonna go listen while you pay, if that's okay? I'll get the next round."

I make my way to the counter, pay for our meal, and pluck a free after-dinner mint from a bowl at the register before grabbing a second for Shelby and meeting her at the truck. She's already sitting in the driver's seat and the engine's running, warming the cab.

"Bad news. Well. Awkward news, anyway. That was the B&B. Their last guests flooded the attached bathroom by accident, so *my* room is a sodden mess. We can stay, but we'll have to share a room."

I freeze. "You're kidding."

"I'm not, but it's okay!" she offers brightly. "They switched us to a room with two twins. So technically, we won't have to sleep together."

"Oh," I say, knowing this is somehow going to be worse. "Good, then."

"I'm really sorry. If it's terrible, we can find a hotel for tomorrow night."

"No!" I cough. "No. Of course it's fine. I've been sleeping in tents for the last six years. A twin bed will feel like luxury." And sweet torture. Sweet, luxurious torture. I will not be telling Kevin about this.

"You're sure?"

"Positive. Although," I joke, "I do know that you snore . . ." *And it's adorable.*

"I'm a maniac in bed, actually," she confesses, and I die a little inside at the images unwittingly flickering past in my brain. Shelby next to me, twisted in my sheets. Shelby's long, toned leg thrown over my hip. Shelby underneath me, her soft blond hair spread out on a pillow and . . . "I kick everywhere and wake up facing the wrong direction. It's a good thing you'll have your own space, really."

"Yeah," I say weakly. "Good thing."

• • •

Shelby is, in fact, a maniac in bed. I know this because I don't sleep a wink. Not one iota. For the eight hours Shelby snores, tossing and turning, her long legs tangled in her quilt, her hair flopping over her face and across her pillow, I am on high alert. A world-renowned CIA-level assassin could blink the next room over and I would know. That's how alert I am. And hard. So painfully hard it's not even funny. Well. Someone would find this funny. My enemies perhaps. Lyle, the fucker, would piss himself.

Initially, everything was fine. We made it into our room a little after ten o'clock and decided it wasn't even worth it to turn on the television. Besides, we wanted to get an early start at the flea market.

Party animals we are not.

I took the bathroom first to get ready for bed, thanking Jesus, Mary, and all the saints I brought a pair of old sleep shorts because boxer briefs leave nothing to the imagination, and I still get sprung like a fifteen-year-old if Shelby so much as sneezes in a cute way. She's fucking adorable when she sneezes, so it's a whole thing.

I crawled into my twin bed approximately one inch bigger than my frame in every direction and picked up my phone to scroll through sports scores while Shelby ducked into the bathroom.

"You can turn off the lights," she said. "I'll be a few minutes."

"It's pretty dark. I don't mind."

She muttered something under her breath and closed the door. I read scores, checked the weather app, and ignored another email from my agent before the bathroom door opened. Shelby was holding her clothes in front of her chest, but I barely noticed because all I saw were her legs. Miles of legs under a T-shirt that barely covered her spectacular ass. I inwardly groaned and shifted in my bedding, pooling the quilt near my waist. She cleared her throat, turning pink.

"So. This is awkward." She dropped her arms and I choked out a cough.

"Is that my shirt?"

"Yeah."

"Still?"

"Yeah." She tucked her hair behind a glowing-red ear. "Well. It's really soft."

"I bet. It's, like, twelve years old."

"Yeah," she said again, biting her lip. "I swear I have other sleep shirts."

"The evidence says otherwise," I said, willing a teasing tone past my bone-dry throat.

"I should give it back to you probably."

"No!" I said. Christ that's the last thing I need. "It's fine. It's yours. Possession is nine-tenths of the law or whatever."

"Okay," she said and tucked her clothes in her suitcase before scrambling under her covers and hiding her bare legs away.

That should have been the end of it. So what if she was sleeping in my shirt? If she's been sleeping in my shirt for twelve years? It's fine. It's not like she's touched herself thinking of me while wearing my shirt. It's not like it smells like me. For fuck's sake, I barely owned it. It's honestly *her* shirt at this point. I turned over in the dark, facing her, and closed my eyes. Within seconds I heard her breathing even out. I thought I was about to follow her into sleep when the softest, most breathless little whimper echoed into the silence from her bed.

My eyes shot open.

She was asleep. She didn't mean anything by it. It's a noise she makes.

Another tiny moan and she turned, her leg slipping out of the covers, moonlit and perfect and close enough to reach. A whimper, followed by a long, shuddering exhale.

This time I groaned, rolling to face the opposite wall and tugging my pillow over my ears. Those were definitely sex noises. Shelby was making sex noises in her sleep while wearing my shirt. I will never sleep ever again.

• • •

The moment the sunrise cracks through the top of the ruffled buffalo-plaid curtains, I throw back my quilt, more than ready to end the torture. I'm greeted by my own morning wood (or all-night-long wood), but if the snores coming from Shelby's bed are any indication, she's still plenty asleep. I don't bother covering myself as I trudge to the shower. I don't even have it in me to be embarrassed. The cold spray will fix me right up, scaring away the boner to end all boners, and hopefully waking me up long enough to make it down the stairs and into the dining room to find some coffee I can inject directly into my veins.

In fact, I almost hope she does see me in this state. A man has his limits, and they include when your beautiful ex sleeps three feet away from you while wearing your old T-shirt as if she hasn't just ruined you for all other women.

I groan, tilting my head against the freezing cold shower tiles. When I am old and gray and barely able to shuffle my way from my La-Z-Boy to my microwave to make my Cream of Wheat laced with MiraLAX, I will *still* have a hard-on.

Less than twenty minutes later, I'm sitting on the front porch of the B&B in a flannel shirt and jeans with a thermos of steaming black coffee, watching the late-season frost get chased into dew by the sun. I have to admit, it's pretty up here. It's not the wild plains of Africa, but it feels like home.

"Danish?"

I look up, surprised to see Shelby. She's fresh-faced and pink-cheeked, wearing a chunky knit sweater over jeans and brown boots laced to her shins. She is sufficiently more covered than the last time I saw her, but I *know* things now. Things I can't ever unknow. And there's only fourteen hours and twenty-three minutes until I see her in my T-shirt again.

She's still holding the plate and I take a pastry without

looking too closely. After a bite, I realize it's raspberry. My favorite. Shelby sits in a rocker next to me and takes a bite of hers, balancing a coffee in between her knees.

"I couldn't remember if raspberry or blueberry was your favorite, so I took a guess."

"Good guess," I say, lifting the danish. "This is perfect."

She makes a noise of agreement and leans back, looking out over the acres of woods in front of us. "It is, isn't it? The house-flipping market isn't great up here, but I would love to settle down in the U.P. one day. It's so peaceful."

"The market isn't good, but they still host this giant flea market?"

Shelby nods and swallows a bite. "That's part of what makes the market so great. It's an untapped resource. When I first moved back and started working for my dad, I wasn't really sure what I wanted to focus on, and all the thrift stores and antique hot spots downstate are pretty touristy. They're super picked-through and cater to the trends . . . lots of shiplap and farmhouse sinks and that kind of thing. Those have merit for sure, but it was being done already, you know? I needed to find my own niche."

"You realize if this show takes off, your niche will become the next trend, right?"

Shelby makes a face, brushing her fingers off on her pants. "I've thought about that. It's part of the reason I didn't want the cameras around this weekend. The last thing I want is everyone making this a tourist destination next spring. I have to keep some of my secrets."

"It's that great, huh?"

"Better, Cam. This is like Disneyland for thrifters."

I laugh at her enthusiasm and finish my coffee. "I'm going to refill. You ready to go?"

She stands up. "I'll top off my cup."

• • •

We spend the morning weaving in and out of tents stuffed with musty-smelling bookshelves, dinged-up rolltop desks, and all sorts of knickknacks ranging from unusual to absurd. Apparently, flea markets are one part farmers' market, one part As-Seen-on-TV infomercial products, two parts beeswax-hemp candles, and infinity parts Christmas crafts. But if you know where to look, which Shelby obviously does, you are sure to find at least a pickup truck's worth of early twentieth-century furniture worth rehabbing.

And two more items besides to be shipped.

"I knew I should have driven separately." Shelby sighs after signing her address to the dotted line. "Four to six weeks. I miss her already."

I bite back a laugh at the forlorn expression on her face. "I think it will take you that long just to make the room for a Hoosier cabinet this size. How will you fit it through the door of your shop, even?"

"Duh. I have a garage door off the side."

"Of course you do."

"I might keep this one, though. I don't think I could sell her."

"Do you also have a garage door off the side of your house that I don't know about?"

"No. But I do have a sliding door in the back. I just need

someone strapping to help me get it up the deck steps . . ." She taps her chin, smirking.

"I'm not sure Daniel's knees are up to it. Better hire movers."

She smacks my arm as we turn away from the tent. "Ouch, woman. If you want my biceps to bring in your giant-ass Hoosier whatsit, you really ought to treat them better." I lead us toward the food tent where I can smell something fried, probably twice, calling to me.

Shelby wraps her arm through mine and tips her head to my shoulder as we walk. "I'm sorry, Cam's Biceps, please forgive me." She rubs the flannel covering my upper arm and I work at keeping a bland expression on my face as my whole body burns under her ministrations.

My. T-shirt. For Christ's sake.

"I'm sure all will be forgotten if we can take an ice-cream break. My treat."

"Deal. It's finally warming up." Shelby lets go of my arm to slip out of her heavy sweater and tie it in a bulky knot around her waist. "Let's get some lunch first. I think there's a small folk band playing, so we can sit and listen to music."

We end up ordering a plate of loaded nachos and a couple of lemonades and sit at a picnic table near the edge of a gathering crowd that's huddled in front of a small stage. For a few minutes, we eat in comfortable silence, but once the music starts up, Shelby's boot starts tapping and before I know what I'm doing, my hand is outstretched and a smile quirks on my lips.

Shelby's blue eyes sparkle with humor. "Seriously?"

"Dare you."

"Well, hell. I haven't been dared in years." Shelby takes my hand and I tug her to her feet, leading her out toward the middle of the crowd. We sway side to side, connected by hands and hips and shoulders. The song is a cover of a country hit, and I can't help but sing along with the lyrics. Shelby giggles and joins after a few beats. I twirl her around, growing more comfortable. We aren't anyone here. I spin her out and pull her back in and she follows my lead seamlessly in a modified kind of two-step. I meet her eyes and can't look away. I'm lost in a memory of us, the sun setting on an open field while I clumsily kiss my way down her body, giddy with nerves and lust. I knew that night I could love this girl—woman. That I would always love her.

God, I'm an idiot for ever walking away.

I can't do it again.

What if I didn't? What if I stayed? What if we sold the season? Could I stay here, working so close to Shelby, loving her as I do, unrequited?

But would it be unrequited? She told me to stop running, but I can't tell the real from the fake anymore. We kissed at the Caroline Street house. That was real. We fought and I stormed off, but then we talked and worked things out. That was also real. We flirt. On camera. Maybe not real. Well, okay, real for me, but . . .

She brought my T-shirt to sleep in.

Too fucking real.

No. It's not unrequited, but things aren't progressing either, and I'm starting to realize why.

I take a chance and pull Shelby closer. Her scent is nearly my undoing. She smells like lemons and springtime. She wraps her arms around my neck without hesitation, her cheeks rosy and her hair shining gold in the midday sun.

I can't leave her again.

14

SHELBY

BACK TO YOU

After *The Dance* (a.k.a. the dance heard round the world or at least in Shelby Springfield's best Nora Ephron–fueled day-dreams), Cameron suggests grabbing soft-serve ice-cream cones before continuing on to the next tent. Not like I have room for more furniture finds, but I haven't even made it through half the vendors yet, and well, we're here.

As if I could concentrate, at any rate. I'm basically a puddle of hormones and incoherent reason at this point. Sleeping practically within reach—close enough to hear his breathing. I mean, if I hadn't taken that Tylenol PM, I'd probably be staggering through my day like, well, like *he* is, if I'm honest.

Poor guy.

I didn't mean to pack his T-shirt. Okay. Yes, I definitely meant to pack it. I rarely sleep in anything else because I'm pathetic. But I absolutely meant to take that secret to the grave and I couldn't very well sleep in my jeans.

But then there's how he's oh-so-casually paid for everything so far. Like a date. Like a date weekend. I should probably fight him over it, women's lib and all, but hell, it's been so long since anyone tried to pay for me.

Again. I'm tragic. We covered this.

And maybe I'm just a little bit hopeful. As if when added up to a whole, these things could mean something . . . because at first, we were only dancing, and it was all friendly and cool, and then it was more. Like, *more* more.

And this time, when our fingers dangle between us as we stroll along the center aisle of the tent, his catch mine, and I swear the clouds clear overhead and an angel chorus breaks into jubilant song.

Halle-fricken-lujah.

I watch as his tongue darts out to capture the chocolate sweetness. "Is this okay?" he asks. *Which part?* I wonder, sardonically. The strong, calloused man-hand wrapped around mine or the talented tongue flexing?

Because, option C. ALL OF THE ABOVE.

I squeeze his giant hand in mine. "Remember when we couldn't do this?" I swing our hands between us, choosing to stifle my overly enthusiastic pheromones. "Nothing but dark corners."

"Not that there was anything wrong with dark corners," he admits, and I feel my face flush. Cameron's pheromones clearly missed the stifling memo.

Fuck it.

"I prefer open fields."

He throws his head back with a groan. "Peaked at eighteen."

"You did have a pretty strong game," I admit.

"Did I ever tell you I got my first speeding ticket that day?"

"No!"

He nods, squeezing my hand once and licking around his cone before swallowing. "Earlier. Lyle was such a tool that day, I swear he knew something was up. He kept messing up his lines and we got out super late."

"I remember."

He continues. "Well, to top it off, I'd already told you I had a spot worked out, right outside town. And I did, but I freaked out that it would be taken, so I wanted to run out after work and save it."

"With a blanket?"

He shrugs. "I was nervous."

"Me, too," I admit. "So, you drove out?"

"I did. Floored it the entire way. I made it, laid the blanket down, and then on my way out, I was pulled over for speeding."

"Were you speeding?"

"Hell yeah. I was out of my mind. I was about to have *sex!*" he stage-whispers the last word and I burst into giggles. "With Shelby *fucking* Springfield!"

I'm laughing-crying at his pure expression. I can just picture him, ten years younger.

"I didn't even try to get out of it. I was all, 'Yes, officer. Go ahead. I messed up. Do your worst.' But the cop must have been able to tell I was in a hurry and thought I wasn't taking it seriously, so he gets pissed."

"Oh no."

"Yeah." His expression is churlish. "So, I'm trying my best to look contrite." He points his cone to his chest. "Child actor, right? Should have been cake. Meanwhile, I probably have a raging boner because . . ."

"Because you're about to have sex for the first time!" I'm dying.

"Exactly. *Now* I have the self-awareness to be humiliated, but right then, I just wanted to get back to you before you changed your mind."

"I wasn't going to change my mind."

"I can't believe you didn't," he admits.

"Cam," I say softly. He turns to me. "I made my mind up about you basically the moment we met."

He swallows. It's the barest of movements, but I can tell he's finally starting to see.

Thank Jesus, because I'm laying this on pretty thick. Like, *weeks* of pathetic Shelby being all *"Hello? Over here! I AM YOURS."*

"Did the cop know who you were?" I ask.

"Oh yeah. He asked me for an autograph for his daughters."

I shake my head. "Unreal. If it's any consolation, I had zero idea. You came off completely calm and collected by the time you showed up at my trailer."

He shakes his head. "You're just remembering the good parts."

I bite my lip. I know I need to take this slow. I don't want to freak him out, but also, *how can I?* I've been waiting possibly my whole life for this man to get a clue. "I remember *all* the parts."

He clears his throat. "Me, too."

I finish my cone and let go of his hand to throw the wrapper in a trash bin. "I still think of all the parts," I say, over my shoulder.

He freezes momentarily before following and throwing his wrapper away.

"So." His voice cracks in an adorably familiar way. "There's a recycled barn-wood vendor in the next aisle I wanted to check out."

"Lead on."

He grabs my hand again, hiding his grin. "Yes, ma'am."

• • •

Cam drops me off at my B&B room door hours later. We were notified a second room opened up this afternoon and I (graciously) offered to keep the twin beds and allow him the queen in the opposite suite.

Let the record show, I deserve a Presidential Medal of Restraint and Second Virginity for letting him walk away.

Especially after he wrapped my body in the cocoon of his strong arms and his delicious smell and his thoughtful gaze. For a full minute. And then he whispered that he "had a good time today." And *then,* when he tightened his embrace, I felt him press against me everywhere but especially *right there,* and he didn't shy away but let me feel it all the way in my bone marrow and—holy hell can you come to completion from a hug?

(Maybe we could call it dry humping? Maybe that would be somehow less pathetic?)

(Is dry humping less pathetic, though? In what universe?)

I close my door and immediately start an ice-cold shower

before giving it up for lost, turning the nozzle to hot and closing my eyes, imagining his tongue.

Before I fall asleep that night, he texts me a single line orchestrated to ensure I never sleep again.

CAMERON: I still think of all the parts, too.

• • •

The following morning, we get an early start. The drive will be slower on the way home, due to our extra cargo, and we have to be back to film bright and early tomorrow at the Caroline Street house. Besides, I was up at sunrise, coffee in hand and belly full of the most delicious mini eggy pancakes called Dutch babies with lemon curd and fresh berries. It's going to be so sad returning to my own cooking. After we're settled in the truck, Cameron passes me his phone since I forgot to charge mine. My dad's truck is too old to have a charger, but it does have a lighter/adapter.

"I can't handle another five hours of Eddie Money. Can you find a podcast or something? I don't care what you pick, but please no more classic rock," Cameron says, pulling out on to the highway. Apparently, he slept better last night (wonder why?) so he's back to driving.

"You got it." He tells me his password is his birthdate and I type it in easily.

"Crap."

His brows raise, but he doesn't remove his eyes from the road. "What? It's not charged either?"

"No, it is. It's Lyle. He's been texting. All caps and everything. Should I open it?"

He sighs. I know exactly what he's thinking. The bubble has officially popped on our weekend away from reality.

"Might as well. He won't quit."

I skim the messages first, as if I'm screening them. "Looks like it's to both of us . . ."

"And?" he asks tersely.

"And you better pull over."

Cam eases the truck off the next exit and turns on the hazards.

LYLE: ANYONE WANT TO EXPLAIN HOW THIS SHIT ENDED UP ON TMZ THIS MORNING? <<video file>>

LYLE: NICE LITTLE COZY WEEKEND AWAY? DID YOU HAVE FUN?

LYLE: DON'T ANSWER THAT. I DON'T ACTUALLY CARE EXCEPT YOU COMPLETELY OUTED YOURSELVES.

"Oh, for fuck's sake," I grumble. Cam clicks on the video and it's a grainy cell-phone clip of us dancing at the flea market. Honestly, it's kind of cute. Cameron reads the caption in a dull voice.

"'Is this who I think it is? Is that Shelby Springfield? And . . . is that grown-up Cameron Riggs with a beard? XOXOXO #OTP4EVA #jacksonsworld.'"

"Hashtag," I correct him when he's finished.

"Huh?"

"You said 'pound sign.' It's actually a hashtag."

He blinks and I bite back a grin. For being a former child star, Cam is refreshingly unimpressed with social media. I imagine it has something to do with filming in remote locations the last six years.

"Never mind."

"I guess I don't understand what he's upset about? I mean, it's our privacy that's been violated here."

"And we were in a public space, so even that is negligible."

He nods, distracted, and rubs tiredly at his whiskers. "Did we sign a nondisclosure and I forgot about it?"

I sit back in my seat. "Definitely not. And it's not like we were walking around telling anyone we were filming a pilot. For all anyone knows, we were just . . ."

"On a weekend getaway?"

I feel my cheeks heat, even though I don't really understand why. "Right. Antiquing. For my business."

"I don't even want to respond. Can we just not respond?"

"We can, but he'll keep texting and calling. Do you mind if I fuck with him a bit instead?"

Cam brightens. "Not at all."

I take back his phone where, as predicted, Lyle is still going.

LYLE: DON'T EVEN TRY TO DENY YOU TWO ARE FUCKING NOW.

Ugh. I wish.

SHELBY: Sorry, Lyle, this is Shelby. I forgot to charge my phone on account of all the crazy hot public sex Cameron and I were having while wearing our new "HomeMade" merch with your name featured prominently on the back. Won't happen again.

I read it aloud to Cam before hitting Send and he snorts. "Serves him right. The fucker." He turns off the hazards and pulls us back into traffic. Before we're even on the highway, Lyle responds, blessedly without the caps.

LYLE: I hate you, guys. You're both fired.

I snicker.

SHELBY: Oh no.

LYLE: The clip is all over the internet!

I give a mental shrug. Cam gives a physical one.

SHELBY: I fail to see the problem. Free publicity?

LYLE: A heads-up would've been nice. We have people who can mitigate that shit.

SHELBY: Like the heads-up you gave me about Ada Mae?

SHELBY: You aren't the boss of me, Lyle Jessup. We didn't bring cameras, and this wasn't for the benefit of the show.

LYLE: So, you two are a thing now?

SHELBY: What we are is none of your business.

LYLE: Same old shit, Shelby.

SHELBY: I'm leaving now. It's Sunday, Lyle.

I try to tuck Cameron's phone screen down in the center console, but we're stopped at the bridge toll, so he picks it up, glancing at the messages. I watch as his face darkens and wait him out.

"I expected better of him," he confesses wryly. "Clearly this was about more than a leaked video."

I huff out a sigh. "Lucky you. I have five more years of experience in suffering through his up-and-down, back-and-forth, manipulative bullshit."

"Okay, but why is he so intent on hurting you?"

"I told you. He wasn't first."

"I thought you said he didn't know about that."

"Not *that* first. I mean . . ." I stare out the window, unseeing, to avoid his shrewd green eyes. "He wasn't ever first with me. Cam," I say softly. "Who did I call the moment he broke up with me?"

"Me."

I trace a raindrop on the window with my fingertip. "And what did you do?"

"I flew out to L.A."

"From Alaska, for fuck's sake. I had no idea you didn't like flying at that time." I turn to him, my palm open between us. My heart may as well be resting on it—an offering. My breath is extra loud in the small space of the cab, but this needs to be said. After all this time, Cameron needs to understand. "He never had a chance."

His dark brows meet together. "But he cheated on you. You were a wreck over it."

"He was always cheating on me, Cam. Like *always.* Marcella just happened to be my closest friend at the time, so that part was painful. He was forever making sure I knew I wasn't *it* for him, and while I knew he wasn't *it* for me either—that we'd been pretty much holding on to the pretense for the sake of our careers—I was still loyal to him. I still cared about him. I thought he cared, too, until his secret album was ready, with his one-sided version of the narrative. I was completely blindsided."

"Why did you stay with him so long, if you knew all of that?"

"Well, I didn't know *all* of it," I concede, chagrined. "It was more like I stayed *in L.A.* I didn't know what else to do. All I was good for was acting and singing. I was typecast in my own life." I grimace. "They kept giving me roles and singles and I took them. Why wouldn't I? But Lyle was only a small part of that, and he knew it and resented me for it. He must resent me even more for calling *you* and getting out of there. It sort of stole his thunder when I went into hiding."

"Good old Cameron," he jokes half-heartedly.

"Yes," I agree sincerely. "Good, decent, handsome Cameron. Who came when I called and refused to take advantage of me even when I threw myself quite literally at his feet."

"I thought about it," he admits with a sly half grin.

"Thank God. I'm not too proud to admit my ego has been bruised for years."

"How could I not? You were wearing my T-shirt. Which, by the way . . ."

I press my lips together in an attempt to hide my smile at his expression. He shakes his head. "You're evil."

"I'm—" *crazy for you.* "Okay. Listen. That was not planned. But I see how it looks." I release a long, slow breath, giving myself plenty of time to back out. But I don't. "Cam, if the whole wide world was on fire and I had to give up everything I owned, I would still have your T-shirt."

He sucks in a quick breath. "You should've had me."

"What about now?"

I watch as his grip tightens on the steering wheel, waiting for him to say something—anything.

"Now I don't want to leave you."

"Then don't."

"It's not that easy, Shelby. My job isn't here. My life isn't here." And to his credit, for the first time, he seems torn up about it.

It could be, I think. But things feel too fragile between us to push it so instead I say, "Well, you're here now."

"I am," he says, resolute.

"So, I have you for now."

"If you want me."

"Don't you mean if you want me? Lest we forget the pathetic T-shirt pining."

"I listen to all your pop songs still," he says in a rush.

"What?"

"Look for yourself," he offers, passing me his phone.

I scroll to his music app and click on it and gasp in delight. "Cam, it's only my music!"

He shrugs. "Pining at its finest."

"They aren't even very good singles."

"They're *you.* And when I was traveling the world, it was the only thing I had."

"Oh my God, you even have the Courtney Love cover."

"My end-of-year Spotify list is mortifying."

I put down his phone and turn to him fully. "Cam"—my tone is gentle—"what have we been doing to ourselves?"

He sighs. "I don't know, but let's start over. Again." He holds out his hand. "I'm Cameron Riggs. Massive fan of yours. I have all your albums."

I'm beaming. "Wow, Cameron, that sounds kind of obsessive. My name is Shelby, by the way, and I'm going to need you to remove your T-shirt before you drop me off so I can sleep in it every night like a teenager."

"You're on."

15

CAMERON

ONLY ONE

It's a relief to be back at the Caroline Street house. I arrive to work early Monday morning, telling myself it's only because I want to see what progress had been made while I was gone, but knowing it's more complicated than that.

Or maybe it's simpler. Everything has been made much clearer since Lyle's freak-out. We've always known he's had his own angle in this, and he was definitely irked that we slipped from his control this weekend. What's less concrete is if he's serious about this pilot becoming a show, or if this is just an elaborate, overpriced scheme to further manipulate our lives.

This, admittedly, sounds insane. And yet, this is the guy who created a real-life scandal by cheating on his famous girlfriend with her best friend while writing a song about it, and then winning a Grammy after the breakup.

The obvious solution is to avoid anything that could be construed as drama-worthy for the duration of filming on the Caroline Street house. But even that's left up to subjectivity. For example, Shelby and I awoke this morning to a hundred different flea-market sightings plastered all over the internet. Who knew so many Yoopers were amateur paparazzi in their spare time? There were plenty that rehashed our past, dragging Shelby more than me (typical), before getting to what we are up to lately. Or at least the speculation of what we are up to.

Speculation Lyle is loath to confirm.

We could hide, but it feels better to control the narrative by just showing up, being happy, and trying our best. And amid all the gossip about what happened ten years, five years, or even three weeks ago . . . there seems to be this sincere wish for us to make it.

I even saw a few articles refer to the *World According to Jackson* kiss.

I can't imagine this is going to fly with Lyle. People always like a happy success story, but they *love* a fall from grace, and I have my suspicions on which version he'd prefer go out ahead of our pilot.

This is why I'm here early, tool belt strapped in place and ready to go over the plans for the second-story addition. It's also why I called my agent, Peter, on my way in and told him to give Dominick Rivera the green light on the Fiji project. I can be a joke, or I can be better, but I can't be in two places at once. There's a chance this pilot will fail, and the network won't order the season, and I'll be fucked. But there's a chance it won't, and for once in my life, I need to commit totally.

To myself *and* to Shelby. This weekend was enlightening,

to say the least. I don't have a place or direction or even a real clue as to what I'm doing, but I do have her and I'm not fucking *that* up again.

Even if it means studiously ignoring the voicemail from Paul Riggs I can't seem to delete. Despite not bothering to care for seventeen years, he sure knew the second I found myself back in the limelight. If I didn't know the man hated technology, I'd wonder if he had a Google Alert set for my name.

Hey, son. Just reading about your latest exploits on the internet. I didn't even know you were back in town. Had to hear it from your mother. Seems nothing's changed on that front. Call me before you fly out for God-knows-where again.

It's fine. I'm not panicking. There's always the spare room at my mom's house. Just shuffle around the treadmill and stair-stepper and I'll be set. No problem.

Daniel is the next to show up at Caroline Street, still early, two coffees in hand. He passes one to me.

I raise my eyebrows, surprised. "Thanks."

"Thought you might be here already."

"Just reviewing the addition."

"Plumbing guys are coming this morning."

I take a sip and nod. "As planned."

"I met with the electrician yesterday."

I knew this, too. "We still on track?"

Daniel chuckles low. "We're ahead of the game and you know it. By a week at least. But . . ."

"Oh no. What?"

Daniel scratches at his silvery stubble. "Steve got a call from Lyle last night. He wants to mess with the deadlines a little. For dramatic integrity or some BS."

"He wants to mess with the deadlines on the construction of a *real* house with *real* owners paying *real* money for dramatic effect?"

"That's what he said. He canceled the order on the tile."

I groan. "Backsplash or bathroom?"

"All of it. We need to reorder today, obviously, but it's likely we'll be put back in the queue for that Spanish backsplash."

"We can order something else, though. Something that fits our schedule."

"We can."

"Fucker," I mutter.

"You aren't supposed to know any of this, by the way. They wanted your reaction live."

"I wouldn't expect anything less. Fair warning, this won't be the last of the garbage he's gonna pull." I tug out my phone and show Daniel the clip of Shelby and me from this weekend.

"It's all over the internet, apparently."

Daniel watches in silence and passes the phone back without comment.

"Aren't you going to say anything?"

"I better not. Shelby's her own woman."

"I really care about her, Daniel. I want you to know that."

He laughs, shaking his head, and gestures to the phone. "I

know you do, kid. Everyone knows you do. Does this mean you're sticking around for a while?"

I exhale, fidgeting with the brim of my ball cap. "I'm trying. I told *Nat Geo* I wouldn't take a project this fall, which means I'm jobless. So . . ." I put down my coffee cup and spread the plans out on a makeshift sawhorse table, moving on. "I want to give Shelby plenty of time for her nook. That dining room table is a masterpiece, but it's been a huge time suck for her."

Daniel looks like he wants to say something more but allows the subject change. "She'll be fine. Not the first time she's worked under pressure."

I straighten with another groan. "That's why they asked her to do that table, isn't it? To create more drama if she's rushed."

"Probably, but she's risen to the challenge. Just like you have and will."

I hunch over the blueprints with a frustrated scowl, tracing the lines of the floor joists I'll be installing on the second floor as soon as I get the go-ahead from the building inspector this afternoon. "Do you think you might be able to help with the joists today or tomorrow?" I ask. "I've been reading up, but I'd feel a lot more comfortable if you were there to start me off."

"I can come by first thing tomorrow morning. Before I hit the Thompson Street house."

"I'd rather she not be under pressure on this one," I say, returning to Shelby. "It means too much."

Daniel places a large hand in the center of my plans,

prompting me to look up. His blue eyes, so like his daughter's, are piercing. "Riggs. Shelby's good for this."

I shake my head. "That's not what I mean. We know she's capable, but I get the feeling Lyle's banking on her failing. I just want to make sure she has every opportunity to prove him wrong. Not only that, I want her to blow everyone away."

"And what about you?"

"What about me?" I ask tersely.

"Do you have something to prove, too?"

It feels like the air has been knocked out of my chest.

"Call me before you fly off to God-knows-where again."

Instead, I wave him off. "I'm here for the comic relief."

"You're the hardest-working comic relief I've ever seen, then."

"I told you, I want her to be taken seriously."

"She will be."

I release a long, slow breath, but my shoulders are still tense as I press my palms into the table. "Good."

"You will be, too."

I shake my head, disbelieving. *"You'll never be taken seriously as long as you keep hamming it up for the cameras, Cameron."* "It doesn't matter."

Daniel places a hand on my shoulder. "It *does* matter. You deserve this as much as she does. I don't know what had you running for so long, but you're here now, and we're all better for it. You're doing good work, son."

My throat is thick, and I can't speak. Can't look up. Can't move. Daniel squeezes once and pats my shoulder before taking his coffee.

"I'm going to check on things. Cabinets should be delivered today. Don't forget to act shocked when they tell you about the tile."

• • •

Unsurprisingly, Steve wants to get some footage of Shelby shopping for her furniture pieces, even if she's not shopping for the Caroline Street house, and he tells me I'm supposed to go along.

"It's for filler," he explains. "Something fun and light for in between the bits that are too construction intensive." I love how at least Steve thinks furniture shopping is "fun and light." Shelby swings by the house to pick me up. I'm all sweaty and covered in a layer of sawdust, but Steve said it added to the "authenticity of the thing," which is a trip because this is very authentic work grime I'm wearing right now.

Shelby laughs at my peeved expression when I apologize for getting her car dirty.

"I have some baby wipes in the back, if you want."

"Do I even want to know?" I ask, even as I reach an arm back and fish the package out, tearing it open and scrubbing my neck and forearms down with a wipe.

"Believe it or not, they remove all sorts of things, like permanent marker and finish, in a pinch."

"I'll take your word for it."

"You're welcome."

I make a face. "My beard smells like baby soap."

"Don't be so dramatic; they're unscented."

"I promise they aren't."

She smirks. "Poor Cameron Riggs, brought low by baby wipes."

"I preferred the sawdust. At least that was manly."

"Don't worry," she quips, wrinkling her nose. "You're still plenty manly smelling."

I lean over in my seat, rubbing my sweat on her. "What was that?"

"Cam! Gross!" She makes a show of gagging.

"Gotta cover you in my masculine essence."

"See if I ever share my baby wipes with you again."

It's then that I notice the red light on the car camera and curse under my breath. Shelby grins, full of glee. "Oh yeah. You just said 'masculine essence' on television."

"Fucking Lyle," I say.

She taps her chin with a fingertip. "I wonder if we could make that the working title?"

She winks at the camera right as I'm flipping it the bird.

A few minutes later, Shelby pulls up a gravel drive and parks behind a dozen other pickup trucks.

"This is a farm sale?" I ask.

"Barn sale, actually. And yes. Steve is here already, so I guess we walk up like everything is normal . . ."

"Totally."

"And shop."

"Act natural."

"If you can manage it, Riggs?" Her eyebrow arches in a challenge and I'm tempted to kiss it.

"Oh. I can manage it." We walk up and I see the camera crew standing outside the barn, waiting. I continue in a low voice, only for her. "It's just, you don't really realize how ridiculous reality television is until you are out and about in reality."

"And everyone is staring at you."

"Right."

"At least I didn't just take a bath with baby wipes."

I growl and lunge for her. She shrieks a little and skitters out of reach.

"Professional truce." She holds a hand out.

"Professional time-out," I concede and shake her hand once before striding toward the camera crew.

• • •

The barn sale is pretty incredible, but it's nothing compared to Shelby *at* a barn sale. She's meticulous and knowledgeable and I probably look like a complete himbo next to her, but I can't even be mad about it. I'm too busy admiring her and following behind, carrying a box of iron hardware like a lovesick puppy.

It's a distinction I wear with pride, believe me.

Every farmer knows her by name and not because they listened to her pop singles. She knows the complete history of the county, including the family farms. She understands the equipment and implements, even if that's not what she's in the market for. They all keep aside items for her—piles of barn wood and signs and hardware and ancient woodworking tools.

"Hey there, young lady," one old guy says. He's dressed in a flannel and Dickies, even though it's gotta be close to eighty degrees in here.

"Mr. Jenson!" Shelby reaches out to hug the man and he pats her back with a laugh.

"I was hoping I'd see you today. I brought you something."

Shelby's eyes glitter with excitement. "I can't wait. Do you mind if my partner Cameron Riggs comes along? He's my muscle today."

Mr. Jenson looks me up and down behind smudged glasses. He raises a hand, showing off his gnarled joints and scratches at his nose. "Sure, sure. Come on." He waves us out toward the trucks. The camera crew follows at a slower pace, giving Mr. Jenson space. If he's bothered by them, he doesn't show it.

He rounds an older model Chevy pickup to the tailgate. Shelby pops the handle and lets it drop with a low whistle. Waiting for her is a solid-oak church pew, scuffed and magnificent. Shelby hops up on the truck bed to examine it closer.

"The scrollwork is fantastic," she says with a reverence that has Mr. Jenson standing taller.

"My dad did it. The church burned down a few years back, but this was in our barn at the time. I was trying to restore them, one by one. Then the fire happened, and I couldn't bear it. Ever since, it's been collecting dust."

Shelby slides her hand along the curled top. "It's masterful, Mr. Jenson. Your father was a true craftsman."

"Do you think you can find a good home for it?"

Shelby's eyes are glittering, but this time, it's with emotion. "Are you sure? What if I restore it for you?"

Mr. Jenson shakes his head. "I don't have a place for it. Hospice has moved in for Maggie, and after . . ." He swallows. "I won't have a need for it. But you could take care of it . . ."

Shelby brushes her hands on her pants and jumps down off the truck bed. "It would be my honor. I'm not sure I could give it away, though. I'm too selfish. I'll be keeping this one for myself."

Mr. Jenson looks pleased as Punch. They haggle over price, but I can tell whatever answer they come to, she's going to find a way to pay him extra.

"Hey, Muscles," she says to me at last. "Think you can help me get this onto the truck?"

"That's what I'm here for, isn't it?" I say, pretending to grumble.

Mr. Jenson chuckles low, his eyes red-rimmed but crinkled at the corners in a fond smile. "It's not a bad job, young man. I've been my Margaret's muscles for fifty-eight years."

I grin at him. "That sounds like it might be the best job, actually."

"You take care of our girl, Mr. Riggs."

"That's my plan."

Shelby beams and gives him another hug, pressing her lips to his weathered cheek. I enlist the teenaged son of the farmer hosting the sale and together we move the solid pew to our truck. After, I retrieve the box of iron hardware and walk back inside to pay. There's a whole crowd of geezer farmers around Shelby now, trading stories and working hard to win her musical laugh. I imagine they're here to look at old tractors, too, but she's the highlight. They don't care about her history or the television crew. I doubt they'll even watch our show, if it gets to that point. Scratch that, I doubt they'd be able to find the channel in the first place.

But it doesn't matter. As improbable as it is, she's earned their respect. They trust her with their memories. They believe in her skill. Long before Lyle came sniffing around, and long after the camera crews leave, Shelby will have a place in this community.

And I'm finding, the more time I spend here, with her—with them—I want to find my place in this community, too.

16

SHELBY

WRECKING BALL

Oh, Shelby and Cam from two weeks ago. You're so hilarious and naive to think you might be able to secretly date while renovating a house and also hiding it from the video cameras and your ex-boyfriend-slash-former-costar-slash-boss.

In the ten days since our trip north, Cam and I have kissed in two (unfinished) closets and spent four nights whispering dirty talk over the phone until the early-morning hours.

The thing is, we're adults—with homes and beds and Egyptian cotton sheets. And I don't understand *why* we aren't spending every (any) night together. I suspect it has something to do with Cameron's sweet, if misguided, sense of honor. He keeps saying he wants to take me on a proper date first, to differentiate between before and now and the kids we were versus the adults we are.

This is all well and good and really very charming, and when I'm eighty, I'll probably look back at his insistence with fondness or whatever. But right now, I really need the man to press me into his mattress and make me forget my own name. Repeatedly.

We have a lot of ground to cover. Years and years of ground. And his thighs are, like, *right there,* taunting me.

Cameron squats, bending to pick up one end of a slab of countertop, and from my perch on the bottom step, I greedily take in every line and clenching muscle. I'm technically on break, waiting on literal paint to dry. My dad directs the crew to drop the countertop against the recently smoothed drywall, and Cam places his end with careful precision, his biceps bulging and his full lips pressed together. I swallow hard, sweat trickling between my breasts, before a flying napkin smacks me across the forehead.

"Lunch!"

I take the Panera bag from my best friend, and she passes me a large iced green tea with a knowing smirk. "Looks like you could use something cold."

"Thanks. It's a hundred degrees in here."

"Yeah," she snarks in a low voice, settling next to me on the stair and cracking open her salad container. "That's what I meant. Still waiting, I see."

I nod, pouring some goopy green dressing over my chopped salad. "Ten years of unrequited lust will do that to a person."

Cameron maneuvers to lift another slab, this time angling himself so that I have a perfect view of his perfect ass.

"I feel a little guilty," I murmur distractedly. "I'm obviously objectifying him. He's more than his body."

Lorelai snorts, stabbing at a chunk of avocado.

"But I can't help it. He keeps wearing those jeans." My voice slips into a stage whisper. "It's like he knows."

Just then, Cam, his back to us, clenches his glutes, making his low-slung carpenter belt hop. My stomach flips reflexively, and I probably drool a little. Then he does it again. And again.

Cameron looks over his shoulder, catches my eye, and winks.

My fingers press to my lips, but it's too late to hide my giggle before he turns, giving my dad his full attention.

"Oh, he *knows,*" my best friend says. "He definitely knows. And I'd venture to say the rest of your crew knows. And probably your audience. And your dad? Even he can pick up on the stifling sexual tension in this place. Y'all are swimming in it."

My face burns red-hot and I smack her arm. She laughs. "I'm happy for you, Shelby."

"Thanks. Me, too."

After we finish our salads, Cameron saunters over and I pass him what's left of my iced tea. He gulps it down gratefully and I try not to stare. His gaze captures mine, and it's like I can literally feel my clothes peeling off—until our eye fucking is interrupted by a commotion at the front door.

"What the—"

Lyle Jessup stands in the rough-hewn foyer, shit-eating grin in place and his arm wrapped around the bony shoulders of my former best friend.

"Someone order a reunion?"

"I'd like mine without the narcissistic dickhead," Lorelai

mutters next to me. She glances nervously at the cameras suddenly in our faces. "Goddammit, I don't even have my lashes on today."

I crack a smile, taking her in. "You're beautiful, as always. But it's okay if you leave. Thanks for lunch."

Lorelai slips out the back door while Cameron crosses the room toward Lyle and Marcella, but Marcella glides past him in enviable steel-gray kid leather booties, aiming for me.

"Heyyyy, bitch!" she shrieks, all plastic smiles and glamorous hair extensions. Before I'm ready, she's wrapped her arms around my shoulders and is swaying side to side. I imagine her eyes are squeezed shut in feigned sincerity, just to really drive the moment home.

"Congrats, Shelb!" she says, pulling back and cradling my face in her tiny hands. "Your hair is so fab! You look so much older!"

"Thanks."

She spins around, her high-waisted skirt flaring just below her butt cheeks. I hear a collective groan from my crew and Lyle chuckles. *Settle down, boys.* I aim a glare at Cam, but he's got his eyes on me.

I try to communicate a mental Morse code of "everything's fine," which is a lie. It's not remotely okay, but I've seen worse.

That is, until Marcella spins toward him and clasps her manicured hands together under her chin. "Oh my God! Cameron Riggs! Look at that beard! And those biceps! Woooow . . ." She drags out the word and struts over to him. She runs her fingers slowly down his arm and I want to slap her hand away, but the camera is rolling. Honestly. She's so *obvious.*

Instead, I slap her with my eyeballs. In my brain. Where I can replay it over and over before bed tonight.

"You're coming with us, right?" Marcella is asking, her glossy lips in a perfect pout.

"Where are we going, exactly?"

I don't know how Lyle can stand it. Well, I do, actually. Marcella isn't as fake as she's acting. That was the worst part when I found her literally and metaphorically in bed with my boyfriend. She was my *friend*. And she had been a good one. She knew my secrets. She loved me, or so I thought. But she's also one hell of an actress and chock-full of ambition. My stomach still twists uncomfortably when I remember how she said to me: *"You don't want him, anyway, Shelb. Not really. And you aren't good enough to cut it out here. So, let him go. Let me have him."*

And she was right. Well, maybe not the part about not being good enough. I was damn good at what I did. My heart just wasn't in it.

"Out," Lyle answers with a broad smile that flashes all his teeth. "Marce and I want to treat you two to a night out on the town. You've been working too hard!"

I meet Cameron's eyes over the top of Marcella's head. He looks as resigned as I feel. There's really only one way to handle this. We'll have to play into Lyle's hands, which means pretending I'm not annoyed by them showing up out of the blue, flirting with my secret-boyfriend costar, and effectively cockblocking us *again*.

In other words, we've got to *act*.

We always were better actors than Lyle. Cameron gives the tiniest nod of understanding and flashes an easy grin at

Marcella, deftly removing her hand and walking over to pull me close and tuck me under one arm. "I know just the place. My friend owns a bar not too far from here."

I can see it already . . . a night out at a bar . . . Lyle, plying us with drinks; Lyle, playing the happily married man to our restless and wandering single selves; Lyle's generosity as a showrunner providing this spectacular opportunity for his oldest friends.

A real philanthropist, that Lyle.

I don't love it, but I don't see how it can be helped. There's too much at stake with our pilot, not the least of which is Cameron staying. He told *Nat Geo* to give his project to another documentarian. He put himself out on a limb for this and I need to do the same. I only wish it didn't come with the feeling that Lyle is giving us just enough rope to hang ourselves on camera.

Cam turns to the rest of the crew. "Shut it down early, fellas! The weekend begins now!"

Decision made, I raise on my tiptoes and press a quick kiss to his bearded cheek, mindful of my mic, and offer a blinding smile at the camera, waggling my brows. "Think they have karaoke? I've been dying to get this guy on a stage!"

. . .

Two and a half hours later, Lorelai, Maren, and I are walking up to Kevin's distillery. The early-June temps have me finally feeling like summer, so I pulled out one of my favorite gauzy white sundresses and a denim jacket. My flat, metallic gold sandals maybe don't do a whole lot to show off my calves, but I'm cute and comfortable. I've twisted back a chunk of my bangs off to the side, and Maren lent me a pair of gold hoops that have me feeling like Cleopatra. I press my lips together at the door, and Lorelai's grin is soft and reassuring, just like last time. "You look like a queen, Shelb. Let's get this bitch."

Maren squeezes my hand between hers and Lorelai opens the door. The noise level is quite a bit higher this time. College students out celebrating the end of the semester, maybe. The distillery is packed to the gills, but Kevin catches us walking in and waves a ginormous hand, calling us over.

"Where's Cam?" I ask.

He nods to the far end of the bar, where a small temporary stage has been set up. "Setting up karaoke."

I choke on my breath. "You're kidding."

"I'm not," he says with a mile-wide grin, rubbing his palms together. "I haven't been this excited since freshman year of college."

"Can I get you gals a drink?" Kevin's adorable and very pregnant wife, Beth, asks.

"Go ahead and start a tab," I say, passing my credit card. "I'll take a ginger ale, please. Extra cherries, if you got 'em."

She grins. "You bet. And you two?" Maren and Lorelai order their cocktails and settle on stools next to me. A moment later Beth returns with our drinks.

"Where's the snake at?" Lorelai asks, stabbing at a cherry in her whiskey sour.

I don't bother to look. "Not here yet. We'd know if he was. The cameras would be here. They'll come together," I say dryly.

"Hey, ladies," Cameron says over my shoulder, raising his brows at my drink. "Liquid courage?"

I grin sheepishly. "I wish. Someone decided to set up karaoke. It's just ginger ale."

He scoffs good-naturedly and my stomach does a tiny flip that has nothing to do with singing and everything to do with the way his fitted gray-green V-neck sets off his eyes. "You owe me a duet. Besides, Lyle won't be happy if there's not any action. This is the best way to fend off the wolves."

My thought exactly.

He elbows Lorelai. "Can you be convinced, Miss Country Music Icon?"

Lorelai lifts a coy shoulder. "Perhaps."

"Oh, please. She's been begging for the chance. Besides, she's got no excuses this time." I bat my lashes, tellingly.

Her Carolinian drawl is on point as she says, "Well, I most certainly won't turn down the chance to belt out a little Reba."

"Here we go," Maren says with a smile. "Last time we had to practically drag her away."

Lorelai narrows her dark brown eyes, perfectly winged in black liner. "That was nearly three years ago, and I was in my Carrie Underwood stage."

A bunch of guys dressed in Michigan State colors come in and sit on the other side of Maren, distracting her from any response. It takes them approximately thirty seconds to offer to buy her next round. It's the closest thing I've ever seen to real magic, honestly. Maren attracts attention in a pair of baggy overalls, but in a minidress and espadrilles, she's irresistible. She looks to me as if to check.

"You're not driving. Go for it."

"Wow, that was fast," Cameron says, impressed.

"That's Maren," I reply. "She's like frat-boy catnip. It's the heady combination of beauty queen and park ranger. There's no stopping that train."

"I think it's safe to say, it's all three of you." He gestures at where Lorelai is flipping through a binder of song choices, two more frat-boy types jumping over themselves to catch her eye. She idly flips her dark waves, revealing a tanned, bare shoulder. I hide my smile. She knows exactly what she's doing.

I shrug, taking a sip from my straw. "I have hot friends." I let my eyes linger on his muscular form. "Have I mentioned today how well you've grown up, Cameron Riggs?" He reddens under his beard and I continue, teasing. "Like, have we discussed this beard recently? Because"—I make a show fanning myself—"it works for you."

He shuts his eyes, as if he's in pain, then shakes his head, raising his voice to Kevin. "Excuse me! I'd like to file a claim for sexual harassment in the workplace!"

Kevin nudges his glasses primly. "You don't work here."

"Beth! Help!" Cameron tries.

"Oh no," Beth apologizes dryly. "Thoughts and prayers." She passes him a drink. "If it helps, I'll put it on *her* tab."

I grin. "Cheers, Beth." Turning to Cameron, I pat the stool next to me that Maren left open when one of the guys she was talking to asked her to join them at their table. "Looks like you're stuck with me."

He makes a show of covering his glass with his palm. "Okay, but I'm watching you."

Fair.

He presses close, his voice low and making the little hairs on my arms stand up. "You look delicious tonight."

I inhale sharply at his suggestive tone and cross my legs at the knee.

His hand reaches forward, his finger tucking a strand of hair behind my ear before dragging down my neck, dipping just under my collar and playing with the skin there. He licks his lips, and I smell the slightest whiff of seven-and-seven on his breath. "You walked in with this sexy flippy dress and your legs are all smooth and they're like 'Oh, hello, is there a Cameron Riggs in the building?'"

I giggle at his aggrieved expression. "My legs were talking to you, huh?"

He groans playfully, turning to lean back on his elbows against the bar top. "You wouldn't believe the scandalous things your legs tell me when you aren't listening. They haven't shut up since the B&B. All day long, it's 'Cameron, don't you want to feel how smooth we are? Cameron, don't you want a little taste?'" He tilts his head toward me, his voice hoarse, his eyes darkening. "'Cameron, we'd fit perfectly around your hips . . .'"

"Gah—stop!" I cover his mouth with my finger, trying and failing to tear my eyes away from his lips. "Right now, there are parts of me, parts just north of my chatty legs, that are telling me to make you stop before I spontaneously combust and take you on this bar."

Cameron's eyes widen, but his grin is way too pleased. He takes a sip of his drink. "Fair enough. Though my parts reserve the right to return to the conversation about bar-top combustions at another time."

I smirk. "The conversation is hereby tabled."

He snorts into his glass. "Very punny, Springfield."

We continue to sit at the bar, sipping our drinks, and Beth keeps us company, showing us pictures of her and Kevin's first two babies, all dark curls and toothy grins, who are spending the night at their grandparents'.

"My goodness. They're beautiful!"

Cameron shakes his head. "I still can't believe a Viking monster like Kevin could produce something so cute. You must have strong genetics, Beth."

"Oh now," I say, giggling at the affronted expression on his best friend's face. "Ignore him. He's just jealous."

The corner of Cam's mouth lifts in an easy smile. "Now, that's true. If only I'd met Beth first . . ."

Beth's eyes sparkle and she lifts up, pulling her giant husband's mouth down to hers for a quick but tender kiss. "Wouldn't have mattered, Riggs," she says, clearly lost in Kevin's smitten gaze. "He had me from the start."

My cheeks hurt from smiling so hard and the fizzy ginger ale does a little swirl in my stomach. These two make it look so simple. You meet, you fall in love, you get married and have babies, and you spend the rest of your life with that one person who likes you best, who *you* like best.

They're kissing again, and I look away to give them privacy, even though we're in a bar. Cam clears his throat. "It's a wonder they're only on baby number three. I walked in on them so much in college, I figured they would end up like one of those prolific Baptist families with fourteen kids in jean skirts all lined up in a row."

Kevin smirks against his wife's lips and straightens. "I'm not Baptist."

Beth pats his butt and spins for the kitchen. "Thank God

for that," she throws over her shoulder. "Your babies are enormous."

Kevin stares after her and Cameron chuckles low.

"What?" I ask.

He shakes his head. "Nothing. It's just that I can practically hear his brain trying to figure out a way to sneak out of here and join her in the kitchen."

Kevin's lips spread in a smile and he snaps his suspenders. "You wouldn't hop back here and cover for me, would you?" Just as quickly, his eyes widen as he looks over our shoulders and leans forward on one massive hand. "Never mind."

We spin in our seats and Cameron grunts under his breath, knocking back the last of his drink. I follow suit, sipping mine until it gurgles against the ice, empty. I probably should have gone for a gin and tonic. As quickly as the thought comes, I shake it off. I don't need the buffer. Not really.

"No matter what anyone says, only ginger ale from here on," I remind Kevin. "Please."

Cameron steps off his stool and I jump down alongside him, smoothing my dress. The cameras are here and so are Marcella and Lyle. Marcella makes a show of squealing my name and the entire bar turns, taking notice of the cameras and, undoubtedly, the reason for the cameras. Up to this point, we've flown pretty under the radar in northern Michigan. People know we're around, and sure, we might be the most famous people in a town of zero celebrities, but generally people respect our privacy. With the exception of the odd dental hygienist or grocery store employee, I rarely hear my name in whispers.

Until tonight. Until the four walls of this space echo with our whispered names. Lyle, you fucker.

Cameron's hand presses to the small of my back, warm and grounding. I take a deep, cleansing breath and prepare to act as if my heart depended on it.

17

CAMERON

DESPACITO

Fucking Lyle. Always playing the good guy on TV. Like a duck on a pond, pristine and collected on the surface, webbed fucking feet paddling like crazy and mucking up shit underneath.

I've done some thinking though, ever since Marcella teetered in this afternoon, her perfect manicure feeling up my arms in front of her husband and my boss. This is a home-improvement show on a family network. Sure, they'll show what they can of our lives outside the Caroline Street house, but they're ultimately limited by time constraints. My years at *National Geographic* have taught me that much.

They get maybe *minutes* of airtime to spend on this bar. Editing can be a shady occupation, so my plan is to give them only the best kind of footage to pull from. This is why I'm here, after all. Shelby brings the skill. I bring the charisma.

And if that means I have to sing every single song from my teenybopper repertoire and consequently face down shit from Kevin for the rest of my life, so be it. We need this pilot.

However, I hadn't counted on the power-couple Jessup and just how cruel they could be. I've been out of the industry too long. I knew Lyle wasn't here to make friends, but he's generally looking for whatever angle puts him in the most optimal light. I don't know a whole lot about Marcella, but I imagine like attracts like.

Marcella, in her painted-on thousand-dollar jeans and fake smile, downs her cosmopolitan, passing the glass to Lyle, and grabs Shelby's hand, dragging her to the tiny stage. "My turn! And I want my bestie up here with me! Ladies and gentlemen! Your favorite party girl and mine, Shelby Springfield!" Within seconds, the screen behind Marcella glows with the lyrics to a song titled "You Chose Wrong" by, *shocker,* Lyle Jessup.

Lyle glows in the camera light, and he pulls a face like "Oh, you girls!" and that right then and there is when I know this shit was planned.

Next to me, Lorelai hisses like a wildcat. Shelby squeaks, and all the color drains from her face, but in a flash, she's composed. Because the cameras are rolling. What else can she do?

"Isn't this—" I start.

Lorelai scowls. "Yup."

My teeth clench together, but I wipe my face clear of any expression. To the casual observer, I'm indifferent; I've never heard this song and I don't know what it's about. *Because what the fuck else can we do?*

Shelby spins onstage, her dress flaring around her toned

thighs. As angry as I am at the situation, I still have the presence of mind to notice again just how delectable she looks.

She beams, waving and brilliant. Marcella tries to hug her, and Shelby allows her a side embrace as Kevin passes her the mic. She's straight-up grace and a good time.

The beat hits and I know what's coming. I remember the first time I heard this song. I was laid over in Paris, in civilization for twenty-hour hours. Long enough to shower, eat hot food, and hear Lyle's song about his breakup with Shelby played a hundred times. The one where he plays the victim and makes *her* out to be some devious cheater.

Marcella sang backup, if I recall. No one even knew she could sing. It launched her mediocre pop career.

"Sing your heart out, Shelby!" I glance to the right and Maren's back from her table of guys. Her fan club cheers and whistles along with her.

"Fuck that fucker!" Lorelai shouts, and even though it'll be cut, I'm grateful. Shelby holds her hands up to see through the lights and winks.

The first verse starts up and Marcella takes it. Swerving her hips, pouting her lips, and playing to the crowd. She's not a great singer, but she makes up for it in showmanship. My hands squeeze at my sides and my shoulders tense. I lock eyes with Shelby, willing her to shine. Pointing to her and then my chest, I mouth, "Just you and me."

She takes a deep breath and raises her mic, not bothering with the lyrics. Because of course she knows this fucking song. It's probably tattooed on the jagged pieces of her heart.

Except she's not broken anymore, and those jagged

pieces are my responsibility now. Shelby pulls off her denim jacket, swinging it around and tossing it to Lorelai, revealing sexy shoulders, carved from all the heavy lifting and sanding she does. She's dancing along to the lyrics like she's memorized the choreography, better than any backup dancer. She shimmies, sways, and pops, all while belting vocals like the sunshine child star she was. Marcella tries to take back the spotlight, but if Shelby notices, she doesn't show it. The crowd is losing their minds. She gets to the instrumental break before the final verse and she's looking through the crowd. "Where's Cameron Riggs? This song requires *real* vocals."

The insinuation that Lyle's original vocals weren't that great isn't lost on me or anyone else, if the tight expression on Lyle's face is any indication.

Or maybe that's the Botox.

I'll be honest. I don't care if they ever use this footage. All I want is Lyle to see me sing his stupid fucking song and sing it better.

I jump the steps and Marcella, knowing she's beat, passes me her mic. Kevin whistles like a fangirl as I roll my sleeves up and stand next to Shelby.

I lean over, and in a low voice, I ask, "Remember that 'Best Girl' choreography?"

She snorts. "How could I forget?"

The beat picks up and I step forward, also not needing the lyrics. Because I'm a goddamn professional. It's been a while since I sang in front of a crowd, but it's not like I could forget how to do this. Shelby next to me is a bonus. Working together day in and day out is one thing but performing with her is another.

I'm not saying I want to get back into singing and dancing. I'm just saying this is the most fun I've had in a decade and it's because of *her.*

Shelby and I move in synchronized steps, jumping with legs spread and crisscross our hands, raising the roof like it's 2010 as we spin. The room goes wild and I laugh, losing my ability to sing the last bit. Shelby takes over, lowering her voice in a super douchey way, perfectly imitating Lyle's over-the-top vibrato, and collapsing in giggles when the song ends. I pull her close and kiss the top of her head before taking her hand and raising it above our heads and taking a deep bow. Shelby blows a kiss at Lyle and Marcella and neither moves a muscle. Through the dim light of the bar, I see a hundred different phones recording us along with the cameras from the show.

Good. Let Lyle work that shit out. If he didn't want footage to leak, he shouldn't have flown out to Michigan and meddled. It's in the back of my mind that we may have completely fucked our chance with the pilot, but for the moment, I can't seem to care.

We jump off the stage and make our way back to the bar. Beth is holding out a few drinks. "On the house," she tells us.

"Shelby, that was incredible!" The crowd parts and Marcella is walking up, followed by the glow of the cameras. She leans in to hug Shelby. "And Cameron! You sound even better than I remember. It's a wonder you never made it big!" She presses herself into me, her perfume a choking cloud of *expensive*.

I take a small step back, unnerved by the way she hugs with *all* of her body. I was joking earlier about the sexual harassment, but I get the feeling that Marcella would be plenty happy to show me what real sexual harassment looks like, despite her husband glaring over her shoulder.

"Marcella," Shelby says. "This is my best friend, Lorelai, and my other best friend, Maren, is around here somewhere . . ."

"Of course. I know Lorelai Jones. I used to be such a fan of yours! Talk about scandalous!" she stage-whispers.

Lorelai grins, all glossed lips. "Well, my momma always said it takes one to know one."

Shelby chokes on her drink and I pat her back. Marcella narrows her eyes. "Should you be drinking?" she snaps, some of her shimmer wearing off. "Remember the last time you overindulged? Wasted your entire career."

Shelby's eyes flicker to the camera and back to her old friend. "It's ginger ale."

Marcella sniffs. "Looks like a gin and tonic to me.

"And it looks like you're almost out," Lyle interjects. "Another gin and tonic for the woman of the hour!" he shouts to a startled Beth. "And"—he turns to me, raising his brows—"what is that garbage you're drinking, Riggs? Cheap beer? You're not a frat boy anymore. He'll take a whiskey neat. On me."

I consider letting this play out. I could accept the drink, put on the show, and give Lyle what he wants. The cameras are rolling, and everything is, well, not congenial but civil enough, and I think that maybe, just maybe, this is salvageable.

But then I glance around the room and see that Marcella

has Shelby cornered against the bar, and suddenly whatever she says makes all the blood rush out of Lorelai's face and Maren hop off her stool. The group shifts and I see Shelby falter, reaching for the bar. Marcella cackles and in a raised voice says, "My God, Shelby, how drunk are you?!"

Beth shouts, "Hey!" but is roundly ignored. Lorelai, who *has* been drinking, steps between Shelby and Marcella and looks ready to strike, but Maren reaches for her two friends just in time. "I love this song. Let's dance!"

Beth is quick and is already waddling over to the stereo system to crank it up as Maren is dragging Shelby and Lorelai to the middle of the floor. Her crowd of Michigan State fans are quick to clear the area, either out of courtesy or hoping to gain points.

Enough is enough.

The camera spins to capture Shelby dancing and I round on Marcella. "What did you say to her?"

Marcella rolls her eyes. "Nothing she didn't already know. She's just drunk, Cam. She'll be fine in the morning."

"Shelby doesn't drink anymore," I bite out through clenched teeth. "And she's definitely not drinking tonight. So, what did you say?"

Lyle puts his hand on my chest. "Easy, Cam. Watch your temper when talking to my wife."

I smack his hand away. "What are you two playing at here? Why did you come? Haven't you fucked with us enough?"

"Oh, you're admitting it's 'us' now, are you? I'm not fucking with anyone, Cameron. But maybe you two need to grow up and be a little more responsible. I'm putting my neck on the line for you, and for what? Missed deadlines, a half-done project, an alcoholic costar, and you two sneaking off on my dime to hook up?"

My fists clench and I'm seeing red. Actually, I'm seeing white. The blinding white of the cameras. A heavy hand falls on my shoulder, and I turn to see a grim-faced Kevin.

"Not worth it. You!" He points to Lyle and Marcella, not caring about the cameras. "Get the fuck out of my bar and never come back."

"Whatever," Lyle grumbles, placing his empty glass on the bar. "This place is so cliché. It'll be closed in a month."

He and Marcella leave, and the cameras follow them out.

My eyes slide shut, and I slump against the bar. "Fuck."

"Yeah. That was not ideal."

"Is Shelby okay?"

Kevin gestures with his bearded chin to middle of the dance floor. "Considering the circumstances, I'll forgive them this once for turning my distillery into a dance club."

I stifle a reluctant smile at his grumbling. "Business is booming, though."

Kevin gives a dry chuckle.

"What are the odds we'll sell the season after tonight?"

"Perhaps the better question would be: What are the odds *Nat Geo* will take you back?"

I groan.

"It's bullshit, man. I'm sorry. I know for a fact Shelby hasn't had a drop of alcohol tonight, and you two are working your asses off on that house. You're getting a raw deal all around. Jessup's a petty dickhead."

I sigh, running my hand through my hair. "Yeah. I knew he was. We both did. Did you hear what Marcella said to Shelby?"

Kevin looks uncomfortable. "Something about using Lyle to be famous and insinuating that Shelby was trying to proposition her husband. The words 'drunken slut' may have been used."

A growl escapes my throat and Kevin nods. "Yeah, man. Me, too. Pretty sure we'd have to get in line behind Lorelai, though. She looked ready to yank off her stiletto and stab Marcella with it."

All this time, being careful and trying to do the responsible thing, and look where it got us. Fuck it. I'm tired of holding back. I cross the dance floor in three strides.

"Dance with me," I say without thinking, holding my hand out to Shelby.

"Really?" Her blue eyes go wide.

"You scared?" I challenge, pulling her flush against me. This song has a Latin backbeat, and it's been a minute since I've tried to roll my hips the way they're meant to, but muscle memory is a magical thing, and it's not long before we're completely aligned; forward, backward, side to side, up, down, wherever my body leads, Shelby's follows. I take her hands and drape them over my shoulders, and she does me one better, sliding them up and clasping them around my neck, her fingers playing in my hair at the nape.

I meet her eyes, surprised, and she smirks. I step my leg forward, in between hers, sinking my grip low on her waist, splaying across her hips. For a second, I think she's going to call my bluff and put space between us.

Instead, her navy irises darken with interest and her body slithers against me from hip to shoulder. Her dress swings loosely between my fingers, and I know if I don't pull back, I'm going to end up lifting it and carrying her off to the bathroom.

Honestly, maybe I should.

The song changes and I spin her out once, pressing a kiss on the back of her hand. She laughs, but it's as breathless as I feel.

You're playing with fire, Riggs. *Good.*

The next song is slow, and Old Cameron would walk her back to the bar. To our friends and our drinks. Our sanity.

Instead, we're magnets. Without even deciding to, I flick my wrist, spinning her back toward me, and she slips into my arms. Her fingers don't waste any time finding my hair, sending sparks flickering across my skin. I don't even bother with her waist, my arms circling her so completely so that I can feel every intake of her breath press against my own. This isn't anything like the flea market. That was sweet and easy. This is sensual and heady.

We barely rock, barely spin, barely notice anything outside of ourselves. I know more people are dancing; I can feel the curious stares.

But I don't give a single fuck about anything but her.

I bend my neck, curling over the place where her head rests in the space between my neck and my shoulder, and tighten my hold. I've never felt anything so perfect as this. Not even *before.*

"Cameron?" I feel her whisper against my skin.

I raise my head so I can see her face. Her cheeks are

flushed; her eyes are alight with a quiet hunger, and I swallow, her fingers driving me mad as they stroke the skin of my neck.

"Ask me if I want to go upstairs."

My heart races, a heavy thudding in my chest, almost painful. I need a minute. To think, to decide. She raises up on her tiptoes and presses a soft, closed-mouth kiss to my lips. I used to think I was calling the shots when we were kids. But I'm starting to see that it's been her all along. She's always been the brave one.

"I want to." This whispered confession feels like it's being ripped directly from my chest. "So much. But I—"

Her eyes slip shut, but not before I see the flash of hurt.

"There are eyes everywhere," I say, putting space between us. I can't think with her pressed against me. I shake my head, trying to clear it. "And Lyle. On the small chance we haven't completely fucked ourselves, if he knows we snuck off together . . ."

"What if I don't care?"

"*I care.* I don't want him to make you out to be—"

Her eyes snap open, blue and fiery.

"To be what, Cam? What am I?"

"Stop," I say. "That's not what I meant." And it's not. I definitely, *definitely* want this to happen, but stealing away from a bar full of people with cameras . . . Well. Okay, it's probably not any worse than rubbing myself all over her on the dance floor. Shelby spins out of my arms and makes her way through the crowd. I see Lorelai near the stage, and she tries to catch her, but Shelby waves her off, with me close behind. I shake my head at her best friend, letting her know I got this. This time, *I got this.* We end up in a dark hallway, but it's not nearly enough privacy, so I reach for her hand and tug her out into the night. I wait to make sure we aren't followed before heading for the back of the building near the outside stairs that lead to my apartment. I pull her under them.

She starts in immediately, eyes flashing, her pale blond hair falling in her face. "You're so determined to save me, Cameron. To save my reputation. We're not children anymore. We don't have to sneak around in closets and dark fields."

"I know that, but Lyle is just waiting to—"

"Fuck Lyle!" she shouts, before lowering her voice. "Seriously. Fuck him. I don't care about Lyle. Not even when I was supposed to did I care about him. I care about *you*. I *love* you. How dense can one man be?" She slaps her hands against my chest, accentuating her words. "I'm stupid for you and your stupid beard and your stupid tree-trunk thighs and your stupid flannel shirts and your stupid dancing and your stupid kind eyes—"

It feels like all of the blood has drained out of my brain. "Wait. You love me?"

Shelby freezes, her mouth open. She collects herself. "I—"

"You said it," I say, breathless. My heart is thudding out of my chest, a runaway train straight off the tracks. "You can't take it back. I heard it."

She shakes her head. "I wasn't—I just—" She clears her throat and tries again. "I was—"

"You love me."

She swallows. "Yes."

"You *love* me."

She glares. "Maybe a little less now than when we started this conversation."

"I love you, too, you know."

She softens, ever so slightly. "I didn't. I hoped, though."

I brush my fingers across her furrowed brow, tracing down the side of her face to cup her jaw. I lean in, my voice husky. "I do. I always have."

She smacks my chest again. "Then *why* won't you take me upstairs?"

I roll my eyes. "*Because I love you* and I don't want Lyle or Marcella or anyone else to twist it into something gross."

"What if I don't care?" she asks again, slowly bucking her hips against mine.

I groan even as my hands find her hips and hold her against me. "You should care. You're lucky I do. I was ready to throw you over my shoulder and haul you off to the bathroom not more than twenty minutes ago."

She smirks, her palms smoothing a path up my chest and around my shoulders. "Now *that* would have been a scandal."

"I don't want it to be like that between us. I mean," I clarify. "I definitely do, but not publicly. I don't care who knows that I'm in love with you. It's not like I can hide it. But they don't need to know when I take you to my bed."

Shelby's eyes are molten. "No one's here now."

"True."

"Take me to your bed, Cam."

I instantly harden at her whispered words.

"Please."

18

SHELBY

UNTOUCHED

We ascend the back stairs to Cameron's place a few minutes later, his large hand wrapped completely around mine, tugging me along. Owning me, if I'm honest. I almost laugh at how fast we went from me trying my damnedest to seduce him to him practically dragging me, caveman-style, up to his place.

I swallow the giddy feeling when he unlocks his door and swings it open, pulling me in and kicking the door shut with his boot. In a near-desperate flash, he spins me around and has me pressed against the door and oh.

Oh.

My eyes slip shut as if they understand they're not needed right now. I only want to feel, feel, *feel* as he kisses me hard, his mouth, ruthless, and his tongue, caressing. I twine my fingers in his hair and yank slightly, causing him to groan, breathless against my lips. I'm starving for this man. My hips take over, shoving fiercely off the door in a slow, intentional grind, the friction making me dizzy with lust. His hot hands tease my waist before sliding along my curves and gripping at the edge of my dress, slipping underneath and clearing a searing path for his calloused palms against my skin, up and around, just brushing the sides of my breasts. I buck and feel his smile against my lips.

"In a hurry?"

"Planning on taking all night?" I retort.

He nibbles at my neck, scraping his teeth along my collarbone before tasting me there. "All night, all weekend, the rest of our lives, maybe." One calloused hand slips under my bra and cups my breast, his thumb flicking over my sensitive peak, and I gasp, already feeling the edges of my vision darkening.

Not yet. I gently push him away. "Cam. Maybe you could show me that bed you kept going on about earlier."

He grins, his eyes flashing in the dim light from the streetlamps outside his windows. "You mean earlier when you told me you love me?"

Gah. He's cute.

I reach for his whiskery chin, tugging his mouth to mine and kissing him softly. "I do love you."

"Me, too."

"Can we *please* have sex now?"

He picks me up and I wrap my legs around him, tempted to nix the bedroom when I feel his muscular thighs underneath mine. Merciful saints.

Next time.

In seconds, we're in his bedroom. He lays me on his bed,

running one hand down the side of my face, my neck, passing between my breasts and stroking me once, his clever fingers dancing ever so lightly against my center, causing my breath to catch in a gasp. "Be right back," he whispers hotly against my skin, and I whimper when he moves off.

I'm just lying there in a daze when I recover and remember myself. I toe off my sandals and pull my dress over my head, tossing it to the floor. Next, I unhook my bra, flinging it toward the dress. I'm reaching for my underwear when Cameron returns, his arms full of something. I hear a clatter near his dresser, then the flare of a match. He spins around, holding the match between his fingers and his mouth falls open at the sight of me, nearly naked and on his bed.

"Christ. I love you," he breathes followed by a strangled, "Shit!" He waves his fingers as the match burns out and I choke on a giggle. He ignites another, and this time concentrates on lighting the candles he's collected on the dresser. He tosses the matchbook on a shelf before ripping off his shirt, kicking his boots away, and diving onto the bed next to me. I pick up his injured finger and suck it into my mouth, swirling my tongue around the tip, before saying, "Very smooth, Cam."

He growls and reclaims his hand, before sinking down between my legs and pressing hot open-mouthed kisses to my bare stomach. "I was trying to be romantic," he grumbles.

"Well," I say as he creeps lower, his tongue making little circles along the edge of my underwear. I squirm. "It's no starry field."

"Take me to bed, Cameron," he says in a teasing falsetto,

his deft fingers slipping my underwear down my legs. He presses his mouth to the inside of my knee, licking up my inner thigh. "Make up your mind, woman."

"I guess this will have to do," I say. His beard tickles in the most fascinating and delicious way and my fingers reach for his hair even as my legs spread, helpless against his ministrations.

He slides between them, his hands wrapping around my hips and pulling me closer. "God, I could live here."

"You do live here."

"Not here," he says. And then his tongue takes me in a long, slow, curling lick. "Here," he says meaningfully, and my fingers grip his hair as I call out. He licks again, suckling at my most sensitive spot and twirling his tongue. "And here." He slides his finger, dipping it into my center, and pressing more intently as he sucks harder, nibbling and devouring. "And here." His hot whisper destroys me, and I rock into him, holding his mouth in place and crying out.

"That's it," he says, before sliding his tongue flat against me, eating me whole. "Come apart for me. Come apart on me. God, I love you. You're so beautiful."

And then he's quiet. His tongue diving and scooping and tearing me to pieces, his fingers filling me, curling and nimble. I gasp and shudder and buck against his mouth, wild and completely out of my mind before I finally shatter into a million glistening shards with his name on my lips. He gentles his touch, guiding me back to earth, and presses achingly soft kisses to my thighs until I'm boneless and wrung out.

"Damn, Riggs," I whisper, hoarse, as he crawls up to meet me on his pillow. "You didn't know how to do that last time."

He runs a fingertip down my neck and traces it along my breast, circling the tip.

"That's not the only thing I've learned."

I press myself closer to him, stretching my knee over his thighs, and capture his lips in a long kiss, tasting myself on his tongue.

This might be the hottest . . . ugh. I slip my hands down his flat stomach, feeling the ridges of muscle taut beneath me. I lay him back on the bed.

"You're wearing too many clothes."

He stacks his hands under his head and grins, boyish and too pleased with himself. "You could take them off."

I slip his fly open and tug, pulling his jeans down his thighs, my mouth watering. Glorious, glorious thighs. I press a kiss to his quads just because I want to. *Mine.*

"Tree-trunk thighs," he muses. I look up and his eyes are sparkling in the candlelight.

"They're the sexiest thing I've ever seen," I admit. "I've dreamed about these thighs." I tug off his jeans and his socks before reaching for his boxer briefs, tented with desire. Very tented. With generous desire. I swallow and pull them down.

"I want to climb these thighs," I say. And I do, straddling him where he's sprung for me.

Cameron Riggs is a beautiful man.

Lightning quick, he pulls my hips to him and scoots us back against his headboard. "You can climb me all you want, as long as I get this view." He cups my breasts in his hands, his fingers deftly pinching along my peaks. I place my hands on his shoulders, gripping at the intense muscle there. His tongue darts out and he sucks my pink tips into his mouth, rolling and scraping his teeth until I'm heavy and aching for his touch. I jerk against him, already feeling my control slip, and panting with need.

"Cameron. I want you inside of me."

His tongue makes a lazy circle around my nipple and I clutch at him, my nails dragging along his skin. "*Now,* Cameron."

His eyes darken and his grip on my hips tightens almost painfully. He reaches across his bed to the nightstand, opening the drawer and pulling out a condom. I steal it from his fingers, ripping it open with my teeth. He sucks in a breath as I roll it down his hard length.

He raises me, guiding my hips over him and thrusting once, his tip immediately finding where I am wet and aching for him.

I spread my legs farther, sinking to the hilt, allowing him to fill and stretch me completely. He closes his eyes, his forehead falling to my chest.

"Holy shit, Shelby. You feel unreal. So tight. So wet for me."

I start to ride him, rocking my hips and raising myself nearly completely before sinking down. He gives a shuddering hiss, his hands nearly frantic as they cup my breasts, squeezing and plucking. "Kiss me, please. Distract me."

I take his jaw in my hands and kiss him hard, swallowing his moans and rolling my hips harder and harder. I've never felt so complete, so full. I can't tell where Cameron ends and I begin.

"I love you so much," I whisper, even as I feel myself begin to unravel again.

"Look at me. I want to watch you come."

I open my eyes, locking on his. His hands are on my hips now, kneading me, his breaths short.

"I'm so close," I pant, writhing against him with a loud whimper.

"That's it." He takes my nipple in his mouth with a hard suck and I cry out.

I'm reckless and spastic with want, until I'm consumed, inside and out, sobbing my release and convulsing around him, my hands buried in his hair. Cameron thrusts up once, twice, letting me ride out my pleasure before following me over the edge with a magnificent, seizing groan. We collapse together, deliciously sated and curled into one another, and we stay there for a long time, pressing delicate kisses and whispering soft words.

Eventually I climb off his glorious lap and slip away to the bathroom to clean myself up. In the mirror I'm all flushed skin, wild eyes, and ruined hair.

And love. I'm so full of love, I may as well be bursting.

I climb back into bed, sliding under the covers, and watch Cameron doze. Jesus, I'm gone for this man. Just like I was gone for the boy he used to be. I nudge him awake. His lips spread into a smile before he opens his eyes.

"I just had sex with Shelby Springfield," he says, and I smack his shoulder lightly with a laugh.

"You sure did. And now you should probably go take care of that."

He rolls to his feet and I soak up his tall, lean silhouette in the shadows of the candlelight before he goes to the bathroom.

A moment later he's out and curled around me once more, our bodies fitted together and exactly matched, his face buried in my hair. "I love you," I whisper again. It's like now that I've said it out loud, I can't stop.

"I love you, too." He runs his wide hands purposely down my side, dipping them between my legs.

"You're still wet," he says, his tone, hungry.

I spin to face him, my fingers tracing his beard and slide my knee over his hip. "Only for you."

He thrusts against me, hard, and I moan even as my thighs open farther, welcoming him all over again.

"Mine," he says, capturing my lips. His possessive growl zings right to my core and I pull him on top of me.

"Yours," I promise.

"I might need to find other locations besides my bed, at this rate," he teases.

"I hear open fields are lovely this time of year."

"Timeless, that one."

"Worked on me."

"Let's see if I can figure out what else works on you."

"*You* work on me, Cam."

"Until the day I die, I suspect," he offers with a half grin.

"There's no way we can hide this from the crew. They will take one look at my face and know I'm lost over your . . . thighs . . ." I say, dancing my fingers along his firm muscles and squeezing his backside.

He presses against me.

"Who said anything about hiding? I'm getting custom T-shirts made."

I giggle.

"You think I'm kidding. Which do you prefer? *I did it with Shelby Springfield* or *Shelby Springfield owns my Riggs*?"

This time I cackle. "The second, please."

"I'm not joking."

"Good."

"We could get Lyle one for Christmas."

"Please don't speak his name while we're naked."

Cameron smirks, thrusting against me again, and I gasp. "I had you first, and I'll have you last."

"You'll have me forever."

"It's only fair. I've been yours since the moment I saw you."

• • •

I wake to Cameron's long, blessed fingers teasing another rolling orgasm out of me. I haven't even opened my eyes and already today is the best day. His beard tickles, sending the most perfect shivers down my skin as he places open-mouth kisses across my breasts and down my stomach, but before he can get any farther, I wake fully and pull him up.

"One more," he whispers, his smile all brilliant white teeth and damnable charm.

I giggle, still breathless. "Get real, Cam. I won't be able to walk as it is. We don't have to make up for all ten years in one night."

"It's a new day," he points out, and I kiss him hard because, suddenly, in the light of morning, I am feeling too, too much.

We pull apart and I trace a fingertip along the side of his handsome face. "How about we shower, and I return the favor and start your day off right, and then, if you want, you can wash my hair?"

He sprints out of bed and I laugh, even as I take a long, lingering look at his behind.

The man has a spectacular ass. On top of spectacular thighs. And in between?

Heaven. A personal heaven created just for me. If this is my reward for all those years of misery and meltdowns?

Worth it.

• • •

Cameron drops me off at home later that morning and I see a car waiting in the drive. *Lorelai.*

"Want me to come in?"

"I thought you had to get to your mom's?"

"I do," he admits. "But I feel like I'm leaving you to face the firing squad alone."

I snicker. "It's just Lorelai. She's mostly bark." I release my seat belt and lean forward, intending to give him a quick kiss, but his lips chase me down and his hand slides up, grazing the side of my breast, setting me on fire all over again.

He slips his thumb back and forth, teasing, and I arch automatically against his palm, seeking more contact. Right when I'm considering how much room I have to straddle his lap in his truck, there's a rap on the window. We pull apart and Cameron's smile is sheepish mixed with adorably proud. He tries to subtly adjust himself while waving out the window. "Hey, Lorelai."

I close my eyes, squeezing my knees together and trying

to calm down my racing heart, not ready to face my best friend.

"Heyyyy, guys. What're you doing out here in the driveway?"

I reach for the door, climbing out with a huff, and Lorelai leaps back, guilty grin in place.

"Looking good, Shelb . . . real glowy."

I smirk, shoving at her shoulder. I turn and blow a kiss to Cam, who catches it before reversing out of the drive.

"Blech," Lorelai grouses. "You are just as fucking adorable as I always knew you would be." She wraps an arm around my shoulders, leading me up to the house. Her dark hair is in a messy knot at the top of her head, and she has bags under her eyes. The overall look is *tired* in a way I'm not used to seeing. "I'm really happy for you, Shelb."

I tilt my head to hers. "Thanks."

"Now get your ass inside. I want all the gory details. I've always wondered what it would be like to sleep with a lumberjack spliced with Fred Astaire."

I laugh. "You have not."

"Well, maybe not always, but since last night I sure have. So, spill. I called Maren. She's bringing donuts."

My stomach growls in response.

"Didn't he feed you?"

I smirk and waggle my brows. "Not with food, no."

Lorelai's eyes widen and she holds open my front door. "I slept in the guest room. Alone," she adds. "In case you want to feel sorry for me."

"I don't."

"Just tell me how many times."

"I . . . lost count."

Lorelai passes me a mug full of coffee. "I want to hate you, but I can't."

I slump into a chair and take a sip, finally looking around my living room and choking out a cough. There's pillow stuffing everywhere.

"What happened? I thought you said you slept alone."

Lorelai waves it off, walking over and grabbing up handfuls of stuffing and throwing them in the trash.

"I owe you a new pillow."

I raise my eyebrows over my mug. "Okay."

"Drake drunk texted me last night."

"You sure it wasn't the other way around?"

"Positive. I wasn't drunk. I drove Maren home, then on my way here, my phone blows up." Drake is Lorelai's ex-fiancé who broke her heart three years ago and still occasionally texts her when he's drunk. But she also texts him. And sometimes they sext. It's . . . complicated.

"And?"

Lorelai tosses the last of the pillow in the trash. "And nothing. He was horny and between girlfriends and thought he could rile me up. But I told him last time I was done with this shit."

"Did you tell him that again this time?"

"In so many words."

"And?" I repeat.

"And"—she releases a long breath—"he told me he still loves me."

I inhale sharply. "And?"

"And what? I told him to fuck off. He doesn't love me. He's bored."

I shake my head. "You don't tell someone you love them out of boredom, Lorelai."

Her expression darkens. "Drake Colter does."

I leave it at that. I know from experience that we could go round and round all day and night, but Lorelai is a locked-down fortress when it comes to her ex.

I find it interesting that he's telling her he loves her. I wonder if he was even drunk. First, the "Jonesin'" song, which is so obviously about my best friend, and now this. If I didn't know any better, I would think maybe Drake Colter was trying to make amends.

"Knock, knock!" Maren walks in, holding donuts. "I come bearing gifts."

"Excellent." I reach for one and she pulls back.

"Ah, ah, ah, not so fast. First. Did you and Cameron Riggs have sex?"

"We did."

"She lost count," Lorelai says, reaching for an apple fritter.

"No!" Maren gasps.

I pull out the Boston cream and take a huge bite. "Oh, yes."

19

CAMERON

GIVE ME LOVE

On Monday, we're back to work on the Caroline Street house, as if nothing has changed, because, on camera, nothing *has* changed. We're still here to do our job and restore this place before (hopefully) selling it, regardless of the fate of the pilot. But off camera, I haven't had my mouth on Shelby since yesterday morning and I'm crawling out of my skin with want.

This is kind of inconvenient when working alongside her *dad,* who also happens to be a man I respect—maybe more than anyone on the planet.

Suffice it to say, it's been a long day. I'm not positive Daniel hasn't picked up on something between Shelby and me. It's five o'clock, though, and Daniel is nothing if not punctual, always kicking the crew out first and following right behind, presumably to not think about this place for the rest of the night. Daniel has the healthiest work-life balance of anyone I've ever met.

I'm not there yet. The thing is, the film crew leaves at five, too, or sooner, so that means if I want to work without the eyes of the world studying my every move, I have to do it at night.

If I'm making mistakes, I'm doing it alone, healthy work habits be damned.

"Can I ask you about something upstairs, Cam?"

Well, mostly alone. Shelby's working late tonight, too.

"Be there in a minute," I say, casually, pretending to smooth some drywall as I wait for her dad to pack up. He seems to be taking an inordinately long time this afternoon. Or maybe I'm just more than ready to be alone with the woman I love.

Both, I figure.

"Sand that any more and you'll be replacing that section," Daniel observes dryly from over my shoulder.

"There was a rough patch."

"I don't think so. I did that piece myself. Smooth like a baby's butt."

I grimace to myself, standing. "Felt like there was a rough patch."

"Shelby needs you upstairs."

"I heard. I'm just wrapping up."

"Sanding?"

I brush off my jeans and remove my goggles. "No, I guess not. Seems ready to go for the painters tomorrow."

"I'd say so." The corner of his mouth twitches.

"I'm nervous," I admit.

"About the painters or my daughter?"

I ignore his obvious attempt to wind me up. "The painters. I don't feel like we're ready. Like I've done enough."

"We're ready."

"The addition—"

"Is *ready*. It looks great. It cost a chunk of money, but it was worth it. We'll recoup it and then some. She was right, as usual."

I release a slow breath and he grins, reassuring.

"You were right, too. I know she was stubborn about it, but you backed her and you were right to do so. The nook is perfect, and you did a fine job on that master bath. You two make a good team."

"Well"—I scratch at my beard, feeling my face prickle—"I guess that's why they hired us for this show. We do well together on-screen."

Daniel shakes his head, reaching down to pick up his lunch pail and belt. "Not only on-screen, Riggs." He widens his arms, gesturing to the house at large. "You did this. She has the vision. Shelby always has. But you make things happen. You bring her visions to fruition. That's special."

I swallow hard. I've been floating a long time. Trying this, chasing that, never quite finding anything to tie me down.

But this? It's something I could do. Maybe I wasn't looking for *something* to tie me down. Maybe I've been looking for *someone,* an anchor. And not just any someone. Not like the proverbial "someone," but *her.* As in, she is the only one.

As if that first day, when I knocked on Shelby's door and helped her finish those shelves, her soul entwined itself with mine, holding me down and passing me a brush loaded with varnish, and said, *Stay with me and we can build something together.*

I've never really delved into the whole "soul" business

before, but if we do have souls and those souls have mates, Shelby's soul is mine. After all, I am hers in every literal iteration. Why should my soul be any different?

I don't know how long I stand there thinking, but it's long enough that I'm snapped out of it when Daniel shuts the front door behind him. With everyone gone, I take the stairs two at a time up to Shelby.

She's varnishing, looking gorgeous in her holey jeans and an old Clay Coolidge concert tee with the sleeves cut off. Her hair is pulled back in a red bandanna, and she's singing low to something pretty and Italian—which I happen to find very, very attractive.

"I didn't know you knew Italian."

She doesn't look up from her work. "I don't. Not really. But I've learned a few songs. I know a couple in French, too," she says, turning her head to wink, "if you're into that kind of thing."

I lean a hip against the banister and tuck my thumbs in my tool belt before removing them and placing them on my hips. "I might be."

"Do you know any other languages?"

"I took a few semesters of Spanish in college. Conversationally, I do okay. It was a lot like memorizing scripts. But don't ask me to conjugate anything."

"Fair enough."

"You called me up here?"

"Grab a brush. We'll get this done twice as fast."

I pull out a brush and a mask and squeeze on a pair of latex gloves. Then I move to the row of shelves next to her and get started.

We work without talking for a long time, until the sun is sinking in the sky and I can hear her stomach rumble. We've been leap-frogging each other's progress on our way down the nook, which runs the length of the house, minus the bedrooms on either end. I get to my feet, carefully placing my brush down on the edge of a can of varnish and taking off my mask before drawing to my full height. I crack my neck side to side and stretch my arms over my head to soothe the bunched muscles in my shoulders.

"You sanded the railing, too," I say, surprised that I hadn't noticed before. Opposite the shelves is an intricate loft railing that was sturdy enough to keep as is, but pretty beat-up, aesthetically speaking. It was one of those improvements we initially put in the "leave for the buyers" pile.

Shelby wipes her forehead with her forearm and puts her brush down, then removes her gloves and pushes off her knees to stand. My eyes study her movements, drinking in the fit of her jeans: the contour of her strong thighs, topped by the flare of her hips. Wood finishing should not be sexy.

Nevertheless.

She drops her mask around her neck, sliding her fingertips along the railing. "I wasn't going to, but it felt unfair. The bookshelves are so pretty. Don't get me wrong; it was as much a pain in the ass as we assumed it would be. Took me most of the day, and I might need a second round to clean up the little crannies."

I raise my brows. "Crannies? Is that the technical term?"

She continues tracing her hand along the grooves, memorizing any trouble spots, and grins. "Nook." She gestures to the grand expanse of bookcases. "Crannies." She thumbs at the railing. "There's like seventy years of grime in these. It will be worth it, though."

"Always seems to be."

"You learn quick," she quips, but her eyes flash with something extra that shoots straight to my groin.

"I aim to please," I say, definitely not talking about home renovation, and stifling a groan at how ridiculous I sound. I'm basically panting after her.

She clears her throat and pulls off her mask completely, tossing it to the ground. "So. Are you free for dinner?"

"Sure," I say.

She steps closer. "Pizza and beer?"

My stomach rumbles and she laughs, pressing forward to place a soft kiss on my mouth. "I'll take that as a yes. Do you have any more work here tonight?"

"Nah." I hook her by the belt loops and tug her closer. "We're all ready for the painters to start tomorrow. My place or yours?"

She rests her hands on my chest. "I need to check on the chicks. Do you mind coming to mine?"

"Not at all."

"Should we drive one car? Conserve gas?"

I stand still, forcing myself to be cool. *Quick. Channel someone smooth.* The coolest person I know is Daniel. *Don't channel her dad!* "Are you offering to drive me back tomorrow morning?"

Because, yes.

She smirks. She's so much better at this than I am. "Or you can drive me. I'm not one to presume."

"I have to stop at my place and shower and change," I say. "I'm covered in drywall dust."

"I could come with and supervise."

Jesus.

I pretend to think it over. "But then you won't have clean clothes."

She purses her lips, her eyes twinkling. "You're right. Then I'll need to shower *again* at my place."

She loves me. That's the only explanation. "And I'll have to supervise *that*. To make sure you're being safe."

"Conserve gas to waste water?"

"Oh, don't worry." I draw her close enough that my words are a whisper against her pink lips. "That water won't be wasted."

• • •

The next morning, I'm late to work. Well, not late, exactly, but I'm not early, and Shelby is one hundred percent the reason why. My best efforts to beat the camera crew were fumbled when my insatiable girlfriend accosted me at the coffee pot and insisted I take her against the countertop.

The things I suffer through for her. Some might even call me a saint. Canonized and blessed in the glory of Shelby's breasts.

Somewhere, eighteen-year-old Cameron blacks out completely.

I pull up to the curb in front of the Caroline Street house, behind a large landscaping trailer.

"I didn't know we were at the point of landscaping," Shelby says, impressed.

"We're not," I say, squinting against the blaring yellow sunshine pouring against my windshield. "Maybe they're here for a different house?"

Shelby unbuckles her seat belt and reaches for the door, but she hesitates, her hand pausing on the handle. "Hm."

"Hm?"

Her blue eyes narrow and she tucks her hair behind her ear. "Yeah. Hm. We aren't that late, but the camera crew is waiting for us at the front door."

I grunt. "That figures. Lyle will love getting footage of us arriving together first thing in the morning."

"Undoubtedly," Shelby says, sounding unconvinced. We'd kind of assumed Lyle had washed his hands of us.

I grab her other hand, giving it a squeeze. "If you'd rather, you can drop me off, then take my truck for coffee and circle back."

Her lips quirk in a half grin. "Didn't get enough caffeine this morning?"

"Someone distracted me," I admit.

Her brow arches at me in challenge. "Someone distracted *you*? That's not how I remember it. I was minding my business, filling my cup—"

"While naked."

She shrugs lightly. "I forgot pajamas. Whoops."

I bite back a groan. This woman.

She smirks and gives up the act, reaching for the door again. "I'm good if you are, but we should get going. There's some kind of congregation happening on the porch and my dad's looking flustered. He needs you."

The sun is still preventing me from seeing much, but I

pull my keys out of the ignition anyway and follow Shelby. Once I'm out of the bright light, I can read the side of the landscaping trailer. My chest instantly deflates like I've been kicked in the diaphragm.

RIGGS & SON

Son. As in singular.

Derek is here.

Shelby takes in the wording and her hand finds mine. After a beat, I allow her to pull me along toward the porch where a full camera crew is ready to catch my reaction.

Fucking. Lyle.

My brother's back is to me, but I'd recognize him anywhere. Tall like me, but more lean, angular even, same as my dad. His hair is longer, with a soft curl. He's dressed in durable khaki pants and a burgundy polo. The uniform of generations of Riggs men, but not me.

My heart is pounding a staccato beat and my hands are clammy. I try to pull away from Shelby, but she doesn't relent, and I'm grateful she's so stubborn.

What I really want is to leave. To get in my truck and call in sick. I don't care what Lyle makes of that. All I know is I don't want to do this, and I especially don't want to do it on camera.

Shelby's fingers squeeze mine and I have the sense to squeeze back. "Can you do this?" she asks in a low tone.

"I don't think so. I can't . . ." I scramble for the words. Can't face him? Can't think of what to say? Can't imagine what Derek must think of me? "Act," I finish. "Not with him."

"No," Shelby agrees. "And you shouldn't. I got this one. Just stay close and let me take the lead for once."

I manage a stiff nod and Shelby pulls us up to the porch, her face bright and eager. She releases my hand, clapping hers together. "Morning, everyone! Derek Riggs! What an amazing surprise! It's been ages. Come here, you handsome devil! Give me a hug."

Derek looks gobsmacked, and I can't tell if it's because of Shelby's words or if he's stunned by the megawatt movie-star smile she's offering.

They embrace, and she kisses his cheek in a brotherly way, before looping his arm through hers. She pulls him to face the crowd, which includes the camera guy, Steve, and me. Shelby beams in my direction, making a show of waving me off. "I know, I know, you boys have catching up to do, but I'm not ready to let go yet. It's not every day a girl gets twice the Riggs. Imagine the hate mail I'd get if I didn't take advantage." She turns to my brother, affecting a sweet pout. "So, Derek, please, please, *please* tell me you're going to work some magic on our poor excuse for a front yard? This project is crying out for some curb appeal."

If I hadn't already been in love with Shelby, I would be a goner. I see what her dad meant about watching out for each other—holding each other up. He meant this right here. Because when you care about someone, you know just when they need you to step up and take the reins. Like jumping on stage to sing karaoke. Equal partners. A team.

Costars in life.

To his credit, Derek doesn't flinch at the full-force blast of Shelby charm. Much. After a blink, when he's undoubtedly trying to decide if Shelby is real, my brother goes on to describe his plans for the front acre. His tone is confident and knowledgeable, and once I'm able to move past the fact that he's even here in the first place, I'm nodding along with his vision.

"I like it," I say once he's finished and I've recovered my ability to speak.

His green eyes, the same shade as mine, widen slightly but he grins, relieved. "Yeah?"

I studiously ignore the pang in my chest. "Yeah. Like Shelby said, the lot is a mess. It's got gobs of potential, but it's been left wild for too long. It's a shame to do all this work inside and leave the outside looking like this."

After that, they pull Derek aside for a talking head about his plans, and I go inside and bury myself in bathroom tile work.

Twenty minutes or so later, there's a knock at the door.

"We have mudders for that," Daniel says.

"I don't mind. I've been watching some videos on YouTube. Wanted to see if I could do it."

"Apparently, you can," he says, his tone approving.

"I'm slow. Professionals would have had this laid down already."

Daniel grunts noncommittally.

"Your brother left. Said he'll be back in two weeks with a crew to get to work on the terrace."

This time *I* grunt noncommittally.

"He seemed to linger longer than necessary. Like he was waiting for you to come back."

I plop down a tile, adjusting it carefully along my string level.

"He wanted to talk to you, Cameron."

I sigh, getting to my feet and brushing my hands together, shaking off some dried mud. "I'm sure he does. I imagine he has all sorts of things to say about how he's glad I finally came home and found a real job, even if it's in television. I bet he'd even like to point out how old his kids are and how I'm a terrible uncle for only sending them Amazon gift cards for Christmas because I have no idea what a five-year-old likes. He, for sure, wants to mention how he's taken care of our mom, since I desert her time and again to travel the world in search of stories."

I slump, embarrassed at the emotion strangling in my throat. I know exactly how childish I sound, but I can't seem to help myself. "He's better off without me. They both are. Lyle's just fucking with things for drama's sake."

Daniel moves farther into the space and leans a hip against the vanity, crossing his arms. "That's true. Lyle's pulling the strings, and he shouldn't have brought in your brother without asking. Much like with Shelby's mom. But I think you're wrong about everything else. Derek wasn't here to lecture you. He was here to see his brother. I know things are rough between you and your father. I get it. Both sides, if I'm honest. I never really understood Shelby's career either and certainly never approved of so much exposure and responsibility so young. I should have stepped in, but I didn't. I let Ada Mae do what she wanted, and that was my fault. I was the dad, and I didn't do my job. But I wasn't there with her in L.A. I didn't have control of the day-to-day things, like what she ate for breakfast or what time she went to bed.

"In a way, I understand how Paul felt. He was on the periphery of his own kid's life. He watched you grow up on television like everyone else, and it's hard to love your kid from afar. So, instead, he poured all his love into your brother because he was around, and he needed it, too. And that *hurts.* It's fair for you to be angry about that. You should be." The edges of his blue eyes crinkle in memory. "You should have heard the way Shelby screamed at me when everything came to a head with us. She let me have it. You haven't had the chance to do that, but you should. As angry as you are, you need to accept what's between you and him isn't the same as what's between you and your brother, or even you and your mom. All that about Derek's kids getting older and you traveling the world instead of coming home? He didn't say that. *You* did."

I swallow hard, my face burning and throat tight.

Daniel straightens off the vanity and steps carefully over the cardboard covering the subfloor toward me. He places a hand on my shoulder and squeezes. "You're here now, though. And if I'm not completely off base, you're not going anywhere anytime soon."

I shake my head. It's all I can manage. Daniel squeezes my shoulder again, nodding once, as if that decides something for him.

"Good. Then you know what to do next."

20

MAD LOVE TO BAD BLOOD

By Jocelyn Bennett

Last month, we reported on the long-awaited reappearance of L.A.'s favorite child-star darling turned ruined pop princess Shelby Springfield. Five years after the release of Lyle Jessup's "You Chose Wrong" (rumored to be written about the dissolution of their fairy-tale romance), and ten months after her mother's scathing tell-all, Ms. Springfield turned up with a new man on her arm.

But is he really new? Certainly not to us! Springfield, 27, was seen painting a small-town flea market in starlight, feasting on ice-cream cones, and dancing a two-step with *the* Cameron Riggs, 28. The two costarred, along with Jessup, on the über-popular tween show *The World According to Jackson* and, at the time, were rumored to have a secret love of their own (in case you're wondering, that sound you hear is the banger vocals of Katy Perry belting "Teenage Dream").

Of course, the duo always denied any attachment, and in a shocking twist, it was heartthrob Lyle Jessup who Springfield spent the next five years on-again, off-again dating, amid perpetual personal turmoil. Rumors of alcohol abuse, mental instability, and cheating (recently bolstered by her mother's bestselling memoir) followed the young starlet everywhere. It's no wonder she turned tail for the Midwest in 2017 after Jessup released his self-proclaimed autobiographical album.

But trouble couldn't stay away forever, it seems. Shelby and Cameron turned up in L.A. in early spring, reportedly entering into discussions regarding a television opportunity with Jessup, a successful producer with an endless reserve of generosity for his down-on-their-luck costars.

"They're doing the pilot," Springfield's bestselling mom, Ada Mae, confirmed over the phone. "I went to visit the set and lend my support, but I'm not so sure this will stick. Shelby never could commit. She's spent her whole life making excuses and playing the victim. I just feel bad for Cameron Riggs! Poor guy doesn't even know what he's gotten himself wrapped up in."

After the pair was spotted canoodling at a flea market in the middle of nowhere, Jessup himself spoke to *Hollywood Hotwire* last month to confirm that Riggs and Springfield are filming a pilot for a new home-renovation show for HLNW, aptly titled *HomeMade,* which all sounded very reserved and aboveboard for Springfield, until, that is, a series of unfortunate (and familiar) events last weekend.

In a land far, far away (or Michigan, as it were), cameras were on hand to catch Shelby behaving badly, this time with a (bearded and muscular) Cameron Riggs by her side. Hollywood's favorite power couple, Lyle and Marcella Jessup, reportedly flew all the way out to the tiny Midwestern town, in the hopes of celebrating the green-lighting of the duo's home-repair show. To say they had a cool reception would be an understatement.

When we reached out about the situation, Springfield's former BFF confessed her concern through her publicist. "I'd hoped she was past this, but when I asked her to quit drinking, she practically laughed me out of the bar, insisting it was only a ginger ale. But I know what I saw, and I know Shelby. She needs help. She was drunk and belligerent. She and Cameron Riggs are wasting this opportunity. I only hope this time she gets the help she needs before it's too late."

Then, of course, there was the moment when Jessup tried to mend fences with her old friend, jumping onstage and inviting her to do karaoke. Readers might remember the days when these two songbirds shared many a stage, delighting L.A. clubgoers and pop fans alike. Turns out former good-boy Cameron Riggs might have a jealous streak running through those golden veins. He reportedly hopped onstage, midperformance, to steal the mic from Jessup. Why would he make such a crass public gesture? Apparently good manners mean nothing when you want to duet with your new love.

The song choice? You guessed it. None other than Lyle Jessup's Grammy-winning hit, "You Chose Wrong." Talk about rubbing salt in the wound!

The dastardly duo didn't stop there, however. Michigan clubgoers were also treated to some dirty dancing between the (presumably intoxicated) costars, causing this reporter to wonder just how wholesome this television show of theirs promises to be. Will we be witnessing home improvement or home *wrecking*?

I hope for the sake of Springfield, Riggs, Jessup, and child stars everywhere, it's the former, but reality-television viewers will be on board for the latter, regardless.

Comments (1,804)

Margie_78: who cares Springfield is a whore

Lester-the-collector: Once again the fake news media is more concerned with the activities of cokehead celebrities . . . (329 replies)

SuperChick: Dude. Lester. You're reading an online gossip rag.

The Lorelai Jones: Damn right they sang Jessup's weak ass lie of a song and they sang it BETTER

QuirkyLibrarian: I've always liked Shelby Springfield. I hope she gets the help she needs.

Ginnifur01: Marcella Jessup is way hotter than Shelby. Lyle leveled up.

(reply to Ginnifur01) **IheartCameronRiggs:** Actually, Cameron Riggs is hotter than Lyle Jessup. Have you seen his thighs?

(reply to IheartCameronRiggs) **IheartShelbySpringfield:** Like tree trunks, one might say.

JunkInDaTrunk: Lyle Jessup eats ass. I hated that Beauty and the Barber show he did.

The_Local_Idiot: I was in rehab with Shelby Springfield. Girl was a mess. Gave good head tho.

MYHEARTWILLGOON: I used to love The World According to Jackson! Watched it with my grandpa before he died. So many good memories. I really hope Shelby's okay.

TwerkIt: I did an acoustic cover of "You Chose Wrong" and would really appreciate it if you could head on over to my YouTube channel and check it out!

21

SHELBY

INVISIBLE STRING

I should be angry. Throwing a fit, punching walls, screaming into the void, and drinking myself under the table. No one would blame me. At least no one who knows me. By the time I woke up this morning, the *Hollywood Hotwire* article had been picked up by a zillion other outlets, each one more nefarious and far-reaching than the last. Even if I had a real publicist to navigate such things (which I don't anymore), it would have been too late to make a dent.

So, I got up and went to work. In my shop. Because even if I'm not angry, I *am* hurt, and I need twenty-four hours to cry it out by myself before I turn up on camera. I'm lucky I have that option. After calling to check in this morning, Cameron had to report to the Caroline Street house to meet with the bath fitters. In an effort to apologize for the grief and aggravation I've caused by being named Shelby *mother-effing* Springfield, I sent the entire crew lunch via Lorelai. She called me on her way home, pleased to report everyone seemed offended on our behalf, to the extent that the camera crew left early, and when Lyle called to smooth things over with Cameron, he apparently cut him off saying, "Not fucking today, Lyle," to thunderous applause.

It's a small and short-lived victory, but it feels good to know our crew believes in us. That's the thing about Midwesterners. We're a polite and generally pleasing people, but fuck with one of us, and we'll take that offense to the grave, then cremate it and sprinkle it in your coffee with maple syrup.

I don't make the rules, but I am grateful for them.

At any rate, I fully intend to head in first thing tomorrow to finish my railing. It's not the nook's fault I made poor decisions in my early twenties, and I refuse to allow one teeny, tiny damning article to *derail* me from my deadline. Heh. Furniture pun.

As for today, I have my pew. Thank you, Mr. Jenson, for your sentimentality and decades of sticky varnish. My fingers ache from the seven straight hours of precise effort exerted to sand it new. So much so, I can barely raise my middle one in righteous indignation. It's been a healthy compromise.

"I'll be honest. I was expecting Josh Groban."

Cameron.

My heart can't help but skip in my chest. Wonder if that will ever go away? Hasn't in fifteen years, so I kind of doubt it.

"When I'm in my feelings, I like my country singers salty. It's a side effect of being best friends with Lorelai."

"This is Miranda Lambert, right?"

"She's verrry salty," I say, nodding. "All that angst with her ex." I tilt my head, pretending to consider. "I wonder what that must feel like."

Cameron snorts, making his way over to where I'm working, and squats down with a reverent intake of breath. "Shelby."

"Cam," I respond mildly.

"This is the pew?"

"The very same," I say, pleased at the obvious approval in his gaze.

"It doesn't even look the same. Well, no. It *does.* It just looks brand new is all."

"She shined up real pretty," I say, standing and taking in my work. "Turns out I had some elbow grease to spare this morning, so this was the perfect project. I think I want it in my foyer."

"What's this?" Cameron picks up a block of wood and shakes his head back and forth with a low whistle. "The scrollwork is . . ."

"Magnificent, isn't it? I didn't do it. That was all Mr. Jenson's father. I was able to remove it without destroying the integrity of the pew." I pick up the decorative slab of oak and place it on the top corner to show him. "They sat on either corner. I have a set, and I want to refurbish them for Mr. Jenson. They could be great bookends, but really, he can do whatever he likes with them. The attention to detail is phenomenal. Things just aren't made like this anymore, and I think he would appreciate having a piece of his father's work in his home."

Cam rolls the wood in his hands, turning it this way and that, studying it. "I'm sure you're right. He seemed pretty broken up about giving away the pew, insistent as he was."

"His Maggie is dying," I say with a soft sigh, brushing

loose sawdust from the scrolled arm of the bench. "A whole life together, and now, he's not sure what to do with himself if she's not there. They have grown kids, one works with him on the family farm, but it won't be the same without her."

Cameron is quiet. "No. I don't imagine it will."

"So," I say, straightening and taking the piece from him. I wrap my arms around his neck and pull him close. "I love you."

He huffs a laugh, stirring the hair at my neck. "I love you, too. And I love that I can say that now."

"You could have said it before."

"I tried to."

I take a half step back, arching a brow.

He laughs again. "What? I did! It was just with my eyes. And, like, my . . . intentions."

"Your intentions?"

"Whatever, I can say it now. I love you." He takes a deep breath and yells, "I LOVE SHELBY SPRINGFIELD!"

I giggle, lifting on to my toes and kissing his cheek. "You're a dork. You don't have to use my last name all the time, you know."

His eyes twinkle with mischief. "Oh, I do, though. I want to make sure there's no confusion with all the other Shelbys."

I sigh, taking in his open, handsome face. He's so steadfast and strong. Solid, like this oak pew, ready to take on the test of time.

"I'm sorry for the things they said in the article, Cam."

He furrows his brow.

"I know," I say at the exasperation in his expression. "I didn't write it and had nothing to do with it, but you can't say this didn't happen *because* of me. I brought this on you, just by being with you . . . That's how this is always going to be. Twenty years from now, they're gonna dig out my mistakes and pin them to your name. No matter what we do, my past will haunt us."

"Twenty years from now, huh?" he asks, his face transforming and his white teeth flashing in an easy grin.

"I'm serious, Cameron. There's no way the pilot will sell after this. And what about *National Geographic?*"

"What about them? I'm being serious, too."

I take a deep breath. This needs to be said. Before we go any further. "Cam, I'm the same girl I was five years ago, and you didn't want—"

His gaze darkens and he steps out of the cradle of my arms. He reaches for my hands, opening them faceup and pressing a gentle kiss to each palm. I bite my lip against the sudden rush of emotion cutting off my breath.

"Listen to me." His voice is low. "Never for one second have I ever *not* wanted you. And I don't mean physically. I mean with all of me. When I was eleven, and you amazed me with the way every emotion painted your face during a scene; when I was eighteen, and you tucked my note into your back pocket, blushing; when I was twenty-three, and you said you'd framed my shitty *Nat Geo* pictures in the apartment you shared with Lyle.

"And that was *before,* Shelby. Before you opened that door three months ago and let me back into your life. Trusted me with your work and your friends and your dad. Before you showed me your workshop and sang and danced with me and made my entire fucking *life* when you shouted at me that you loved me before beating me up." He sinks to his knees on the dirty sawdust-covered floor and presses his forehead to my stomach, whispering to my hands. "I have never not wanted you, and I never will. Never. You are stuck with me. You told me you loved me and I'm all in, Shelby. No take-backs."

I slip to my knees beside him, tears tracking down my cheeks as I lift his face to kiss him, hard. After a minute, I pull back. "Jesus, Cam. That was a good speech."

He cracks a smile. "Are you sure it wasn't too much? I feel like it might've been too much."

I shake my head, sniffing. "Just enough."

"But the getting on my knees part? That was a lot, wasn't it?"

I shake my head again, laughing, even as the tears keep falling. "Too late. You've done it, and I loved it. Now you'll have to figure out how to one-up yourself forever and ever."

His head falls back, and he whispers, "She said 'forever and ever.' Let the rafters be my witness. She said it."

I reach for his jaw and pull him down to my lips, kissing him softly, taking my time. When his lips part, I worship him with my tongue. My fingers dive into his hair, holding him to me, anchoring him, anchoring *us* to this place, to this moment when we promised forever.

And then we're promising more. Our kisses become frantic and fiery, and Cam's hands are moving with purpose, sliding up and along my sides, back down and curving to cup me, while his hips crush against me, sending fissures of pulsing heat to my center.

Without even meaning to, I shift my legs wider, trying

to capture the sweet friction, but he has other ideas. In one swift movement, I'm scooped to my feet, and in another, I'm placed on my workbench.

Fucking tree-trunk thighs. I love 'em.

I sweep my hands behind me right as Cameron's lips latch onto my breast through my tank, his tongue dampening the cotton with the most incredible friction, making me gasp out loud when he bites softly.

"Tell me you have a condom."

"Are you kidding?" he says, tugging at the hem of my shirt and pulling it over my head. "Ever since that first night, I have at least three on my person at all times." He reaches into his back pocket and passes it into my waiting hand.

I snicker. "Ambitious."

He deftly unhooks my bra with a smirk. "Prepared."

He palms my breast, lifting and weighing, letting his thumb flick over the sensitive tip. Once. Twice. "Cam . . ." It comes out on a moan, and he grins, teasing.

"Yes, Shelby?" Three times. His tongue gives the slightest lick, leaving me bare and cold and desperate. He steps closer, pressing himself against me. I can't keep from bucking against him.

"I hate you," I pant.

"You don't."

"I might."

He removes his shirt, painstakingly slipping the buttons of his plaid work shirt through one by one.

He takes me down, lays his shirt on the bench. *"Oh,"* I say and kick off my shoes. He slips my zipper south, peeling off my jeans before I gracelessly wriggle out of my underwear.

He places me back on the bench, his shirt spread out beneath me. Feeling midway between caught and bold, I spread my legs apart, opening myself to him and meet his stunned gaze straight on.

"Christ, Springfield," he says with a growl. "If I had a camera. I've never seen anything so . . ."

"Impatient? Turned on? Deliciously frustrated?" I reach for his belt, hungrily kissing along his collarbone and down his bare chest. My tongue curls, circling his flat nipple, and I drag my teeth until he hisses. The echo of his desire reverberates softly in the open space of my workshop, and I'm done waiting. I spring him free of his clothes and sheath him in the condom, leading him forward.

He captures my lips in a frantic, heady kiss, all tongue and strength, probing and loving me. His fingers cup and pinch my breasts until I'm writhing against him and he grabs my hips, taking me in one slick thrust.

My entire body tightens around the place where we meet, absorbing him and making him mine. When he pulls back, he takes his time, letting me feel the absence, before powerfully filling me again and again, striking against the place that makes stars burst behind my eyelids and sparks ignite in my veins. I'm reckless and undone and practically sobbing with want and Cameron is there. Matching me, protecting me, ravishing me, *loving* me.

His gloriously rough hand traces down my thigh, setting me ablaze as he grips my knee, raising it, and changes the angle of our meeting. I cry out, my nails digging into his back as my walls collapse around him in a ripple of seemingly endless fireworks and heat. Cameron stiffens under my hands and thrusts once, twice, three times more, his grip almost painful on my hips as he crumples forward, his finishing groan buried in my skin. I press soft, open-mouth kisses in a path from his ear over his cheekbones and back. He straightens, pulling from me, and I whimper at the loss of his heat.

"Deliciously frustrated?" he teases, when at last he finds his voice.

"Sorry." I shrug and smirk as his eyes follow my breasts. "I meant to say horny. I was distracted into using big words. Speaking of . . ." I smirk again, self-satisfied, and his lips spread into a grin, even as his green eyes don't stray from my bouncing nipples.

"The lighting in your workshop is impeccable."

"I know," I say. When he finally looks up, I make a point of dragging my eyes over every ridge and dip of his body, noticing the way a certain part of him seems to rise under my attention.

My eyes flicker to his and he grins, almost sheepish. "I told you, I brought three. Once will never be enough."

"I've been wondering about that workbench over there," I say. "Just got it. It's an antique."

"Think it's sturdy?"

"Only one way to find out."

22

. . . .

CAMERON

I'M YOURS

KEVIN: Hey man. You should stop in when you get home.

CAMERON: I'm pretty beat. Rushing toward the finish line on the house. Rain check?

KEVIN: What I meant to say is your dad is here.

CAMERON: . . .

CAMERON: Fuck.

KEVIN: Sorry.

I pull my truck into my reserved parking space behind the distillery and shut off the engine. The darkness covers me, and my ears ring from the sudden quiet. There's no way my dad is here for a good reason, and I don't have the energy for anything else. I contemplate sneaking up the stairs to my apartment and leaving him high and dry.

But that would be the old Riggs. Running away is something I don't do anymore, for better or, it seems, for worse.

I swing open the truck door, slamming it harder than necessary behind me, and stride in through the employee entrance of the bar. Normally, I'd stop and chat with the dishwashers or Beth, but I'm all business tonight. Any interaction with Paul Riggs is always business. I come out from behind the bar and Kevin nods toward a dimly lit corner of the seating area.

"What's he nursing?"

"Water."

Figures.

I consider mixing myself something strong for fortitude but decide against it. He's my dad. *Stop being such a tool and walk over there and sit down.*

"Hey, Dad."

My dad lifts his head. He looks the same, but older than when I saw him the last time, four years ago. He has a beard. Maybe we do look alike after all.

"Cameron. Have a seat."

I slide into a booth and clasp my hands in front of me. He wraps his around his untouched ice water.

"Your mom told me where to find you."

I nod.

"Thought I'd better stop by before you took off."

There it is.

"I'm planning to stick around, actually. I like it here."

"Living above a bar?"

"It's a distillery and it's not half bad. The rent is reasonable, and it's close to work."

"Right. The reality show."

Strike two.

"It's a home-renovation show, actually."

"Can't imagine there's too much home renovation happening in the rain forests."

I suppress a sigh. "Cloud forests. And you're right, but I'm a quick study. I've been apprenticing under Daniel Springfield and learning a lot. He thinks I have a knack for it."

"Oh, well, if *Daniel Springfield* thinks so . . ."

This time I let my sigh out. Because, fucking-A, I'm tired. "What exactly did you come here for, Dad?"

"I wanted to see how you're doing. You're my son, and I care what you're doing with your life. I tried calling you."

I swallow my guilt. The time never felt right to call him back. Honestly, I didn't want to deal with him poking holes in my already-shaky plans. "Well, then, you should be pleased, Dad. I'm doing well. I'm living in one place, working a job where I'm making something worthwhile, dating a girl I really love . . . everything is going well."

"And what happens if the show isn't picked up? Are you just going to keep renovating houses and living above a bar?"

"Distillery, and maybe! I don't know yet."

"I looked you up online." I grimace. *Christ,* here we go. Leave it to Paul to pick at every single one of my insecurities until they bleed. "I read the articles. Hot-mess costar, Hollywood drama. It doesn't sound real stable, Cameron. What happened to *National Geographic?*"

"I thought you hated me traveling the world doing docs."

"I did, but at least it was a respectable, steady job."

I scrub a hand down my face. "For fuck's sake, make up your mind! First of all, that article and any others you read online are garbage. Shelby doesn't even drink and she's ridiculously talented at what she does. Her commissions make more in a month than I'd venture the landscaping business makes in a year. The only reason we have this show is because of her. Lyle Jessup is fucking around and holding the pilot over us because he's jealous that she moved on and made a name for herself outside of Hollywood.

"Second of all, I love her, and I want to stay. I don't know how I'm going to make it work yet. Ideally, the pilot would get picked up, but even if it doesn't, I don't know. I like working with my hands. Flipping houses wouldn't be terrible."

"It's a hard living, Cameron."

"I have some savings, Dad. I'm not completely irresponsible. I've been living in and out of tents for six years and was able to bank my paychecks." Some, anyway. It's not ideal and definitely not enough to buy a house, but it's enough to keep renting from Kevin. I shake my head. "And anyway, I don't even know why I'm justifying myself to you. You've literally never approved of anything I've ever done. Why would you start now?"

"That's not true."

I level him with a glare.

He sputters. "I don't even know you! You're my son and I know nothing about you. Everything I know I read online and now I learn not even that is real."

"Ask me!" I lower my voice when I notice Kevin look over at our table. I wave him off. "Dad. I'm right here. Just ask me. All I've ever wanted is to tell you about myself."

He sits back in his seat, his hands flat on the table, and presses his lips in a thin line. He sits there for so long, I start to wonder if he's going to talk or leave, or if maybe I should leave? But then he reaches for his water glass and takes a long sip, clearing his throat.

"Okay. Fine. Tell me what's going on with *National Geographic* and the house-flipping show."

• • •

An hour later, I say goodbye to my dad and sit on an empty stool at the bar. Kevin walks over, handing me a beer. It's a weeknight, so the place is basically empty at this late hour. He grabs another beer for himself and leans his forearms on the bar. "So?"

I shrug and take a sip. "In all honesty, it could have gone worse. I thought it might at one point, but we actually talked, and that was okay."

"He give you grief about it being a reality show?"

"Of course. And my alcoholic girlfriend and leaving the steady job at *Nat Geo* . . ."

"I hope you corrected him about Shelby."

I glare at him.

"Well, he does have a point about *Nat Geo*. From what you've told me, that's a pretty sweet gig. And you don't have to deal with Lyle."

"It's a great job if you don't mind traveling eleven months out of the year and being single forever."

"Which you are not."

"I am not."

"How not single are you, exactly?"

"It's only been a few weeks," I hedge.

This time Kevin is the one who glares, pointedly, his lenses flickering in the firelight. I fess up. "As I've been in love with her for over a decade, pretty fucking not single."

"And she knows?"

I grin like an idiot. "Yeah."

"Then there's your answer. *Nat Geo* is out. You said yourself: it's a single man's job, and you, my friend, are attached."

I take another drink and let that wash over me. It feels right. "Huh. You're good at this. Is it because of the whole bartender thing, or . . . ?"

"Probably the suspenders," he quips. "If *Nat Geo* is out, what will you do?"

"Hope for a miracle."

Kevin barks out a laugh. "Cheers to that."

. . .

"So, what's the plan? Are you ever going to respond to the article? Are you going to hop on CNN and give an exclusive or something?" Kevin asks the following weekend. Apparently, he's really taking this wise-man-in-suspenders thing to heart. We're sitting on his deck, overlooking his wooded backyard, tasked with supervising his two kids as they toddle around their playset. A hundred yards away, Beth is showing Shelby the abandoned woodshed that came with the property.

I lean back in an Adirondack chair and inhale the sharp pine-infused air into my lungs before sipping my beer. "First of all, CNN? That goes to show how much you watch the news if you think CNN gives a shit. And second, I don't think we're doing anything."

"Nothing?"

I shake my head.

"So, you're going to let them publish lies. Isn't that slander? Or libel?"

I make a face. "Not really. If you read carefully, they didn't *actually* lie about anything." Kevin makes a noise of disbelief and I continue, "No, really, that's how they can get away with it. They tell a colorful version of the truth. It makes us sound bad, but the facts remain."

"You guys didn't pick that song to sing."

I roll my eyes, taking another sip. "True, but I can't call up Howard Stern just to be like, 'Let me set the record straight, I didn't want to sing Jessup's fucking song, but I did, and I thought it turned out okay.'"

"Better than okay," he grumbles, legitimately offended on our behalf. No one will believe us, but it's enough just to have people in our corner.

"Thanks, man."

"You should be able to defend yourselves is all."

"We will. In our own way, we'll set the record straight. Through the pilot, assuming they go through with it, test audiences will be able to see how talented Shelby is and how respected she's become over the years."

"And they'll be able to see how you look at her," he offers mildly.

I narrow my eyes over my bottle. "And? How's that?"

"Like you told *National Geographic* to fuck off and have a ring picked out."

I grin, my focus drawn to where Shelby is laughing at something Beth is saying while carrying an armful of wood up toward the deck.

"Riggs?" Kevin's tone is stern.

I ignore him and get to my feet. Passing him my beer, I say, "Hold this for me, will you?"

I jump down the steps to meet the ladies halfway and Shelby passes the load off with a grateful smile.

"It's white oak," she gushes, her navy eyes twinkling with happiness. "Old construction. Looks like it's been salvaged from a barn or maybe another shed. It was just sitting in there, all preserved and perfect, like it was waiting for me. Kevin was going to burn it!" She admonishes my friend as if he was going to pee on the wood and then cover it with puff paint.

"Thank God you were here to save it," I say dryly. Beth laughs at Shelby's sheepish expression before hollering after one of their kids, who's shoveling sand into the grass.

"It's not a ton," Shelby says in a low tone. "But it's enough to make something for Beth and Kevin. Like a hanging address sign or maybe something for their foyer? Beth seems to like farmhouse decor."

"They would love that. Or maybe something for the nursery?" I suggest.

Shelby's entire face lights up. "Yes!"

"I'm gonna throw these in the back of my truck, then."

When I return, Shelby's stolen my chair, so I retrieve my beer and settle on the end of the deck in front of her, leaning back against her knees, my legs dangling.

"The thing is," she's saying to Kevin and Beth, "I honestly *was* that bad in my late teens and early twenties. I'm not proud of it, but Cam knows it's true. He saw me at my lowest."

"Highest?" I suggest, and she smacks the back of my head as Kevin and Beth laugh.

"Maybe highest," she concedes. "Either way, it wasn't good. I have entire periods of time that I don't really remember. I was barely old enough to vote and was getting the VIP treatment in clubs and pissing away money. Entirely lost and lonely. Lyle's a fucker," she whispers the last word, being mindful of the little ears in the yard. "But he wasn't in any position to take care of me, and I certainly didn't care about him.

"My point being," she finishes, "the reputation was earned, and they had every reason to say the things they did in that article."

"That's debatable. Mess or no, you were a kid, Shelb. You shouldn't have to carry your mistakes forever," I say.

"But I will," she says, ruffling my hair.

"You don't have to, though." I've been thinking this through, and there is only one way we can guarantee she'll be left alone. That we both will. "We only signed on for the pilot and the house is nearly done. We can walk away."

Her boldness from earlier seems to have slipped away and is replaced by something more tender. "Cam," she starts softly, leaning forward and placing her hands on my shoulders. "I thought you loved the show. Plus, you already turned down *Nat Geo* for that doc."

"I love *you*," I say simply. "And, yeah, I do like the show. But not if it means you get dragged through the dirt at every turn because your ex has a chip on his shoulder."

"What would you do if we didn't have the show?"

I grimace. "Not sure. I'm going to stay in one place for a

while and see how that goes." Shelby's cheeks flush a wild pink, pleased.

"Well, I'm pretty sure my dad would hire you on in a heartbeat, if you're not completely turned off house flipping. That said, I'm not ready to walk away from the pilot," Shelby says. "Don't get me wrong: Lyle is the worst, but I'm tired of letting him dictate the things in my life. It's more obvious than ever that he's only been interested in sabotaging us, but I'm not sure it's working."

"But the article—"

"Was gross, sure, but our crew deserves to see it through. And they support us. So does our community and my dad and our friends . . . there's a whole world outside of *Hollywood Hotwire* and Lyle."

"Except he's the showrunner, Shelb. And if by some miracle the network orders an entire season, he's still the one pulling the strings."

She rolls her eyes lightly. "I know. He's going to keep effing around with us. I realize that. And yet, so far, we've managed to handle everything he's thrown our way."

I meet her grin, turning sideways on the deck. "That's true."

"It's just . . ." She makes a face and huffs. "It feels like this is a good thing we're doing, you know? Like the positive outweighs the negative. My dad's already getting offers for future projects, not to mention a generous consultant fee as long as we keep going. And this is still a really awesome opportunity to bring good press to the area. Remember our first talk? Boost tourism, fight gentrification, make houses pretty for generations of families?"

I consider this. "Okay. But at what personal risk to you?"

Shelby shakes her head. "Nothing I can't handle." She must read the defensiveness in my expression because she narrows her eyes and holds up her hand.

"Cam. Stop. I know you want to protect me from all the bad things, but I don't need it. I'm a grown woman. I can handle Lyle and I really couldn't care less what people say about the mistakes I made years ago." She presses her lips together and crushes them to the side, in a move that's self-deprecating. "Although, Lorelai *is* helping me hire a publicist if things move forward after this. I don't want to be caught off guard again. This means that someone else will get paid to deal with Lyle."

"You're sure?" I check one last time, reaching for her hand.

She squeezes mine in response. "Positive."

"Then, I am, too."

"Me three," Kevin adds. "Not that you asked, but you did mention friends somewhere in that pretty speech. You've always got access to my karaoke machine if you're feeling desperate."

. . .

After dinner, the sun is slipping low, so Beth lights a veritable moat of citronella candles around the edges of their deck. The yard glitters with amorous fireflies, and the shrill cries of cicadas echo in our lazy silence. Kevin returns from putting the kids to bed and asks if I need a fresh beer. I shake my head, raising the half-full bottle I've been nursing the last hour. Shelby settles back in her chair, bouncing a little and propping her pretty bare feet on the railing of the deck.

"I've been thinking."

"Here we go," Kevin mutters good-naturedly.

Shelby pauses her bouncing. Her eyes sparkle in the fading light. "And?"

"About my brother. And him showing up unexpectedly."

"I thought it went well," Shelby says. "And he's coming back, right? Are you okay with that?"

I nod. "I am. He's the best at what he does. I'm annoyed I didn't come up with the idea of bringing him on. But I was thinking about what you said, that good can come from this. What if we took control and not only brought him in, this time prepared, but offered him a regular partnership with the show? If, one, we make it past the pilot, and two, he does well on the Caroline Street house?"

Shelby doesn't even take time to consider. "I love it."

"Yeah?"

"Absolutely. Let's ask him on the show. He doesn't even have to do anything on camera, if he doesn't want, but he adjusted all right that first morning. Maybe he's got a little of your charm inside—"

"Deep inside," I offer wryly.

Shelby bites her lip, hiding her smile. "I'd like to get to know him, and he needs to see what you do, not just the finished product on television, but the real Cameron at work."

"That's a good idea."

"And I think it would go far in patching things up between you two."

I cross my ankle over my knee. "It's not so much patching as maybe we'll get to know one another. We're basically strangers. Maybe I'll bring my mom around, too? I can invite her on set. She'd love to see you again."

"Oooh. I like it," Beth says. "Let the world see you surrounded by the people who love you."

Kevin agrees. "Jessup pretty much forced the last reunion. At least this would be on your terms."

"And," Beth says, gaining momentum, "it would be the perfect way to show how much you've grown, without the gory details."

"Maybe I could bring Lorelai around," Shelby says. "Even let them film in the shop . . ." Her face goes pink. "Or something," she rushes to finish.

"Maybe not the shop," I say with a smirk.

"I said 'or something,'" she grumbles, redder still.

Kevin belts out a laugh and winks at his wife while making air quotes. "I think their 'shop' is the same as our 'stock room.'"

Beth struggles to stand, wriggling in her chair and finally popping up and rubbing a little at her belly. "Careful, Shelby," she warns. "What happens in the stock room doesn't always stay in the stock room."

23

SHELBY

CONFIDENT

A week later, Maren finds me in my workshop. I've finished up my projects for the Caroline Street house, so I've got some time to work on the growing pile of commissioned furniture. Today I'm repairing a buffet from a nineteenth-century farmhouse that was chewed up by an overeager family pet.

I'm listening to Celtic Woman and happily humming under my breath. I'm not saying the universe has been magically restored over the last few weeks, but it kind of has. The thing about living so far away from L.A. is that it's easy to pretend it doesn't exist and go about my everyday life . . . sanding off puppy-teeth marks and listening to vocal standards.

"Good morning. Did you know you have a couple name trending on social media?"

Mostly easy to pretend.

I scramble to my feet and slip my protective goggles to the top of my head. "I'm sorry. I have a what?"

Maren sidles over to me, unbuttoning her park-ranger

uniform shirt and tugging it off. She ties it around her trim waist, leaving her in a white tank. She leans against a bench, her arms crossing over her chest, but holding her phone in one hand.

Her lips are pressed tight, holding in her amusement, but it's still pouring out of her eyes. Maren couldn't hide her feelings if they were huddled away in a cave with one of her hibernating bears.

I take her phone. "What am I looking at?"

"The trending hashtags. Under 'Spriggs,'" she prompts.

I see it, but it's not computing. I try to pass her phone back. "That sounds like a science fiction show. How do you know it's a couple name?"

Maren huffs, snatching the phone. "For a former celeb, you are woefully behind the times, Shelby."

"For a park ranger, you're surprisingly judgmental," I grumble. "Just explain, please. Like I'm a kindergartner. Or, like, I'm me, a person without consistent Wi-Fi."

Maren comes to stand next to me, tapping around her phone with a fluency that frankly surprises me. I had no idea she was so tech savvy. Maybe Maren should be my publicist. "Okay, watch," she says. She pulls up the trending hashtags and clicks on the one that says *Spriggs*. Suddenly her screen is flooded with images of Cameron and me. Most are from when we were teens, freeze-frames from the infamous kiss. Others are from our trip out to the U.P. . . . us eating ice cream and holding hands and dancing like dorks at the flea market.

"They made us into gifs?" I ask, stunned.

"Yeah," Maren answers happily. "People are drooling

over how Cameron keeps stealing looks at you during the leaked talking heads."

I squeak. *"Leaked talking heads?"* Lyle is going to shit a brick.

Maren shrugs. "Who knows how that happened. I doubt anyone will fess up, but look how adorable!"

I'm overwhelmed as his image turns to watch me over and over, a soft smile spreading on his full lips, his hands running down his thighs as if he's nervous.

I don't read the comments, but there are a lot. Like, thousands of comments and tweets and reposts or whatever. Our names, together, and people seem to like it.

"How on earth did this happen? Did I miss something?"

Maren bites her lip. "Have you talked to Lorelai lately?"

"I texted her this morning to see if she wanted to meet us for dinner. She said she was busy."

Maren clicks around on her phone. "It's actually very, very sweet. But I don't think she had the first clue how fast it would go viral."

"Viral?" My voice is slightly strangled.

Maren passes me her phone. By the looks of all the pictures, she's pulled up Instagram. It's Lorelai's page . . . a quick glance at her numbers shows she wasn't kidding when she told us people liked a bad bitch. Her follower count is in the hundreds of thousands, complete with a blue checkmark. Not bad for someone who hasn't had a hit song in five years.

I see the clip immediately and click on the thumbnail. It's maybe thirty seconds long, just Riggs and me sitting on his tailgate outside the Caroline Street house. He's in his typical uniform of plaid shirt and work boots, sunglasses perched on his head. I'm wearing a pair of holey jeans and my varnishing mask is around my neck. I've got a bandanna tied up in my hair. This was from two days ago. Cam shoves my peanut butter and jelly in my face, and I throw a chip that sticks in his beard . . . before laughing hysterically as we crash into each other.

Ah. Yes. That's . . . very cute.

Underneath, Lorelai wrote:

When your best friend finally, finally gets their person, you can't help but be happy for them

I swallow hard, but I don't even bother to hide the tears. "She is so fucking nice," I say.

Maren nods. "But don't tell anyone."

"Right? It would ruin her carefully crafted bitch exterior, but damn she's soft."

"Softer than me, I'd venture. And that's saying something. You aren't mad, right?"

I shake my head. "Definitely not. We were out in the open. I even knew she was there. I just didn't realize she filmed us. She didn't come up with the couple name, did she?"

Maren snorts, echoing me. "Definitely not."

I wipe at my eyes and scroll through the rest of Lorelai's photos, including one from Kevin's bar the night Cam and I admitted our love to each other. "She has a lot on here. I had no idea she was keeping up with this stuff."

"She's definitely gearing up for something, if you ask me."

There are a few photos of her songwriting posted just this morning. "Interesting, so that's what she's up to today."

I scroll around the site. "Should I have an Instagram? Is this something I need to be doing? I mean, instead of Lorelai posting for us, obviously."

Maren tilts her head, considering. "It couldn't hurt. You would control what you put out there, which could be a good thing. I would just make sure you close your DMs, and whatever you do, don't read the comments."

I hum noncommittally, passing back the phone. Maybe tonight, after I get home, I could post photos of my projects and some behind-the-scenes stuff at the Caroline Street house and maybe even pay back Lorelai a bit.

I don't need to hide quite so much. I'm proud of everything I have, maybe it's time I show the world.

• • •

That evening, Cameron and I are curled up on my loveseat. He's watching the Tigers game and I'm tooling around on my phone. I set up an Instagram account and am trying to figure out how the site works . . . all the filters and clips. I follow Michelle Obama and Glennon Doyle and spend a solid twenty minutes watching Jennifer Garner's backlog of adorable farm videos.

I can do this. It's not so scary.

I elbow Cam. When he turns to me, I hold out my phone. "I'm going to take a selfie of us for Instagram, okay?"

"Quick question: Is it called a selfie if we're both in it?"

"Cam—"

He grabs my phone. "I have longer arms." He reaches in front of us and presses a kiss to the top of my head as the camera clicks, before passing it back.

I examine the photo. It's perfect. Cam kissing me, me radiating luckiness. I post it and underneath I write the words:

Love of my life

The next morning, I have a checkmark and a million and a half followers.

Lyle has nine hundred thousand.

(Not that I'm comparing.)

• • •

It's a quiet Tuesday night and we're eating grilled cheese and tomato sandwiches on Lorelai's front porch. My best friend invited me over after work, which isn't unusual, but she's quieter than I'm used to. Not her typical brash self at all.

After several long minutes of near silence, I crack.

"Out with it, Jones. What's wrong?"

She sighs, long suffering. I quirk a brow, and she smooths her napkin, playing for time. Eventually, she says, "I have an idea, but I'm not sure if it's something you'd be into."

I take a sip from my iced sun tea and gesture with my hand for her to proceed.

"I've been writing," she starts with a near grimace. "Kind of a lot, actually. Like, an album's worth, at least."

I know this, but I let it play out because I have a feeling I'm about to get the entire story, finally. I place my glass on the table with a soft thud. "Since when?"

Lorelai shrugs. "Since the bar?"

"You mean since Drake texted you and told you he loved

you?" She doesn't deny it. "That's a lot of songs in a matter of weeks, Lorelai."

"I know. It all poured out. Five years of choking on silence, and all of a sudden, it was like a purge. Anyway, I sent some demos to my old friend, Craig Boseman. Since," she rambles on in an uncharacteristic rush of words, "just because *I* think I've got something, doesn't mean I do, and long story short, he wants to fly me down to his studio outside Nashville to put down some tracks. He thinks I might have something really great here."

My jaw falls open. "You're kidding. Lorelai. That's . . ."

"I know," she says, her face flushed with a happiness I haven't seen from her maybe ever. Certainly not in the last year since Drake started reaching out.

"I'm . . . well. I'm not shocked. At all. I knew it was only a matter of time, but I'm so, *so* extremely happy for you."

"Thank you." She plows on. "So, like I said, I had this idea, after the article. You always talk about how Lyle controls the narrative when it comes to you three and always manipulates things to make himself out to be the fucking hero."

"It's exhausting," I grumble.

"Right. Totally. And you don't have to say yes, but my friend Craig, he's not with a label, per se. He's indie, with a kind of low-key way of doing things. Anyway, it's obviously been a minute since I had a single, so he said I might want to choose a song and do a music video. Something we could upload online and tease out there, to garner some excitement."

"Okay. That makes sense."

"Well, I wrote this song called 'What They Have,'" she says, her eyes suddenly misty. "Um, inspired by you and

Cam, and oh, just, here. I have it on my phone." She presses Play on the link, and it takes me less than three heartbeats to decide it's the most beautiful thing I've ever heard.

"Oh, Lore," I say softly. I'm beyond touched.

"I know, right?" she says, pleased. "I wouldn't mind a soprano to harmonize if you're feeling generous."

"Me?"

She rolls her eyes lightly. "Yeah, you. I've heard you belting Sarah Brightman. You've aged into your tone and it's lovely."

"I'd be honored."

"Fabulous," she says quickly, before flashing a wide grin. "But that wasn't the idea I had. That only came to me as you were humming along just now."

"I was?"

"Always." She shakes her head, chuckling. "Anyway, as I said, the song is inspired by you and Cam and how gross you are, so I thought maybe you two could act out your side of the story in a video. *If* you wanted. You know, maybe hit on the first love and the years apart and then maybe some of the fun B-roll Steve can't use since you two are always fucking it up with your goofing? I don't know if that's legal or whatever, but you get what I mean."

The idea has merit. We could show what Cam and I have going on behind the scenes, and probably a whole lot more effectively than a sad Instagram campaign fronted by an amateur. Not that we owe it to anyone . . . but it might be just what we need. We're hopeful that once viewers see the show for what it is, they'll support us, but we don't know anything for certain. Not when Lyle still gets the last word.

This might be our chance to get the last word *and* a whole season of the show.

If nothing else, I could guarantee that thanks to our drama, Lorelai's song would go viral, and that would be enough for me.

"I have to check with Cam, but it's a great idea. If you're sure."

"Yes, absolutely. Please."

The following weekend I fly down to Nashville with Lorelai to record my harmony on her song. She stays on to finish the album with the mysterious Craig Boseman, who, if I'm honest, seems halfway in love with her, but also wholly in love with her talent. Apparently, he used to be Drake Colter's bandmate and songwriting partner, so that's . . . plenty loaded. I get the impression Lore isn't the only one with something to prove via an artful indie comeback. I'm reserving my opinions, however, as I'm hardly one to talk after this last summer.

As expected, Cam loves the idea of the music video. He practically begs to take over the conceptualization after hearing the song. The challenge speaks to his documentary-making sweet spot, and while he says he's not upset about ending things with *National Geographic,* I do think he genuinely enjoys putting his vision out there for people to experience. Kind of like building houses, but instead of one family, you're reaching *all* the families. At any rate, by the time he finishes drawing up the plans, Lorelai and Craig ask him to work with them on three other songs, assuming the first goes over as well as they hope.

Weird how we started this summer as pop-culture pariahs,

you know? Me, having kittens at the mere thought of working with Lyle and slipping back into the spotlight; Cameron, snubbing reality television and trekking the globe, avoiding his past. Avoiding *us.*

And now look?

Hashtag Spriggs.

24

CAM

INTENTIONS

Derek agrees to take on the Caroline Street project, after I make the trip out to his place and ask in person. He might've agreed without the extra step, but it was well past time I made the effort. I've been stewing in low-key humiliation from the way I froze when he surprised me on camera. I'm sure it looked fine, especially since Shelby smoothed everything over, but I felt like a dick. I admitted to this, in between tossing my niece and nephew around in the air and accepting the Tupperware full of leftovers courtesy of my sweet sister-in-law.

"She's a better cook than Dad, even," Derek confesses. "It means I have a lifetime of dish duty, but I can't complain. You'll see what I mean."

And I do. I really do. Her lasagna will make Shelby drool. No wonder my mom wanted to move closer.

In the end, Derek doesn't love the idea of being on camera. But I've been able to cushion the blow a bit. I'm no longer an awkward asshole every time he enters the room, so he's more at ease on film, and I can admit that I like having him around. He's like me but, in a lot of ways, better. Instead of bothering me, though, it (mostly) makes me want to learn from him and see if I can't figure out how to stick around in one place, even when things get uncomfortable. Like when Derek's kids hid from me because, duh, I was a complete stranger. Or when I accidentally called my brother "Dad" while we were recording a talking head about the driveway.

Yeah. That was *something.*

So, it's not exactly comfortable, but it's a start, and Shelby was right. Derek seems to be looking at me differently after seeing me jump in front of and behind the camera. He even stayed late one night to help me finish the front porch railing.

"You made this?" he asked, impressed, surveying the finished product, his tanned arms crossed over his broad chest where the *Riggs & Son* logo is scrolled.

"I did. Well, I bought the spindles. Shelby can turn these, but it would take more time than we have, and I had to prioritize the nook."

"It looks good, Cam. Michelle is gonna want one after this episode airs. You'll have to come over and help me put it up."

"I'd be happy to, as long as she makes some more lasagna."

Maybe there's hope for us.

Today is Derek's last day on-site, so I brought my mom along. She spent most of the morning weeping over her boys working together and the rest freaking out over Shelby's nook. Steve asked to get her on camera, and unlike my brother, she was thrilled. He shot a really nice segment with my mom and Shelby sitting cozily together in the nook and reminiscing about the old days.

"Is it my imagination," my mom asks me during lunch, "or are you and Shelby getting closer?"

I grin. "I love her."

She throws her head back. "Oh, thank God. And she loves you, obviously."

"I don't know if I'd go so far as *obviously,* but yeah. Or so she tells me."

"You two have been destined since you were eleven years old. Two Michigan kids in L.A."

I laugh. "Well, that would have been helpful to hear a few months ago, but I doubt I would have believed it."

"Probably not," she agrees. "It's one of those things you have to figure out on your own. I'm happy for you, kid. For both of you."

"Thanks, Mom. Don't be a stranger, okay? Shelby's dad is first-class, but her mom . . . she came by a few weeks back . . ."

My mom makes a rude gesture. "Ada Mae Springfield is not a mother to that girl. She only ever saw her as a pay-check or an accessory. There is a special place in *H-E*-double-hockey-sticks for women like that."

"Amen," Daniel says from behind us.

"Oh, Danny, it's so good to see you. Let me hug on you a sec." Daniel accepts my mom's embrace and she's speaking low in his ear as he nods along. A moment later, they pull apart and my mom is wiping her eyes.

"Mom?" I ask. "You okay?"

She gives me a soggy smile. "Of course. I'm just so grateful is all. For so long . . ." She shakes her head, starting over. "You're not old, Cam. You and Shelby are still young, but you also started young. You know? You've lived a lot of life already. More than most. I'm just so happy to see *you* happy and creating something important and loving someone and being loved in return. And you did it all your way. You deserve that." Her smile is soft and fresh tears spring to her eyes. "You might not believe me, but that's all your dad and I ever wanted for you. He didn't know how to help you get it, and I'm not saying he did right by you, though I know you're both working on that. But ultimately, it *is* what he wants. And I'm so grateful to Danny because he was there for you."

"I don't know what's going to happen with the show, Mom," I warn.

She shakes her head. "It doesn't matter. This show is special, and I hope it works out, but everything you got in exchange is more than enough."

• • •

We wrap on the Caroline Street house on a Friday afternoon, right on schedule. Despite the canceled tile order, extra furniture work, and surprise guests, we were able to get it done just as the weather was starting to change. The house is going to be staged next week and put back on the market, but for now, I'm happy to sit in it and enjoy the fruits of my labor.

I went out for a six-pack and am now sitting on a stool at the shiny kitchen island when Shelby texts me.

SHELBY: Want company?

I grin, walking to the front door and flinging it wide open. She's there with a bag of takeout and a grand smile.

"Thought you might be here. I can leave you be, though, if you prefer."

I pull her to me gently and shove the door closed before capturing her lips in mine and kissing her deeply.

After a moment, she pulls back, smiling. "Good. I have something to show you."

I turn for the island. "Please tell me it's something naked."

Shelby giggles, her eyes flashing. "That can be arranged. But first, something else. You'll want to be clothed for this part."

We sit on the island and unwrap food, digging into dinner. After a minute, she pulls out her phone.

"Is it something on Instagram?"

She snorts. "Um, definitely not. This is an email from my agent."

I straighten, forgetting all about my burger.

She reads, "'Blah, blah, blah, how are you? Heard you're wrapping up! Hope the flip sells fast! I've cc'd your new publicist, blah, blah, blah.' But *here,*" Shelby emphasizes, raising her finger in the air. "'Good news, HLNW has reached out, and they've already ordered a complete twelve-episode first season of *HomeMade,* contract forthcoming, blah, blah, blah.'" She stops, her eyes dancing. "What do you think?"

I'm at a loss. "Wait. Really?"

"Yeah, really. You probably have an email, too."

"The pilot's not even done yet."

"I know! Apparently, Steve sent the edited footage, though. They were anxious to see what we were up to after all the recent good press." Shelby points to her phone. "Some of the blah-blah-blah parts were about our net worth and our newfound popularity, whatever, I don't care about that. But we get to do it again!" She bites her lip. "Sorry. I got excited. Do you even want to do it again? I mean, now that it's officially, unbelievably, on the table?"

"Absolutely," I answer immediately. "I'm surprised is all. And a little nervous. But I definitely want to do it."

"Yeah?"

I nod. "Yeah. One hundred percent. Yes."

"Good!" She beams. "Then I want to do something first and I want you with me when I do it."

"Sure."

She holds up her phone and hits Call. After a ringing sound, I hear Lyle's voice as he picks up. She turns the speakerphone on and places it between us.

"Hey, Lyle. It's Shelb. I got an interesting email from my agent today."

Lyle's smarmiest voice echoes off the empty walls of the kitchen. "Yeah, sorry about that. I meant to reach out first, in person, but things got crazy."

"Sure, they did," she soothes. "I guess I'm a little confused. After the article came out, I was under the impression we'd somehow offended you. It seemed like our pilot might be dead in the water. Again," she finishes blandly.

"Yeah, about that article. That was bullshit, Shelb. I didn't want it to go down like that, but you know these Hollywood gossip rags. They're like dogs at the proverbial bone . . ."

Shelby makes a derisive snort. "So, you're saying it was an accident?"

"Yeah. A miscommunication."

"And you didn't arrange for *Hollywood Hotwire* to do a write-up making Cam and me look bad?"

"Well . . ."

"Because I spoke with my old friend Jocelyn Bennett over there at *Hotwire* and she said you were the one to tip them off."

Lyle's tone is flat. "It's business, Shelby. I wouldn't expect you to understand—"

Shelby cuts him off. "I want you to listen to me, Lyle, and then I will tell you our decision about the order."

Silence.

"Lyle?" I prompt, annoyed.

"Jesus, fuck, you're both there? Of course you are. Fine. Go ahead and say what you need to say. I'm listening."

I grin at Shelby and settle back on my stool. This is all her and I've been waiting years for this moment.

She presses closer to the speaker, her fingers tapping on the wooden countertop. "I am tired of your bullshit, Lyle. Exhausted. I made some mistakes when I was a kid, but so did you. I know you don't believe me, but I never cheated on you. I never loved you the right way, though, and that's on me, but that's where my apology ends. I'm sorry I didn't love you. But I'm not sorry I left, and I'm not sorry that I grew up and made something amazing of myself, and I'm especially not sorry for falling in love with Cameron. And you don't get to take credit for any of that, do you understand me? I did that on my own, despite you and your fucked-up sense of importance. We built this beautiful house and this incredible show, and it was *despite you*.

"And we'll do the season despite you, too. But only if you step the fuck back and leave us alone. No more articles or surprise visits from my nightmare mother, and no more fucking with the time line. We will do this our way or not at all. I want it in our contract."

"Yeah, that's not a real thing—" Lyle starts.

"Make it a real thing, Jessup," I say, before ending the call and rounding the island to my girlfriend. She swirls in her stool to face me, her face lit up.

"That felt good."

"I'm not going to lie, I'm pretty turned on right now."

"Really?" she asks, already undoing the buttons on my shirt.

I still her fingers. "We can go back to my place. I know you said you didn't want to have sex here."

She swipes my hand away and continues with my shirt, pulling it down over my shoulders and tossing it to the gleaming kitchen floor. "I said I didn't want to have sex against the wall. Which, as you know, I've reneged on. Several times." She presses forward, her tongue teasing my earlobe and sucking it into her hot mouth. Her hand reaches down the front of my pants, stroking against me with enthusiasm, as she whispers, "And I never said anything about the kitchen counters."

25

SHELBY

THE BONES

I prefer to keep the furniture to a minimum when I'm staging a house. Particularly one as beautiful as the Caroline Street project, letting the polished Craftsman details speak for themselves. But I've managed to come through with some books, fresh flowers, logs in the fireplace, and so forth. I've scheduled an open house with Jazz this Sunday, and I'll be on hand to bake some cookies in the oven, light a cozy fire, and walk the *HomeMade* cameras through, before the public gets its first glimpse of what we've done. I should probably feel nervous, since the entire world will see if we sink this house, but I've been too busy browsing options for the next project with Jazz, my dad, and Cam. We're planning to take on a few this time. My dad always has multiple projects going at any given moment. It's more sustainable financially and pragmatically, and it will help keep things rolling for our camera crew during light weeks. Or so we think. If necessary, I can take on one project while Cam takes the lead on the other, and we can fill in the gaps together.

Everything together.

Meanwhile, as we wait for *HomeMade* to make its debut, Cameron has been in his cave, creating the music video for Lorelai. He's spent the last week collecting footage from a number of sources, working all hours, day and night. He and Lorelai have decided to surprise me with the end result, which is sweet and maybe a little nerve-racking. Plus, I just miss him. Pathetic, I know. In my defense, I've gotten used to having him around after all his running.

He, Lorelai, and Craig have gone back and forth several times about when to release the song. Cam and I feel like, ultimately, it should be whenever Lorelai is ready. Because once it's out there, there'll be no stopping it. My friend has been hiding as much as any of us in Michigan. More so, maybe, because she's not done being a star yet. She's too talented to keep her music from the world. Honestly, if Drake Colter walked through the door right now, I would put on my highest (and only) stilettoes and kick him in the nuts. He broke not only her heart but also her spirit, and he cost her too many years. It could have all gone so differently if he'd stood by her side when everything went south.

I'm not saying you need a man to stand up for you. I'm just saying it's nice to have someone to lean on when things get tough. Someone to take you against the kitchen island after you get done telling off your ex, finally. You know, to be there for you. Lorelai was left to topple on her own, and that's gonna take a long time to forget. This album? It might just kick things off.

I'm glad she's got her spirit back. There's no containing it now.

Lorelai insists she's ready—that she's been ready—which is why she wants to release the single and video ASAP. As in, before the school year begins and she "chickens out and goes back to teaching third grade," and before the pilot of *HomeMade* premieres.

"Everyone will want to tune in for your show after they hear your song and see the video," she explains while perched on a barstool at Kevin's place. It's early on a Saturday evening . . . the last Saturday of the summer. "Plus, Lyle's gonna be so annoyed."

"Lore, it's *your* song. And I don't see any reason for Lyle to be angry. He should want his show to be successful, especially since we signed a contract for a whole season."

"Oh, he does," Cam says, gleefully rubbing his hands together. "But he won't be able to take full credit and that's gonna bug the shit out of him."

"Have you seen the video yet, Shelby?" asks Beth from the behind the bar. She places a basket of hot wings in front of each of us.

I look up at her, surprised. "No. Have you?"

Beth looks guilty. I look at Kevin. "You have, too?" He nods, shoving up his frames. There's something significant flashing behind his lenses.

I turn to Cam. "Has everyone seen it but me?"

He shakes his head, taking a long, lingering sip of his beer, and then he licks his lips, Cheshire-cat grin in place. "Just them."

"It's really good," Beth says.

"You're gonna love it, Shelb," Lorelai says.

"When do I get to see it?"

Cameron lifts a shoulder, lifting a wing to his lips. I shove at him, impatient, and he swallows. "I have it upstairs. Eat. You're starving. I'll take you up after."

The way he says it feels charged, and a little shiver goes up my spine. "Okay," I agree softly.

I eat as much as I can while our friends banter like they've known each other for decades. I've stopped listening, feeling distracted, when Cam finally nudges me to let me know it's time to head up. I hop off the stool on suddenly wooden legs. Not because I'm scared, but I am weirdly hesitant.

He takes my hand. "You look like you forgot your lines."

"I never forget my lines," I say loftily.

He leads me up the stairwell outside and into his apartment, which looks messier than normal.

"Sorry, it's a sty," he says.

"You've been preoccupied," I say. "And I don't mind. It's kind of nice to see. Like a glimpse into Distracted Cameron."

"More like Mega-Focused Cameron. They used to tease me all the time about my messy tent at *Nat Geo.* I would get so absorbed in my work that my tent was basically a drop-off location."

His apartment isn't gross, only scattered. No open food containers or days-old dirty dishes. Just unopened mail and shoes kicked off wherever he settled with his laptop. That kind of thing. And I'm struck with the idea that I want to be the one to pick up after him when he's focused like this. At the end of the day, when he's tired and on deadline, I want to be there to make sure he's eating and cover him with a blanket when he passes out on the couch.

I shake myself.

"So, where's this video?"

He takes my shoulders and steers me to a squishy leather chair that I happen to know is plenty big enough for two and gently prods me to sit down. Then he picks up his laptop and carries it over, making a few clicks on the screen before placing it in my lap. "When you're ready, click Play."

"You aren't going to watch?"

He shakes his head. "I want to watch your face."

"Oh-kay." I take a deep breath and press Play.

Immediately Lorelai's song begins. She's standing in a cornfield, in jeans and a white tank, breeze blowing through her hair. She looks so good. Utterly healthy, graceful, and sharp as a tack. I'm so proud of her I could scream. Then, my breath catches in my throat as the first image, some ancient footage, starts to roll on the screen. It's home video from the set of *Jackson*. We can't be more than ten and eleven, maybe. First season for sure. I'm in between Cameron and Lyle, hamming it up. Gap in my teeth, frizzy hair. We're singing something, and Lyle and I are staring at the camera, behind which I assume is Cam's mom. But Cam is looking at me. There's more home-video footage of our years on *Jackson*, and you see us gradually age. During tutoring, while playing cards, some low-key red-carpet premieres. Sometimes the three of us, but mostly just Cam and me. By the time my vocals layer into the song, we're in our late teens, and it's clear as day that I'm crushing on my costar. Clip after clip of us staring, laughing, blushing, flirting . . . even one of us sneaking off, hand in hand.

It's . . . so sweet, so pure. I can barely stand it.

Cut to Lorelai looking gorgeous, sitting on a dock under the shade of some willow trees. She's wearing a pretty cotton dress and is cradling a guitar in her lap, strumming like she was born for it.

Because she was.

The song changes, and there's a few clips of us apart . . . nothing sinister. More red carpets, *Nat Geo,* even Michigan in those early years when I was still learning and too thin in my overalls. Shadows under both our eyes. Tears prickle hot along my lashes as I realize, for maybe the first time, how forlorn we were apart from each other. Just going through the motions on our way to becoming who we are, together.

Lorelai appears again, this time on stage in Kevin's bar. The place is empty, except for shadows, and she belts it out under the hot lights. She looks fierce and fiery in a pair of dark-wash skinny jeans and a bright-red halter top and matching lipstick. Grown, matured, ready to take over the world.

And then we're in the present. More home footage of Cam and me playing around and flirting on set. I have no idea where or who the video came from, but I'm so grateful, because I get to watch us fall in love all over again. And *wow,* are we obvious. All loaded looks and lingering stares. There's one clip of the first day, walking into the house . . . just up the stairs where you can only see our boots, angled together, as we talk about taking on the project. Hand in hand at the flea market, dancing at the bar, my hands twined around his neck, his eyes on me again and again and again. Joking at the barn sale, hugging his mom, him working with my dad, and finally, a quick, meaningful kiss as he walks in the door and hugs me one morning a week or so ago.

Lorelai closes things out, finishing with a longing look over her shoulder, as she picks up her guitar and walks away down a long, lonely road, and I swipe at my cheeks—hot tears slipping from the corners of my eyes.

"That was . . ." I'm shaking my head, at a loss for words.

The laptop lid comes down with a click and behind it is Cam, down on one knee.

My breath catches even as my heart gives a mighty lurch in my chest. "What are you doing?"

He moves the laptop to the floor and takes my hand. "Shelby, I love you."

"I love you, too."

"I've loved you since I was a kid. Since before I knew what it meant to love someone."

"I know."

He grins at that. "Of course you know. You always knew when it came to us."

I shrug. "I don't know why you're on your knees. We talked about this. You don't need to get on your knees for me," I tease.

"Marry me, Shelby."

I freeze as he pulls a ring out of his pocket.

"Was that there all day?"

"Maybe."

"Just in your pocket, Cam? You have *got to be kidding me.*"

"Shelby." He laughs. "You haven't answered me."

"Yes! Please, yes. I want to marry the hell out of you, Cameron Riggs."

He slumps. "Thank God."

I slip to the floor, getting on my knees next to him. "I've wanted to marry you since the day I met you," I say, pressing my lips to his for a soft kiss. "Forever and ever, you and me."

He slips the ring over my finger and stares at it, whistling low. "Wow. I was not prepared for how hot you'd look with my ring on your finger."

"Oh yeah?"

"Yeah . . ." he says distractedly, rubbing his hand up and down my back.

"I'm never taking it off."

He groans. "Fine, as long as I can remove everything else."

I stand up, taking his hands, and walk us backward toward his bedroom.

"For the rest of our lives, if you want."

EPILOGUE

HOMEMADE:

Child Stars Turned Reality-TV Renovators Build the Happily Ever After We All Need

BY FRESCA BIANETTI

"Furniture restoration saved my life," Shelby Springfield, 27, admits with a smile. She's as relaxed as I've ever seen her, dressed in a pair of jeans, a thickly knit oversized cardigan, and white Converse. She gently shoves off, rocking the porch swing she's sharing with her fiancé and *HomeMade* costar, Cameron Riggs, 28. He takes over as she curls closer to him, natural as can be.

The attractive pair could easily grace the cover of a Lands' End Christmas catalog. Riggs with his rugged charm and lumberjack appeal, Springfield and her sweet girl-next-door sensibilities. The onetime child stars have broken into the reality-TV home-renovation scene and hearts of viewers everywhere, as they quite literally fell in love on-screen and off-.

When I ask Springfield to elaborate on that, she gives a small shrug. "I was definitely in a bad place when I left L.A., nearly six years ago now. Acting and singing—it was all I'd known—but it wasn't what I loved anymore. I felt adrift. I don't know how much longer I could have carried on."

Me: So how did you get from L.A. to Michigan, of all places?

The costars share a look. They do this a lot. One of those easy silent communications that makes everyone else feel like intruders. If I hadn't been invited . . .

Riggs answers. "She called me. I was in Alaska, shooting a doc for *National Geographic*, when I got a text from Shelby."

"He took the first flight out, even though he hates flying," Springfield adds, her expression gooey.

"I did. Thought I was going to die, honestly. It was barely a plane," he jokes. "But anyway, I showed up at her apartment and it wasn't good. I could tell she needed out, but I wasn't in the right place to help her. It wasn't my brightest moment, but before I left, I wrote her a letter encouraging her to leave L.A. behind and save herself. I'm so glad she took it to heart."

Me: You didn't drive her back?

Riggs shakes his head, fidgeting with the rolled sleeve of his flannel shirt. (Yes, dear readers, he really does wear that much flannel in real life.) "No, I didn't live here yet, and I wasn't ready for it. I wasn't ready for us. I was still chasing sunsets."

It's this kind of forthright honesty and down-to-earth candor that has brought about the tidal wave of viewer loyalty showered over the duo during the last few months. Speculation ran rampant this summer while a smear campaign tried to sink the couple before their show even hit the airwaves. But, in a move becoming typical of the pair, they addressed the rumors and skeletons in their pop-star closets with a narrative of truth.

"The thing is," Springfield says, "when you grow up on television, everyone thinks they know what you're about, deep down. They're invested in you the way you would be with a sibling or classmate. It can be wonderful, like when people are cheering you on. But it can also be suffocating. Every mistake I ever made in my teens and early twenties was public record."

Riggs adds, "And it was this catch-22 for us, because we couldn't change while living in L.A. So, we left and did our changing in private, but with privacy comes ignorance. No one knew we'd changed, and we weren't ready to tell them."

"Until we were," Springfield finishes with a wide smile.

I ask if the smear campaign pushed them to tell their side.

Riggs grimaces, scratching at his signature neat beard. "Probably. We had to decide if we were going to let the show speak for itself or take control of our response. So many people were counting on the show to succeed—our families, friends, the crew, and contractors. Even our community. It felt like we owed them a fighting chance."

Springfield and Riggs offer to show me around their workshop. "A little behind the scenes," Springfield jokes. "I don't allow film crews into my sanctuary."

It's a massive barnlike structure with state-of-the-art equipment, a decade-in-the-making treasure trove of furniture castoffs and . . . chickens.

Riggs laughs. "The first time she let me see the place, I was ready to bunk down with the chicks, I was so intimidated."

And rightfully so. This is a warehouse dedicated to craftsmanship. Springfield shows off a few of the pieces she's working on. A Victorian-era sideboard donated from a local farm that she's restoring to its original sheen. A battered rolltop desk with a least a dozen little magical hidden cubbies.

"I don't know if I can bear to sell this one."

"Even though you already have two," Riggs complains good-naturedly.

Springfield shrugs with a sheepish grin. "I like cubbies."

And we like these two. Recently, they wrapped

on filming their first season of *HomeMade*, which premiered in September on HLNW.

Me: So, Cameron, we've really gotten to watch you come into your home-renovation trade on-screen. How was that for you?

Riggs jokes, "I don't know, you tell me. Am I pulling it off?"

Springfield rolls her eyes, smacking his broad chest. "Cameron was meant for this. Every project, every challenge we threw at him, he's tackled with aplomb. He likes to tease that he 'plays a contractor on TV,' but the reality is, he legitimately does it all. He could have taken the easy way out, letting the so-called professionals do the dirty work, but he never has. Early on, he apprenticed under my dad, but after a while, it became his."

When I ask him his favorite part of contracting, his response is quick. "Working alongside Shelby every day. Even as kids, we had the time of our lives working together. Despite all the show-business BS that comes along with being a child actor, I always had fun with Shelb. And this is infinitely better, because restoring homes is something we truly enjoy. This community is one we belong to. Plus, now I get to keep her."

Oh, believe me *I know.* When you're all done swooning, I have more.

The pair invite me into the home they share, a small farmhouse in the middle of rolling green acres of pine forests. There's a squashy-faced cat cleaning herself on the front porch to welcome us.

"She's mostly harmless," Springfield assures me. "But a bit of an asshole."

We settle down at their kitchen table (that Springfield restored, of course), and Riggs offers coffee and cookies. The pair move in a synchronized way, hosting, before sitting across from me.

Me: Tell me about the music video. How did you come to work with Lorelai Jones?

They share another look.

"Lorelai and I have been friends for years, actually," Springfield explains. "We met by chance in Grand Rapids and hit it off immediately. When I moved here, she followed. I never planned to go back to show business, but I always knew Lorelai would return to music eventually. It's in her bones."

I ask about the rumors that Riggs, who developed the infamous "What They Have" music video, layered with footage of the two stars growing up, used it to propose to Springfield.

Springfield flushes. "He did. And before you ask, no, there is no video of that. It was very private and incredibly romantic."

Me: Did you hear the complete album (*Last & Never*) first?

Riggs: Yeah, and we both fell in love within the first few chords. It's phenomenal songwriting. Lorelai deserves every bit of the acclaim she's been getting.

Me: What do you think about Jones's infamous ex, Drake Colter?

Riggs and Springfield, at once: NO COMMENT.

Springfield repeats with a giggle, "Seriously, we can't comment."

Over the course of several (delicious and melty) chocolate-chip cookies, I ask some rapid-fire questions of the lovebirds.

Me: What can you tell me about your upcoming wedding?

Springfield: It will be a simple affair. Maybe in our backyard? Something very small and private and lovely.

Riggs: Soon. It will be soon. Like, yesterday soon.

Me: Shelby, do you ever think you'll go back to singing?

Springfield: Doubtful.

Riggs: What are you talking about? You sing every day in your shop.

Springfield: Well, you sing in the shower.

Riggs: (waggles brows) How would you know?

Me: Cameron, how does it feel to work for your former costar Lyle Jessup?

Riggs: Who?

Springfield slaps his chest again.

Riggs: Fine, fine. I kid. Honestly, we wouldn't be here without Lyle. We've known him as long as we've known each other, and he's the one who brought us back together for this show. I'm grateful for that.

Me: So, no hard feelings?

Springfield: Ehhhh. More like a fresh start.

Me: Speaking of, what's the word on a second season?

Springfield and Riggs exchange smiles.

Riggs: We might have a few properties picked out.

Springfield: And we signed a contract. So, it looks like we'll be back!

And we're betting we won't be the only ones there to watch this sweetly real couple as they navigate their second season of renovation projects and their first year of marriage.

Comments (9,341)

Frankie_11: I heard Lyle Jessup actually cheated on Springfield with Marcella before they were married!

Phil-to-Chill: I went to college with Riggs. He's a super decent guy.

JesusSaves: Fake News

QuirkyLibrarian: When will the *HomeMade* merch be available?

Sheila is my name: Road trip to Michigan planned!

Twihard Fan: Good for them. They deserve to be happy. We watch their show as a family and love them.

IheartCameronRiggs: I heard Springfield named her rooster after Lyle Jessup.

(reply to IheartCameronRiggs) **IheartShelbySpringfield:** "The Fucker" is doing just fine. Ravishing all the hens with his surgically enhanced . . . comb.

Coffee-Drinker: WE LOVE HOMEMADE.

FastandtheTedious: I watched them as kids and watch them now. Congrats! Two child stars who made it out alive!

FantasySweet: I watched that Lorelai Jones music video a million times. So cute. Her entire album is incredible. Best I've heard in years.

(reply to FantasySweet) **The Drake Colter:** Best I've heard ever.

(reply to The Drake Colter) **The Lorelai Jones:** . . .

(129 replies) (cont.)

ACKNOWLEDGMENTS

Since the first time I read *Confessions of a Shopaholic* many, many years ago, I knew I wanted to write my very own rom-com one day. The transition from YA to adult romance has been an adventure, but I've been so very lucky to have the best team behind me, smoothing the way. Authors tend to write these acknowledgments pages pretty early on in the publishing process, and because of that, I don't always know who to thank and inevitably miss people.

Not this time. I've got a list! Firstly, a big thanks to my editor, Vicki Lame, who didn't even bat an eye when I sent her my adult manuscript after years of writing YA stories. Thank you for always pushing me to torture my characters more, but myself less.

Thank you to Kerri Resnick, who designed the cover of *Built to Last*. I've never not gasped in happiness at one of Kerri's covers, but this one in particular made me giddy.

To Alexis Neuville, who I've called my hero at least twice

this month already. Thank you for always being there with a super-quick fix to my tedious marketing questions. Marketing can be pretty awkward for authors, but it's far less so when you have someone so sweet and capable as Lexi advising you.

Mary Moates has been my publicist on my last few books, and it was *such* a relief to hear we'd still get to work together in adult. Ditto on the "sweet and capable." Thank you for your unrelenting encouragement and enthusiasm, Mary!

Thank you, Vanessa Aguirre, for keeping everything running smoothly. With multiple books in multiple stages, I don't know where I would be without Vanessa keeping me on track. You. Are. Amazing.

There're a whole lot of people working on my books behind the scenes that I don't always get to speak with directly but who are making my dreams come true, nevertheless. From SMP/Griffin Books: Michelle McMillian is the interior designer, Hannah Jones is my managing editor, Brant Janaway is the marketing team leader, Jennifer Eck is the production editor, Gail Friedman is the production manager, Lisa Cowley is my copy editor, and Cheryl Redmond is my proofreader. My books wouldn't be here without each and every one of them and I'm so grateful to have you all in my corner. In case I never get the chance to say it face to face, THANK YOU SO MUCH.

To my agent, Kate McKean, who has talked me off many a ledge, always asks even if the answer will probably be no, and has had my back the last *five* years. We've come a long way since that first call when you told me I might have to "remove the fucks for Walmart," and I've been grateful for that candor every day since.

To my husband, Mike. It's weird to be the partner of an author and I imagine even more so the partner of a romance author. It's okay. You can absolutely tell everyone Cam is inspired by you, even in "those scenes." You've earned it.

To my kids, if you ever read this book someday when you're much older, disregard the previous paragraph. I was just kidding.

To my parents, siblings, in-laws, and extended family, *see above*. I love you all. Thank you for being supportive of my dreams even when it means I'm hiding in my bedroom during family vacations to write. Special thanks to my sister Cassie who is always my very first reader. If it wasn't for her, none of this would have ever happened. (So it's her fault.)

A lot happened *gestures around at the world* while I was writing this book. I lost family to Covid, grieved *a lot*, raised two middle schoolers through both of those things, and supported a spouse through loss. Because of this, I *know* I am missing dear friends who read early versions of this story and cheered me through. Please know this is unintentional and I am so grateful for you. Thank you, Ashley Schumacher, for laughing at my "comment sections." Thank you, Trish Doller, for encouraging me in my jump to adult. I'm still fangirling! Thank you, Brigid Kemmerer and Jodi Picoult, for asking to read this book . . . neither of you could know what a boost that was to not only my self-esteem but also my heart. Thank you, Kelly Coon, Lillian Clark, and Laura Namey, for reading and then sending me endless TikToks of men with tree-trunk thighs to spur me on.

Special thanks to my real-life besties, Megan Turton and

Cate Unruh, for reading early versions and workshopping different words for "thrusting." I hope I did you proud.

AND THANK YOU, READERS. Most days I still can't wrap my head around having readers, period. Thank you so much for trusting me with your time and for loving on my characters. I'm the luckiest because of you.

Erin Hahn

Erin Hahn is the author of the young adult novels *You'd Be Mine, More Than Maybe*, and *Never Saw You Coming* as well as the adult romance *Built to Last*. She married her very own YA love interest, who she met on her first day of college, and has two kids who are much, much cooler than she ever was at their age. She lives in Ann Arbor, Michigan, a.k.a. the greenest place on earth, and has a cat named Gus who plays fetch and a dog named June who doesn't.